Son of Saigon

A novel by
David Myles Robinson

Terra Nova Books
Santa Fe, New Mexico

Library of Congress Control Number 2018940375

Distributed by SCB Distributors, (800) 729-6423

Terra Nova Books

Son of Saigon. Copyright © 2018 by David Myles Robinson
All rights reserved
Printed in the United States of America

Published by Terra Nova Books, Santa Fe, New Mexico.
www.TerraNovaBooks.com

ISBN 978-1-948749-00-8

Son of Saigon

PART ONE

Chapter 1

Hank Reagan had recently begun having depressing old-man thoughts. *When and how will I die? Will this be the last pair of shoes I ever buy?*

Not being stupid—and being brutally aware of his physical and emotional state—he knew these downer ruminations were the result of a) his turning seventy a couple of days ago, and b) Becka, his wife of thirty-six years, dying a couple of months ago. He'd been trying hard to "move on," but he was finding it difficult.

Just that afternoon, while playing a game of gin with his best friend, Norm Rothstein, he had looked up in the middle of a hand and said, "Getting old is fucked."

Norm had looked at him with his basset-hound eyes, bags and all, and his big round nose spread with broken capillaries, and said, "Dying is fuckeder." Then he picked up the jack of hearts Hank had finally discarded.

Hank grunted and tried not to think about the concept of no longer existing. Although he still had his memories, which he knew would eventually begin to fade, Becka's living, physical being had simply vanished from his life, just as he, too, would all too soon cease to exist. The only difference was that Becka had someone to mourn her while Hank was pretty sure his passing would go largely unnoticed—except by Norm, of course, who would lose a good friend and gin partner.

Hank discarded a ten of hearts and picked a card off the stack, but he could see from Norm's expression that he'd blown it. He'd been too immersed in his dark thoughts of death to pay attention to which cards Norm had been picking up.

"Gin," said Norm.

"Fuck you," said Hank.

Now the two were standing in line at the dining hall, waiting to be seated for dinner. Hank had lived at the Sunrise Adult Community condos for just over two years, and he still didn't understand why they lined up at 5:45 waiting for the dining room to open at six. It wasn't like there weren't enough seats or enough food for everyone.

Norm was talking up a woman named Matilda. Although she didn't have any noticeable accent, Hank assumed she was British. He couldn't conceive of any self-respecting American parents in the 1940s naming a daughter Matilda.

Hank wasn't inclined to engage in conversation with anyone around him, so he resolutely stared at Norm's god-awful madras sport coat. The more Hank stared, the more the reds, greens, and yellows all seemed to blur together, and he wondered if he could self-induce a seizure.

Matilda laughed loudly at something Norm said.

Norm's last wife, his fifth, had left him shortly after talking him into buying a place at Sunrise four years ago. She was fifty-six, ten years younger than Norm, and within eight months of moving in had hooked up with Vince, the overly tanned fifty-two-year-old tennis instructor. Norm told Hank he tried not to wish melanoma on the guy, but it was hard. Somewhere, the gold-digger dick was banging his ex and spending his hard-earned dinero. To Norm's credit, his conscience ultimately got the better of him, and he told Hank he had modified his curse from melanoma to squamous cell, or when he was feeling particularly charitable, basal cell.

Norm had sent her packing with a one-time alimony payment of $5 million and immediately became the prime target for the plethora of women-vultures who populated Sunrise. Women outnumbered men there three to one.

"The problem," Norm once confided in Hank, "is that I've never had sex with a woman over sixty. I'm kind of scared of what I'd find when she undressed."

"Picture your own pinkish-white, sagging, wrinkled body without the hair covering every square inch," Hank had said. They were on Hank's patio overlooking the Pacific Ocean, smoking Becka's medical marijuana.

"Hey, that's not fair," Norm said. "I don't have hair on my head." He sighed heavily. "Maybe I'll discontinue my Cialis prescription."

As far as Hank knew, Norm had yet to bed any of the grande dames who continued to throw themselves at him.

For a while, after Becka died, Hank had been flooded with condolence gifts of cookies, cakes, casseroles, and such. One woman, who must have been one of the first women named Tiffany to ever move into a retirement home, presented Hank with a beautiful mahogany box filled with exotic teas. She pulled out one tea bag in particular, dangled it in her thin, age-spotted hand, and said in a coy voice, "This green tea varietal is said to have aphrodisiac qualities." Then she winked at him.

"She actually fucking winked at me," Hank told Norm the next day.

Now Hank felt a finger poke him in his back. "You gonna move forward, Hankie? Or have you finally succumbed to dementia?"

Hank knew the finger and the voice belonged to Roger Aikens, who was bitterly bitter because Hank refused to let him play in his golf foursome. He'd caught Roger cheating and had called him on it, but gave him a pass after he apologized. But there was Roger, the very next day, once again surreptitiously improving his lie on the fairway.

For a brief moment, Hank considered doing a fast pirouette, grabbing the extended finger, and breaking it. There was a time, back in the day, when he could have done just that. But, he decided, now he would probably fall down mid-twirl and cause both physical and psychological injury to himself. So, without responding to Roger, Hank took two steps forward into the space that had opened up between him and Norm.

Hank sighed and refocused on Norm's jacket. An upbeat instrumental version of The Doors' "The End" was playing on the sound system. Matilda laughed again and then glanced back at Hank. Were they talking about him? He didn't really care.

The line moved forward another two steps.

*   *   *

In the well-appointed condo lobby, a dramatically beautiful Asian woman sat straight-backed on the plush leather couch. Her right foot tapped lightly to the perversion of the Doors classic.

Chapter 2

Norm invited Matilda to join them at their table for dinner, so Hank lapsed easily into the third-man-out role, letting the inane chatter wash over him as he ate.

He and Norm had met shortly after Hank and Becka bought into the complex, and they'd become fast friends, mostly because of their mutual cynical, dry, biting wit. When Becka had been diagnosed with cancer, Norm was there for Hank every awful step on the road toward her ceasing to exist. It had been Becka's idea to buy into Sunrise, just as it had been Norm's wife's idea, so now here they were, stuck in what Hank referred to as the "death farm," a place where neither would have chosen to be.

Apropos of nothing, Hank broke into Norm and Matilda's conversation. "Do you think it was the developer's idea of a cruel joke to name this place Sunrise instead of Sunset?"

Matilda stared at Hank as if she hadn't realized he'd been there all along.

Norm laughed. "I think some young marketing executive probably got mixed up about what the term 'golden years' really means and tried to spin it as some kind of new start, as opposed to waiting to die."

Matilda coughed into her napkin and excused herself to go to the ladies' room.

"Sorry, man, didn't mean to bum her out," Hank said.

Norm waved his hand dismissively and was about to say something when Jackie, Sunrise's thirty-something receptionist, who favored short skirts and clinging blouses, approached the table and leaned in to whisper to Hank.

"There's a woman in reception who's asked to see you," she said.

He enjoyed her hot breath in his ear.

She hesitated a moment before adding, "She's very beautiful."

Hank's face scrunched up inquiringly. He thanked Jackie, put his napkin on the table, and stood.

"What's up?" Norm asked.

Hank offered a slight shrug. "That's what I'm gonna find out."

There was only one woman in the reception area when Hank arrived, so he approached her without hesitation. She stood as he neared.

"I'm Hank Reagan," he said. "You wanted to—" He stopped short and stared at the beautiful woman.

She had coal-black hair, pinned up and held in place with what looked like black-lacquered chopsticks. He noticed her prominent cheekbones, her thick and sensuous lips. Tall, stately, and dignified, she wore a tight-fitting *ao dai,* the Vietnamese national dress, which was a silk tunic, in this case powder blue, worn over pants, in this case white. There were tiny crow's feet around her eyes, but the rest of her face appeared smooth. Her dark, almond-shaped eyes seemed to bore into him.

"Mai? Is that you?" Hank's voice had gone husky, tentative.

Tran Xuan Mai smiled and bowed her head slightly and said, "Hello, Hank." She had only the slightest trace of an accent.

Neither of them said anything for several seconds as they continued to appraise each other. Hank felt old and beaten down and inwardly cringed at what he imagined Mai was seeing. He had a full head of gray hair and an equally gray beard. His once-handsome face was craggy with lines. Becka used to tell him he looked rugged. At least his body was still lean, he thought. He'd become a gym rat during Becka's illness, as if he could sweat out the unbearable sadness.

Mai, on the other hand, looked ageless. If Hank remembered correctly, she was about ten years younger than he, which would make her sixty, yet she looked forty. Hank self-consciously ran a hand through his hair and smiled, still tentative, still unsure of the situation.

Then, as if in response to an unspoken mutual prod, Hank and Mai moved into each other's arms.

Chapter 3

On one of Becka's last good days, just a week or so before she ceased to exist, she covered her bald head with a maroon knit beret and joined Hank and Norm for dinner in the dining hall. The incessant flow of well-intentioned Sunrise residents stopping by to say hello only served to remind Hank that Becka's days were numbered. They both knew by that time that there was not going to be any miracle recovery. She would be dead and cremated and gone from the earth in a matter of days or weeks.

Once back on their condo's large patio, the three had shared a joint, staring out at the blackness. After a period of innocuous chitchat and several chocolate chip cookies, Becka turned to Norm and said, "Did Hank ever tell you how we met?"

Norm shook his head and smiled. "Hank doesn't talk a whole lot about the past."

Becka giggled, a real honest-to-goodness stoner giggle that reminded Hank of the old days. "That's because he was a spy. He can't even talk to me about a lot of the stuff he's done, and I had security clearance."

"I knew Hank had been with the CIA," Norm said, "but why'd you have security clearance?" He took another cookie.

"Because I worked for the CIA too," Becka said. She paused a beat before adding, "But I wasn't a spook like Hank. I was just a lowly translator, so my security clearance wasn't high enough for Hank to tell me about all the people he assassinated and the end-of-world plots he thwarted." She giggled again, took the roach from Hank, and took a big hit. When she let the smoke out, she coughed and said, "But that's how we met. Hank had some document in French that needed immediate translation, so he came personally to our department, and I guess I was the first translator he found." Becka stopped talking and took a bite out of another cookie.

"And that's how we met," Hank said, as if putting a period at the end of the conversation.

Becka waved a hand, obviously not finished. "I thought Hank was the most handsome man I'd ever seen."

Norm chuckled. "And he thought you were the most beautiful woman he'd ever seen and asked you out?"

Hank sighed heavily. These kinds of conversations embarrassed him, but he saw the huge smile on Becka's face. "Not exactly. She was pretty in an all-American kind of way. She had a lovely face with a great smile, but she wasn't someone I would have hit on."

"So I hit on him," Becka said. "I asked him out and pretty much had to coerce him into saying yes."

"Obviously, we hit it off," Hank said. He reached out and took Becka's hand. "She turned out to be one of those women who becomes more beautiful with age."

Becka laughed and then closed her eyes, still smiling.

The three sat in companionable stoned silence until Norm nodded at Becka, who had fallen asleep. He stood, patted Hank on the shoulder, and left.

Hank sat for a few minutes, staring off into nothingness, and then picked up the wasting body of his wife in his arms and took her to bed.

Chapter 4

Hank stepped out of the embrace with Mai and noticed Tiffany and two other women staring at them from the hall near the elevator banks. He gave them just enough of a glare for them to move out of sight.

"There's a quiet bar around the corner where we can talk," he said to Mai. He looked at his watch, saw it was only 6:35, and realized that normal people probably hadn't eaten yet. "Have you had dinner? There's a little Italian joint nearby as well."

"I am a little bit hungry," Mai said. "I've been so nervous all day about coming to see you that I've eaten hardly anything."

Hank resisted the urge to ask how and why she had found him and instead asked, "Can we take your car? My keys are in the condo."

* * *

Less than five minutes after leaving Sunrise, Hank and Mai were seated in Luigi's Fine Italian Restaurant. The place was about half full. Most of the customers looked like Sunrise residents, out with visiting family members. The décor was a typical American version of Italian: checkered tablecloths, Chianti bottles as candleholders, pictures of Italy on the walls. In a nod to being so close to a retirement community, each table held a small flashlight.

Hank's mind had been spinning since he'd realized the beautiful Vietnamese woman waiting to see him was Mai. Mai, the only other woman he had ever loved. Mai, the lover he had abandoned in Vietnam.

Hank realized that Mai had put down her menu and was staring at him. He thought he detected a hint of a smile. He was about to say something when the college-age waiter appeared.

"Can I get you something to drink?"

Hank looked questioningly at Mai. "Wine?" he asked.

She nodded.

"Red okay?"

She nodded again.

"We'll have a bottle of the Gaja Barolo," he said to the waiter.

"Awesome. Do you want to order now, or shall I get the wine?"

Hank again looked to Mai.

She spoke for the first time since sitting down. "Let's take a minute with the wine first."

"Excellent," the waiter said.

There was a moment of awkward silence. It looked to Hank like Mai was going to say something, but he held up his hand to stop her. "Before you say anything, I want you to know that I *did* search for you. I tried every contact I still had to find you. But you'd left the apartment, and with all the confusion and turmoil, I just kept hitting dead ends." He paused, wondering if he sounded defensive and guilty—*knowing* he sounded defensive and guilty.

Mai shook her head slightly. Then her smile broadened, just a little. It was not a smile of hilarity; it looked to Hank to be a smile of understanding, almost of pardon. Or was that merely what he wanted to see?

"I know," Mai said. "The times were terrible. My friends told me to get away from the apartment in case the landlord told the authorities it had been rented by an American. The restaurant shut down, and we all dispersed into the city." She sighed, as if she didn't really want to remember those days. "After that first awful week, I knew you wouldn't be able to find me." She paused, studying him. "I'm not here for recriminations."

The young waiter reappeared and held out the bottle of wine for Hank to inspect. Hank barely glanced at it and nodded. No one spoke while the waiter went through the ritual of pouring a taste for Hank, who nodded again. The waiter poured the wine glasses too full, almost to the top, but Hank said nothing. He glanced at Mai, who raised an eyebrow in apparent amusement.

"Are we ready to order?" the waiter asked.

Without consulting Mai, Hank said, "Give us a minute, please."

Alone again, the two were silent as they clinked their glasses and took a sip of wine. There was no verbal toast. Hank didn't know what exactly would be the proper thing to toast.

"How'd you find me?" he finally asked.

This time Mai really did laugh. Her obvious amusement made her face look even younger and more beautiful. "I've pretty much known where you were since 1984."

Hank stared at her. "Huh?"

Mai took a sip of wine, the amused look still on her face. "Once I finally got to America and settled down and had made a little money, I decided to try to locate you. I knew you worked at the embassy when we were together, so I figured you worked for the State Department. I hired an investigator to look for you. But your name wasn't on any of the employment rosters at State, so I suggested to my investigator that maybe you were with the CIA." The slender fingers of Mai's right hand toyed with the wine glass while she spoke.

"How'd you make that leap?" Hank asked.

She laughed. "I may have been young and naïve, but I wasn't exactly stupid," she said in a light tone. "It didn't escape my attention that every time you came to the restaurant, you met with my boss, Nguyen, all secretive-like, before sitting down to eat and trying to pick me up. So when we found out you weren't a State Department employee, it wasn't a huge leap to think that maybe you were CIA." She paused again.

"In fact, when I think back on it, I probably should have started there. You were always overly secretive, even for those times. And on that last day, when you hurried into the restaurant with a gym bag for Nguyen and a paper bag full of money for me, had I been a little worldlier, it would have been totally obvious." She took a sip of wine, her eyes never leaving Hank's. "Once we made that assumption, it was pretty easy to confirm you worked for the CIA. My investigator was pretty good."

"Wow! So why didn't you contact me then?"

Mai set the wine glass down, and her look of amusement seemed to Hank to morph into a rueful, almost sad, smile.

"Because we also found out you'd married," she said. "I had no intention of ruining either your marriage or your career."

Hank didn't say anything for almost a minute. Mai gave him time.

The waiter reappeared. "Are we ready?"

Mai ordered the veal saltimbocca.

"Awesome choice." The waiter looked at Hank, who shook his head.

"Nothing for me."

When the waiter was gone, Hank said, "I want to hear everything—about your life and how you are. But let's start from the end first. Why are you here now?" He kept his voice gentle, knowing his words could be taken wrong, perhaps even seem accusatory.

At first it looked as if that was how Mai had taken his question. As her small smile faded and she broke eye contact, Hank thought she suddenly looked very sad.

"Because," she finally said, "I want you to help me find our son."

Chapter 5

Hank's cellphone rang almost as soon as he'd taken it off vibrate. He finished unlocking the door to his condo and went in before answering. The caller ID showed that it was Norm.

"Yo."

"You okay, buddy?" Norm asked. "You just kind of disappeared on us. You were last seen hugging some Asian woman."

Hank tossed his keys on the granite kitchen counter and opened the sliding glass door to the lanai. The cool air coming off the ocean felt good. "Jesus. The death farm's gossip machine is world-class. Come on down."

*   *   *

"I was sent to Vietnam toward the end of 1973," Hank said.

He and Norm sat side by side on the Brown Jordan couch on Hank's patio. Had it been daylight, they would have been looking out over the Laguna Hills to the Pacific. Now they were staring out into brilliant stars. The Sunrise complex was about halfway between Laguna Beach and Laguna Niguel. Los Angeles was to the north, San Diego to the south. South Laguna and Highway 1 were tucked below the sloping hillside, not visible from their vantage point.

"I was low man on the CIA totem pole in Saigon," Hank said. "I was only twenty-eight, and I didn't fit in well from the beginning. Maybe it was because I'd already come to agree with the demonstrations back home. The war was bullshit. We were accomplishing nothing but the systematic destruction of American and Vietnamese lives."

Norm snorted. "Kind of like Iraq, thirty years later. We always seem to learn so much from history."

Hank grunted as he got up and went into the living room. A moment later he came back with a box, which he held on his lap once he was reseated. He pulled out some rolling papers and a tin of marijuana and began rolling a joint.

"I met Mai when I was assigned to handle an older couple who owned a popular restaurant just off Tu Do Street. Restaurants and bars were excellent places to pick up information, and in exchange for nominal consideration, they passed on to me whatever they'd heard and thought was important. Mai worked as a cook and waitress in the restaurant." Hank lit the joint and took a deep hit.

For once, Norm kept silent and waited for Hank to continue.

"I was enamored of her almost from the first time I saw her. She was young—probably too young for me—and she was beautiful. It took a long time for me to get her to open up." Hank let out a big sigh, releasing residual smoke from his lungs in the process. "Turns out she was brilliant. She'd gone to private Catholic schools and spoke pretty fluent French and English, in addition to Vietnamese, of course. Her father had been a famous chef in Saigon, and they owned one of the top restaurants in the city, just around the corner from Lam Son Square."

"Then why was she working in the place where you met her?" Norm asked.

"Both her parents and a dozen customers were killed when the propane tanks in the restaurant kitchen blew up. Mai had been across the street, walking to the restaurant from school when it happened. She saw the explosions as first one tank and then another blew. The prevailing wisdom was that it wasn't an accident, that it was the doing of a Vietcong cell working within the city.

Among the customers killed were several high-ranking ARVN commanders who were regulars at the restaurant."

There was silence as Hank went to take a hit on the joint but then saw it had gone out. He dropped his hand.

"God, that must have been awful," Norm said. "To watch her parents get blown up."

Hank nodded. "The owners of the restaurant where I met Mai had been friends with her parents. They took her in and gave her a job." He pulled a hemostat from the box, clamped it onto the roach, and relit the joint.

"How long were you and Mai together?" Norm asked.

Hank took a pull on the joint and let the smoke sit in his lungs for some time before he breathed out, handed the makeshift roach clip to Norm, and answered, "A little over a year." He smiled and closed his eyes.

Neither man said anything for a full minute.

"The last time I saw Mai was April 29," Hank said. "It was 1975 and the day before the fall of Saigon." His mind wandered back to that day as he absently watched Norm take a hit. "Of course, most of us knew the end had come. General Thieu, the esteemed president, had already fled to Taiwan with a fortune in gold. Two days before, on April 27, General Duong Van Minh had been elected president by the National Assembly. His job was to negotiate some sort of peace." Hank snorted and took the proffered joint. He took a hit and gestured with the roach clip toward Norm. "Want more?"

Norm shook his head no.

"But of course, the North Vietnamese didn't need to negotiate anything. They knew they'd won. Our ambassador, Graham Martin, seemed like the only one in Saigon who thought there was still hope. Some of us thought he'd come unhinged." Hank rubbed his eyes. "But then again, he'd lost his son in the war, so I guess he didn't want to believe it was all for nothing.

"Anyway," he continued, "those last days were surreal, especially the last. We were abandoning the people we vowed never to abandon. We were saving the Vietnamese fat cats who'd done nothing but profit from the war. It was despicable and sad and funny all at the same time. As people saw the writing on the wall, and learned that the airport runway had been bombed, making the airport unusable, the crowd outside the embassy gates swelled into a mob. Those with credentials to get out of the country waved their papers in the air, trying to get the guards to let them in. The monsoon rains had come, so the skies were dark, and there were times we couldn't differentiate between thunder and shelling." Hank coughed, ran his right hand through his hair, and turned his head toward Norm.

"It must have been terrible," Norm said.

"We'd opened the safes in the embassy, and several other CIA agents and I grabbed bundles of money to take to our informants who didn't have enough status to be evacuated. The least we could do was to get them some bribe money. There were millions in the safes. We were damned if we were going to leave it for the Cong. I filled a gym bag with fifty thousand for Nguyen and his wife, and then I stuffed an extra twenty grand in a sack for Mai. Then I slipped out a side gate and went to see Mai for the last time."

A siren in the distance sounded like it was coming up the canyon from Highway 1. The two men were silent. Generally ambulances coming to the ritzy Sunrise Adult Community turned off their sirens before they got to the complex. There was no point in scaring the crops of the death farm. But this siren continued on, heading past the Sunrise entrance.

Hank sighed heavily. "The restaurant was less than a mile from the embassy, but it was the longest walk of my life. People roamed the streets, some running with bundles of possessions, some walking aimlessly, as if in a stupor. I walked by a mangled bicycle with a leg stuck in it. It hadn't been there long, but there was no body to go with the leg.

"Parts of the city were burning. There was smoke everywhere, but it looked like the Chinese section along the river—Cholon, I think it was called—was totally on fire. ARVN deserters looked mean and angry, and some were obviously drunk. I took detours to avoid them whenever I could. I knew they felt betrayed. Non-Vietnamese civilians had been told that a code to evacuate would come on American Forces Radio when the time came. An announcer would say, "The temperature is 105 degrees and rising," followed by eight bars of "White Christmas." Hank shook his head in amazement.

"Outside the restaurant where Mai worked, there was a young woman sitting on the sidewalk. I recognized her from a nearby bar popular with American servicemen. She wore a tight miniskirt that had bunched up almost to her waist, a torn silk blouse, and platform shoes. Mascara ran down her face. Her knees were bloody. I assumed she'd been running to somewhere and had fallen. I knelt down and asked if she needed help, but she just looked at me with dead eyes and said nothing. I left her there."

"Gimme that roach," Norm said in a low, sad voice.

Hank handed the roach clip and lighter to Norm. "I didn't have much time to spend with Mai when I finally got to her. Nguyen and his wife looked scared to death, but they were happy to see the money I'd brought. Mai was oddly composed." Hank stopped for a moment.

"God, she was amazing. We were in love; we'd made that clear to each other. We'd talked of a future. But in those moments, standing close in that small and empty restaurant with the sounds of chaos around us, we both knew the chances of seeing each other again were slim. She didn't cry or cling or beg to go with me. She understood everything, probably even better than me." Hank stopped talking again and breathed in the night air.

Norm took another hit.

"The next day, during the evacuation, we were literally burning money in the rooftop incinerator," Hank said with a wan smile. "Some of it blew away and rained down on the people below, waiting for the next chopper. I was pissed. I should have taken more money to give Mai." Hank looked down at his hands, which he had unconsciously clenched. "I never saw her again. . .until tonight, when she told me we have a son who's gone missing."

"Jesus," Norm whispered. "You tried to find her, I assume?"

Hank nodded slightly. "Yeah, but I've asked myself a million times how hard I really tried. Which, I should add, means I probably didn't try hard enough. Once I started falling in love with Becka, I convinced myself I'd done everything I could."

Norm grunted but said nothing. A slight offshore wind had picked up, making the night air cold. Hank picked up the box of marijuana and paraphernalia, and with his usual old-man grunt, got up and walked into the condo. Norm followed, sliding the glass door closed behind him. The condo was large, an exact footprint of Norm's, two floors up. The open-plan kitchen, dining area, and living room had cream-colored tile flooring with a huge Persian rug under the light-gray leather couch and chrome-and-glass coffee table.

Norm flicked on the kitchen light and got a glass of water. "And she came to see you forty years later to tell you that you had a son? What does she want, money? How'd you leave it with her?"

Hank plopped himself down on the couch and put his feet up on the coffee table. "She's staying at the Laguna Niguel Ritz-Carlton. We're going to meet for breakfast."

Norm snorted. "The Ritz-Carlton? She's got money?"

"Supposedly, she's quite rich," Hank said. "I haven't gotten the whole story yet."

Norm filled a glass with water and took it to Hank.

"Thanks." Hank drank and set the glass down as Norm perched on a barstool. "Frankly, I kind of spaced out after she told me we had a kid, so I don't remember all the details after that. I finally told her I needed to go home and digest everything and that it would be best to meet again tomorrow."

Norm was quiet for a long moment. Then he said, "Okay, Pops, I'll let you get your beauty rest. Give me a shout when you get back tomorrow so I can hear the exciting conclusion of this reunion."

Chapter 6

The king-size Tempur-Pedic bed felt more huge and lonely than at any time since Becka's death. Even when she had no more physical substance than a twig without leaves, Hank had always felt comforted by her presence—by her very existence. When he lost her, when he knew he would never again be soothed by the knowledge that she was near, he'd allowed himself a period of grief before steeling himself against the reality of his new world. He smoked her leftover weed, occasionally took one of her leftover sedatives, and was slowly progressing in learning how to exist without her.

But tonight was different. As he lay in bed, he couldn't help thinking about Mai when they'd been together. He could still picture her lithe, alabaster body with the smallish breasts. When she became sexually excited, her nipples would harden and drive him mad with desire. They would make love in the apartment he rented for her in Saigon, and eventually the ceiling fan would no longer keep them cool. He would begin to sweat and she would begin to glisten, and for some moments there was no war, no fear of the future—only the two of them, joined in a union that felt, at least at that moment, as if it would last forever.

Hank felt himself get hard, and he put his hand on his penis. It had been a long time since he'd had a hard-on, let alone an ejaculation. For a moment he thought about masturbating, but just as quickly, a feeling of guilt washed over him, and he went flaccid.

He turned onto his side so that he faced Becka's side of the bed. Empty, of course. He tried to picture Becka healthy and still sexy, but the only image that would come was the Becka who was dying, decaying into nothingness.

Hank threw the covers off and climbed out of bed. In the kitchen he turned on the overhead light, got a glass of water, and sat on a barstool at the counter. He thought about taking a sleeping pill, but decided not to. Sleeping pills usually made him fuzzy-headed in the morning. The whole thing with Mai was weird enough as it was. He wanted whatever wits he still had for the breakfast meeting.

The kitchen light created a reflection on the sliding glass door to the patio, so all Hank could see was himself, wearing his old pajama bottoms. Would they be the last he ever bought? He wore no shirt, and his hair was disheveled and wild. He was slumped over, and he looked old.

A wave of despair washed over him. He sat up straight, ran a hand through his hair, and turned from the window. He felt as if his life had just been turned upside down. He had a son. What the fuck?

He took another sip of water, turned off the light, and went back to bed.

He thought about Mai again. When they had made love for the first time, she had cried out in pain and there was blood on the sheets. The realization of what an asshole he was had hit him like a blow to the chest. He liked to think of himself as a sensitive, good man, so unlike many of his colleagues who seemed to treat Saigon as their personal playground and the Vietnamese women as their sex toys. He cared about Mai although he was not yet in love with her.

Despite her young age, it had never occurred to him that she was still a virgin. He'd completely failed to differentiate her in his mind from the young barmaids who gave themselves, for whatever reason—money, marital hopes, whatever—to American men. It wasn't that he thought of Mai as a whore. It was more that he hadn't thought of her as something other than a whore, someone with a girl-next-door kind of image. The knowledge that he'd been so self-absorbed, stupid, and racist shocked him.

He didn't let on that he'd been surprised at Mai's virginity, and he hoped the enormity of the event from her perspective camouflaged both his being so taken aback and his shameful attitude.

In the end, Mai never let on that Hank had been anything less than a gentlemanly first-time lover, and he regarded his disgust at his own failings as an epiphany of sorts. So many of his American comrades, black and white, referred to the Vietnamese, even their allies, as "gooks" and "slants" that the effect—presumably intended—was to dehumanize and vilify them, thus making it that much easier to kill them and destroy their culture. Hank vowed never to fall prey to such ignorance and prejudice, and for the most part, he'd held up his side of that personal bargain.

As time passed, and as their lovemaking became more tender and they opened their hearts to each other, Hank and Mai fell in love.

Hank rolled over again, facing Becka's side of the bed. Had he known about the child, he would have moved heaven and earth to find Mai, and that would have been his family. But if he'd found her, there would have been no Becka in his life.

He closed his eyes and did some breathing exercises. Eventually, he fell asleep.

Chapter 7

Hank met Mai for breakfast at the Laguna Niguel Ritz-Carlton. She was already seated at a table with sweeping views of the Pacific Ocean when the maître d' escorted Hank to join her. She stood and they exchanged cheek kisses. Hank noticed that although she still looked young and beautiful, in the light of day, he could see a few more wrinkles and signs of age, and even a few rogue gray hairs. For some inexplicable reason, this cheered him up.

Mai wore tight-fitting blue jeans and a red silk blouse with the sleeves rolled up. Hank couldn't help noticing that it clung to her in all the right places.

They sat, and a waiter appeared almost immediately. Hank ordered black coffee.

"You okay?" Mai asked. "You look like maybe you didn't get a great night's sleep." She took a sip of her coffee and lowered her eyes. "I'm sorry to have sprung this on you, but there wasn't any easy way."

Hank was about to answer when the waiter reappeared, placed a cup in front of him, and poured the coffee. "I'll give you a minute," he said.

When the waiter left, Hank picked up his cup and took a sip. "That's okay. It brought some excitement to an otherwise boring day." He'd meant it to be funny, but instead he thought it sounded flippant, dismissive even. He tried to recover by asking a question. "So, what's your. . .*our* son's name?"

Mai's expression changed, subtly but noticeably. She suddenly looked abashed. "I gave him your name. He was born at Clark

Air Force Base in the Philippines, and I wanted him to have an American name."

Hank blinked. "You named him Henry Reagan Jr.?"

Mai's face changed back to her good-natured look. She even gave Hank a small smile. "My English was good, if you recall, but I wasn't exactly Americanized. I didn't know Hank was a nickname for Henry." She paused, and this time Hank thought her smile looked kind of self-deprecating. "And I didn't know how to spell Reagan. I'm afraid I spelled it phonetically. So his name is Hank Raygun." She spelled the last name.

Hank laughed out loud, almost spitting out some coffee.

"It's pretty funny, but what did I know?" She looked amused. "He hated that name. He took a lot of grief in school for having such a gringo name—and a misspelled one at that."

"Gringo?"

"Sorry," Mai said. "Force of habit. My best friend is a Latina woman, and we fell into a habit of calling white people gringos."

Hank chuckled. Just another thing to love about America, he thought. "So how'd he go missing?" he asked. "It shouldn't be hard to find someone with that name."

Mai's smile faded again, and she looked down at her coffee cup. "I'm assuming he changed his name soon after leaving home when he was eighteen. I have no idea what his name is now. All I know is that Hank Raygun no longer seems to exist."

Chapter 8

Mai brought Hank up to date. With the help of the $20,000 he had given her, she and the unborn Hank had made their way to the Mekong Delta, then to Cambodia and Thailand. Like so many Vietnamese refugees, she was eventually transported to Clark AFB in the Philippines for processing where, almost immediately upon arrival, Hank Jr. was born. After a long and arduous process, they ended up in Seattle, but Mai hated the wet, cold, dreary days of her first winter there. As soon as she had enough money, she moved them to Los Angeles.

"We moved around quite a bit in the early years," Mai told Hank. "I took whatever jobs I could find in restaurants, mostly washing dishes. Early on, I tended to stay close to the cluster of Vietnamese immigrants, but as Hank got older, I became more and more concerned about his education. I wanted him to grow up as an American. So I forced myself away from the security of my compatriots and focused on finding an area diverse enough so we wouldn't stand out as being different, but close enough to upper-middle-class areas where the schools tended to be better." Mai looked off toward the ocean.

Hank said nothing, giving her time and space to remember.

"We ended up in Pasadena," Mai eventually said. "East Pasadena, to be precise. Lots of Hispanic people, but also quite a few Asians and working-class whites. I took a job as a prep chef at a Mexican restaurant. By then Hank was just starting junior high school, seventh grade. The Pasadena school system was great. It was a real melting pot. Mostly excellent teachers. We rented a small bungalow near where I worked. It was our first actual house with a yard." A small smile played on her lips. "Good times.

"The restaurant was owned by a woman named Eva Ochoa. She'd taken it over after her husband died and turned it into a hugely popular place. Even the rich people from Pasadena and San Marino came for authentic Mexican food. Eva and I became friends, and I worked my way up to chef." Mai laughed. Her eyes sparkled with humor. "I loved the reaction I got from people when I told them I was a chef at a Mexican restaurant." She looked into Hank's eyes. "I still make a mean goat cheese and chicken enchilada, if you're ever interested."

"Say the word and I'm there." Hank wondered if there were more to the invitation than dinner, but then rebuked himself for being presumptuous.

Neither said anything for a few moments.

"Anyway," Mai said, "one day when Eva and I were sitting in her backyard drinking tequila, I confessed to her my dream of opening my own restaurant. Over the next few months, we kicked around some ideas and eventually Eva proposed financing me. We leased a small space on Colorado Boulevard, a good location, and I opened a noodle shop. Pho was just catching on in America, and the timing was perfect. Hank worked for me after school and during the summers, and he seemed mostly happy." Mai picked up her fork and absently twirled it in her fingers.

"By the time he graduated from Pasadena High School, I had ten locations around Pasadena, South Pasadena, and Burbank. I'd bought a home. Hank had lots of friends and was talking about going to Cal Berkeley. He seemed so happy and well adjusted." She paused and sniffed. "Or at least, that's the illusion I'd created for him." Mai sighed heavily and looked down at her empty coffee cup.

Hank signaled the waiter.

Neither said anything while he refilled their cups.

"Have you eaten?" Hank asked Mai.

"No, I was waiting for you," she said.

Hank looked at the young waiter. "I'll have the lox and bagel plate."

"I'll have the same," Mai said. When she looked back at Hank, her eyes were wet with tears. "I had no idea anything was wrong with him. Maybe I was working too hard and not spending enough time with him. Maybe he blamed me for his not having a father." She shook her head. "I just don't know. He never seemed angry about anything except his 'stupid' name." She made air quotes with her fingers. "He'd been accepted at Berkeley, but the day after graduation, he disappeared. He left no note. He took some of his clothes and personal effects. He had his own bank account, and it had been emptied."

Hank sat back in his chair and stared out at the view, saying nothing. His son would be over forty years old, a grown man, a life half-lived. He looked around the resort restaurant. It seemed as if most of the guests were in their thirties and forties, probably sales types on some kind of reward boondoggle from their companies. He watched their body language, listened to the patterns of their banter. He knew these young bucks considered themselves the chosen ones, the young princes of a kingdom of money. It wouldn't have occurred to them that one day they'd be the old guy sitting nearby.

It hadn't been so long ago that he'd been there, part of the great American enterprise. After he left the CIA, he started his own security company and ultimately grew it into an empire of sorts. He'd made millions, and had also made lots of other people rich along the way.

Now he lived in a stylish death farm, complete with all the amenities designed to lull him into believing he was still vital, that he still had a life to live.

To his left, a table of six young couples erupted into laughter. He felt a rush of irrelevancy. After a minute, he turned back to Mai. "And your investigator, the one who was able to find me— he couldn't find him? Even back before the trail turned cold?"

Mai shook her head. "I can give you what little he turned up, but the short answer is that he just kept running into dead ends until there simply weren't any leads to follow. Of course, the technology then was considerably less sophisticated. It's like Hank Jr. vanished into thin air."

Hank scratched his chin. "When did you give up looking?"

"After about two years, Pete, the investigator, told me it was useless to keep on."

The waiter appeared and placed their plates in front of them.

Hank picked up a bagel and began smearing it with cream cheese. "Obviously Hank would be able to find you if he wanted to." It sounded harsher than he meant it to be.

Mai hadn't touched her food, and now she looked away.

"I'm sorry," Hank said. "All I meant was to confirm that you were still in the phone book, or that you still owned the restaurant."

Still staring off into the distance, Mai nodded slightly before turning back to him. Her face was tight, controlled. "That's what kills me the most. God knows I've tried to just let him go, to tell myself that he hates me and doesn't want anything to do with me. I've tried to hate him for hating me. I've tried to write him off and forget him."

She leaned forward toward Hank, her arms on the table, straddling her breakfast plate. "He knows where I am. I own over sixty restaurants in five states. He's always known how to find me."

Chapter 9

Mai walked through the large sliding door from the kitchen of her loft condo into Eva Ochoa's identical kitchen in her identical loft condo. Mai wore silk pajamas with an oriental-print silk robe. Eva, in a long, flared denim dress and old denim work shirt, stood at the counter, chopping *serrano* chiles.

At two years older than Mai, Eva's light brown face showed few lines. Hispanic with a hint of Native American, her face had high cheekbones and a soft nose. Her dark, curly hair fell to her shoulders.

"How'd it go?" Eva asked.

They kissed on the lips.

Mai poured herself a cup of coffee. "Pretty good. Pretty strange." She sat on a stool at the kitchen counter and sipped the steaming coffee.

"He gonna do it?" Eva asked. She continued chopping, her back to Mai.

"I think so. He's thinking about it, I guess. He was pretty blown away."

Mai could see Eva's body move in a silent laugh. Her hips and her butt had recently expanded to the point where she'd proclaimed herself officially "pant-free" and traded in her jeans and slacks for long, flared skirts.

"I would think so." She resumed chopping. "So how's he look?"

Mai chuckled. "You mean do I still find him attractive?"

Eva didn't answer right away. She scraped the chopped peppers into a bowl in which she had already cracked three eggs. She beat the mixture with a fork and poured it into a frying pan. "Yeah, I guess," she said, slowly stirring the mixture.

"You getting jealous on me? You're the one who up and married Nick the Dick."

Eva harrumphed. "That *pinche cabrón*."

Mai laughed out loud. "He may have been a fucking asshole, but he was *your* fucking asshole."

"Don't change the subject," Eva said. "You still have feelings for him?" She continued to mix the eggs in the pan and didn't turn around, but Mai could see the slight tightening of her body, the small hunch of her shoulders. Mai let out a quiet sigh.

They weren't supposed to be like this. The two women were best friends and lovers of convenience. Whenever a man came into one of their lives, it was accepted without comment, and the connecting door to their condos would close.

But Mai understood. As time passed, with fewer and fewer men coming into either of their lives, with the door now left open most of the time, it was only natural that one or both of them would fall prey to the jealousy they'd vowed to avoid. Now a new man in one of their lives might be seen as a threat to the comfortable rhythm of their own relationship.

Mai got off the stool and walked over to Eva. She put her hands on her friend's shoulders and leaned in and kissed her head. She felt Eva relax slightly, and after a moment, Eva put down the knife and turned to put her arms around Mai. They hugged and kissed.

"*Lo siento*," Eva said.

"Don't be sorry." Mai brushed back some hair from Eva's face. "I'm not doing this to get back with Hank. I'm doing this as one last shot at finding Hank Jr." She paused and then stepped back. "But yes, old Hank is still pretty damn good-looking." She smiled broadly.

Eva picked up a dish towel and threw it at Mai. "*Puta*."

Mai laughed again. "I may be a whore, but I'm *your* whore."

Chapter 10

"**S**o, you gonna do it?" Norm asked.

The two were walking up the ninth fairway on a cool, cloudless day. Hank was only two over par, and although they'd planned on only playing nine holes, he was tempted to play another nine and try to shoot his age. But he could see Norm was dragging.

"What else have I got to do?" he answered. He pulled an eight iron and hit a fine second shot to the green. Then he waited as Norm shanked his third shot far short and right of the green.

"Good point," Norm said. "The question is whether you'll be doing it to find your son or whether you'll be doing it to get close to Mai again." He paused. "Or both."

Hank didn't answer, and they finished the hole without talking. Hank made an easy par, and Norm made an easier triple bogey.

"Let's get a beer," Norm suggested. "I earned it."

A few minutes later, the two men sat at the grill overlooking the eighteenth hole, which was guarded by a large lake with a spewing fountain in the middle.

"I mean," Norm said, "is there really anything you can do that her private investigator couldn't do twenty years ago?"

Hank took a sip of bourbon and shook his head. "I doubt it. Contrary to what we see in the movies, it isn't all that hard to disappear if you're willing to completely cut yourself off from your prior life. New name. No credit cards. No bank accounts. Low profile."

"What year did he disappear?" Norm asked. "It had to have been in the nineties, yes?"

Hank nodded. "He'd just turned eighteen, so that would have been 1993."

"So before cellphones were commonplace." Norm sipped his beer.

"All I've got to go on is the work Mai's original investigator did. That and a twenty-three-year-old photo."

"Does he look like you?" Norm asked.

Hank shook his head. "I don't see it."

They watched a foursome hit their shots to the eighteenth green. One of the golfers was Roger Aikens, the cheater Hank had banned from his group. Hank smiled when Roger's ball sailed into the lake.

"Let me ask you this," Norm said, "and I don't mean any offense. But do you really want to find this guy? I mean, it's not like you'll have anything in common. He's obviously a dick for running out on his mother. What're you gonna do, find him and play catch with him like a good father?"

Hank laughed. "Maybe he likes golf."

"Yeah, sure. More likely he's a down-and-out dope fiend."

"So maybe he'll know where we can score some good shit," Hank said. He was still smiling, but Norm had hit on the issue Hank had been grappling with since his breakfast with Mai. Did he really give a shit about finding this probable creep? Did he really care about having some grown man in his life who was bonded to him only by genetics?

The answer, he knew, was that he owed it to Mai to try to help her. Hell, he thought, maybe he owed it to the kid. Maybe Junior's disappearance had something to do with not knowing his father. The least he could do was try to find out.

And, he thought, as he'd said to Norm, *what else do I have to do?*

"Let's go smoke a doobie," Hank said.

*   *   *

Twenty minutes later, Hank and Norm were sitting on Hank's patio, stoned into silence.

"I tell you what," Hank said after a lengthy period of thought. "We hate it here anyway, so let's hit the road and see if we can find the little shit." He paused. "Hell, we can buy one of those cool Mercedes vans so we can sleep anywhere we want."

"With a flat-screen TV?" Norm asked.

"Fuck, yeah."

"And built in Wi-Fi?"

"Absolutely."

"Can we get a dog, so it'll be like Steinbeck's *Travels with Charley?*"

Hank choked on the hit he'd been taking. He coughed and laughed until Norm had to pound his back. "Why the fuck not?" he finally croaked.

Chapter 11

Three days later, Hank and Norm sat at the counter in Mai's kitchen. The sliding door to Eva's kitchen was closed. Spread out on the counter were several photos of Hank Jr. and twenty-something-year-old typewritten reports from Mai's private detective.

"Handsome kid," Norm said. "Obviously he got his looks from his mother."

"Ha, ha," Hank uttered. He had been studying one of the earliest reports. Mai had waited almost six months after Hank Jr. disappeared before resorting to a private investigator. She'd filed a missing-person report with the police before that, but nothing had come of it.

Mai was standing at the counter, spreading Brie on baguette slices. She wore jeans and an oversized blue work shirt, the sleeves rolled up.

Hank wondered if the shirt had belonged to one of Mai's lovers.

"He was a great-looking kid," Mai said. "I think he's probably a great-looking man."

Assuming he's still alive.

No one said it, but they all thought it.

"It says here Hank Jr. was—" Hank paused. "I'm just going to call him Junior from now on if that's all right."

Mai nodded.

"So, it says here he was believed to have run away with a female classmate named Dana Clark. Your PI said she was some kind of fanatical born-again Christian." Hank looked at Mai. "Was he into religion?"

Mai shook her head. "We never went to church or even talked about God or religion. I had no idea."

"Well," Norm said dryly, "chicks can make a guy believe in just about anything. Especially at that age."

Mai seemed to grunt an acknowledgement. She placed a platter of bread and cheese in front of the two men and then picked up the bottle of Chianti they'd been drinking and wiggled it slightly in the air. Both men held their glasses out to her.

"Did the private eye know where the kids went?" Norm asked.

"Apparently they went to a Christian retreat up in Northern California," Mai said. "It was a place run by a guy called Pastor Glen. By the time Pete, the PI, got there, Hank was gone. Dana was still there, but she claimed she had no idea where Hank had gone." Mai took a sip of wine. "That was the last confirmed sighting." She gestured at the reports littering the counter. "After that, there were only unconfirmed sightings and rumors."

Hank put down a report he'd been reading and grunted. "Yeah. Mostly worthless. We're pretty much going to have to start from scratch."

Norm rubbed his chin. He'd been a real estate developer, not an ex-CIA security consultant like Hank. "How do you start from scratch from twenty years ago?"

"Slowly and optimistically," Hank said.

Mai looked at Norm. "So, Norm, you going to be Hank's assistant?" A mischievous smile played at her lips.

"Ha," Norm said. "More like his sidekick."

"Won't they miss you boys at the home?" she asked in a playful tone.

Hank laughed. "I think Norm needs a break from all the women who've been chasing him."

Mai switched her gaze to Hank. Her eyes sparkled. "Not you?"

"Too soon for them to have descended on me," Hank said. "There've been a few test forays from some of the more bodacious babes, but mostly there's some kind of unspoken time frame before a new widower becomes fair game. It's a good time for me to take my leave." Hank looked around the kitchen, taking in the eight-burner Viking range and the oversized Sub-Zero refrigerator. "Quite a place you have." He nodded toward the closed sliding door. "Where does that go?"

Mai glanced reflexively at the door. "That connects to my best friend and business partner's condo. Eva Ochoa. I told you about her."

There was something in her tone that seemed a little off to Hank—wary, almost. But it was too faint for him to dwell on for more than a couple of seconds. Mai was offering to show him and Norm the rest of her condo.

As they followed her around the unit, Mai explained that the old brick building had once housed several small manufacturing businesses. The developer kept the brick walls exposed but had gutted the building. There were only two floors, with two units on each floor. Mai's three-bedroom, three-bath condo had just over three thousand square feet.

"All four units have the exact same floor plan," Mai said. They walked from the kitchen into the open-plan living area, which was beautifully furnished with beige leather couches and chairs, Asian rugs, and hardwood tables. The walls were painted a soft white, with pin-spot lighting on the various works of art. On one shelf, there were four Thai puppets on stands that looked like antiques to Hank. On another shelf were several Oriental vases.

It was a formal room, but it was adjoined by a warm, cozy room with slightly darker and heavier furniture in which the center of attention was a sixty-inch television. "This is where I spend most of my time when I'm not in the kitchen," Mai said.

"I can see why." Norm ran a hand across the soft leather couch that faced the TV.

"Do the other two units connect to each other as well?" Hank asked.

"No," Mai replied. "We put that in. We spend so much time together, cooking and watching TV mostly, that we thought it'd be fun to have the units joined. Whenever one of us wants privacy, we just close the door. We'll put the wall back when one of us sells." She led them out of the room. "These are the bedrooms."

*   *   *

Two hours later, Hank and Norm were in Burbank, inspecting a Mercedes Sprinter. Although built on a van chassis, it was best described as a small RV. It was fully loaded with a small kitchen, two single beds, a pull-down dining table flanked by two black leather chairs, and, Norm was happy to point out, a flat-screen TV.

"I love the pull-out awning so we can sit in the shade and have cocktails," Hank said.

"Why do I get the feeling that this search for your son is really just an excuse to hit the road?" Norm asked, stepping out through the van's side door.

Hank smiled a sheepish kind of smile and shrugged. He didn't answer the question. Instead, he asked, "What do you think? Should I buy it?"

"It's over a hundred grand," Norm said.

Hank looked around. The salesman was out of earshot. "So what? We're fucking millionaires."

Norm laughed. "And old. Good point."

It took an hour to complete the purchase ritual, part of which was spent not listening to the manager go through his requisite spiel in which he tried to sell Hank various extras and extended warranties. He rebuffed Hank's attempts to cut him off, saying he was required by the dealer to stick to the protocol.

"I'll be lucky to outlive the factory warranty," Hank said as he initialed all the boxes declining the extra coverage.

"I'm younger than you," Norm said. "Can I have the van when you kick?"

"Fuck you."

Chapter 12

Pastor Glen's Christian Colony, as he called it, was located in a sparsely populated wooded area just outside Eureka, in the northernmost part of California. Hank drove his new van down a heavily rutted dirt road.

"You're getting the van all dirty," Norm said.

"What's a little dirt when you're about to meet a true man of God?" Hank replied. "According to his website, Pastor Glen is Jesus Christ's little brother, whose assignment here on Earth is to decide if God should give up on us humans and simply destroy the planet, or if he should give us another chance and just wipe out some of us in another flood or something."

"Damn," Norm said. "That's heavy. I wonder which way Pastor Glen is leaning."

"Don't know, so I reckon it'd be wise not to piss him off," Hank said.

Norm snorted. "You mean the fate of the world could rest in my hands?"

Hank didn't answer. He pulled the van up to a long, dilapidated wood-frame building. It had once been painted white, but now most of the paint was peeling off, and the exposed wood was dark with dirt and mold. The roof was a sun-faded green metal. The face of the building had large, filthy windows that ran its length on each side of the double front door. Over the door was an expensive-looking metal sign: *Welcome to Christian Colony.*

The building faced a central courtyard of packed dirt. Off to each side, forming a U with the main building as the base, were two other buildings in the same rundown state. Those had curtains in the windows. Hank saw children's faces peering out from the sides of the curtains in two of the six windows.

"You'd think God would give his second son a better allowance," Norm said.

Hank ignored him and got out of the van just as the front door opened and a rail-thin man in dirty jeans and a sweat-stained T-shirt stepped onto the porch. He was bald, with age spots dotting his scalp like countries on a map. Hank couldn't tell how old he was; he could have been a very old-looking sixty or just a pretty old-looking seventy.

Hank walked up to the porch and extended his right hand. "Hi there. I'm looking for Pastor Glen."

The old man stepped forward and shook Hank's hand. "That's me, in all my glory." He smiled, exposing a mouth full of mostly silver teeth and discolored gums.

Hank could smell the sickening musk of body odor. He wanted to step back, but he forced himself to hold his ground. He nodded back toward Norm, who was standing by the van. "That's Norm Rothstein. I'm Hank Reagan."

Pastor Glen released Hank's hand and then squinted toward Norm. "He a Jew? He's got a Jewish name."

"I think his lineage is Jewish," Hank said. "But as far as I know, he's not a practicing Jew." He paused for a beat. "If that matters."

Pastor Glen cackled a creepy kind of laugh. "Don't matter whether he's practicing or not. A Jew's a Jew, and it was the Jews that killed my big brother."

Hank wasn't sure how to respond to that. He looked around at the pitiful buildings. Old-growth pine trees surrounded the compound. Their beauty made the shabbiness of the Christian Colony all the more pronounced.

"What can I do for you?" asked Pastor Glen. "I'm thinking you're not here to worship with us."

Hank smiled. He hoped Pastor Glen would take it as a friendly smile. "Actually, we're looking for someone named Dana Clark. Do you know her?"

It was only now that Hank saw the intensity in Pastor Glen's bright green eyes. Moments ago, Hank would have sworn they were gray. Now they bore into him with an unsettling fierceness.

"What do you want with Dana?" asked the pastor.

"Does that mean she's here?"

"Answer my question." The pastor's tone had turned hard. His eyes were like lasers.

Hank wanted to turn away, but he couldn't. "We're looking for a man she ran off with from Los Angeles back in 1993. They were kids then. I'd like to talk to her if she's here and see if maybe I can figure out where he might have gone." Hank felt as if he were talking too fast, as if he'd been called on the carpet and now needed to justify something. This stinky old man had made him feel like a child.

Pastor Glen maintained his stare, saying nothing.

Hank wanted to stop talking, but he found himself explaining that the man they were looking for was his son, whom he'd never met. Why was he telling the old guy all this?

When Hank was finally done talking, Pastor Glen turned toward the building and gestured with his hand. Hank and Norm started to follow, but without turning around, Pastor Glen held up his right hand. "Just you. Not the Jew."

Hank looked back at Norm, who merely smiled and climbed back in the van. Hank followed the man who claimed to be Jesus Christ's younger brother.

Chapter 13

The double doors, only one of which worked, opened into a church. As he entered, Hank stopped, struck by the sight.

The pews, of which there were about twenty, were a dark hardwood, polished to a beautiful sheen. Smooth, cream-colored tile covered the floor. The altar was draped in beautiful fabrics, trimmed with what looked like hand-sewn gold crosses. On the altar stood two silver chalices and a gold cross. Attached to the wall above the altar was a large crucifix, intricately carved out of wood. A spotlight shone directly onto Jesus's face, which was both beautiful and anguished. A tear fell from his right eye.

Hank stood still, taking it all in, trying to process the disconnect between the ramshackle buildings, the filthy, smelly pastor, and the magnificence of the small church.

Pastor Glen had stopped as well and was watching Hank with a kind of "What did you expect?" smirk. "Come this way," he said after a minute.

Hank followed Pastor Glen across the church and through a door opposite the entry doors. There was no opulence to this next room, a large multipurpose space with a few tables and chairs, and toys stacked along one wall. A wooden credenza along another wall held an old-fashioned coffee percolator.

Pastor Glen gestured toward it. "Coffee?"

Hank nodded.

"Take a seat," the pastor said, pointing to one of the tables. He poured two cups of coffee, set them on the table, and sat down across from Hank. The cups were stained, cafeteria-style porcelain. "So," he said, "what exactly do you want with Dana?"

Hank explained again that he wanted to see if she might have any clues as to where Hank Jr. would have gone when he left the Christian Colony.

"You know there was some guy claimed he was a private investigator who came around asking questions not long after the kid was here. I'm guessing he never found him."

Hank nodded. He held the coffee cup in both hands, close to his nose, trying to block out the pastor's awful body odor. "Yeah. I have his report, and no, he didn't find him. Do you remember the boy?"

Pastor Glen scratched his left armpit and bobbed his head. "Long time ago, but yeah, I remember. There were lots of kids coming through here back in those days." His bright, intense eyes sparkled. "There was a lot going on in the eighties and early nineties. Lots of hijackings and kidnappings and bombings. Mostly Palestinians, I think. Wasn't the first attack on the World Trade Center that same year the kid came here? 1993?"

Hank felt discombobulated, off-balance. The pastor's speaking voice was deep and resonant, and obviously his memory was excellent. Hank nodded. "Yes, it was 1993."

Pastor Glen licked his lips. "Course there's a lot going on now, but I don't think people are searching for the true word of God like they used to. Nobody cares that I'm the true second son of God. Nobody cares that God sent me to decide the fate of the planet and every living thing on it. Now the so-called evangelicals just want to go to megachurches and listen to a bunch of tripe from slick-looking snake-oil salesmen who tell them the more they donate to the church, the richer they'll become." Small dots of white saliva gathered in the corners of his mouth.

"Tell me what you remember about the kid," Hank said.

Pastor Glen focused his powerful gaze on Hank, not saying anything for a moment. Then he blinked, as if he had just comprehended what the question was. "He was different from a lot of the kids. I mean, besides the fact that he was only part white. He was pretty tall for being part Asian. Good-looking boy. He was only here a day or two. He seemed smart enough, but he also had an edge to him, something I couldn't figure out. He had a scared look to him, you know, like a deer caught in the headlights."

"Did Dana ever tell you what he was scared of?" Hank asked.

"No. She didn't seem to want to talk about him once he bugged out on her. I didn't press. She wanted to find the way of the Lord, and I was happy to oblige."

Hank didn't ask what that meant.

"Since then, I've pretty much restricted my congregation to white people," Pastor Glen continued. "They're God's true children."

"Uh-huh," Hank said. He wished Norm were with him. "Do you remember what name the kid was using?"

Pastor Glen scrunched up his craggy face. He absently rubbed his upper gums with his right index finger.

Hank looked away. He thought he heard a television in another room.

"Joe. I think it was Joe." Pastor Glen got up. "I'll see if Dana wants to talk to you." He turned and left the room through a side door.

Hank took a sip of the coffee. It wasn't bad. He noticed a blackboard on the wall by the credenza and got up and walked over to it. "At the behest of God, the fate of the world is now in my hands" was written in beautiful cursive chalk. Underneath the sentence were the initials *PG*.

A door opened behind him. He turned to see Pastor Glen enter, followed by a middle-age woman. Hank walked back to his seat at the table.

Pastor Glen introduced the woman as Dana Clark. She nodded and sat down. The pastor excused himself and left the room.

Hank studied her for a moment. She had greasy-looking, shoulder-length hair with traces of blond, but most of the hair had turned gray. Her face looked bloated, her skin blotchy. Her eyes were a dull blue. She wore a plain brown dress that buttoned down the front. She had huge breasts, which, from Hank's quick glance, hung heavy and low. She might have been pretty a quarter-century ago, but now she was worn down and tired looking.

"Thanks for talking to me," he said.

She grunted. "Not much to talk about. I don't know where he went once he just up and left."

"I understand that," Hank said. "But maybe you can help me understand what he was going through. Why he left home. Why he left here. What was on his mind. That kind of thing."

Dana seemed to study him. "Why you so interested? He's old now. Wherever he is, he obviously isn't interested in going home."

Hank hesitated only a moment before answering. "Because I'm his father." He could see the surprise in her eyes, and he heard her sharp intake of breath.

She brushed an invisible strand of hair off her face. Then the surprise turned to a look of intense suspicion. Her eyebrows moved toward each other as her brow furled. "Hank didn't have a father."

"Of course he had a father. He just didn't know who he was. I didn't know I had a son until last week."

Dana, who'd been leaning forward in her chair as she peered at him, now leaned back. Her eyes were still dull. She rubbed her abdomen just below her pendulous breasts.

"You've been living here all this time?" Hank asked. "Do you have children?"

She nodded. "Six."

"All by Pastor Glen?"

She nodded again. She didn't seem to have taken offense at the blunt personal question. Hank could read nothing in her expression, neither pride nor regret. It was as if her vessel of personhood had been emptied, discarded, and then forgotten. It crossed his mind that she was no more alive than his Becka.

"What name was Hank using when you two left Pasadena?" he asked.

"Joe. Just Joe." Dana almost smiled. "It wasn't very imaginative, but it was temporary. He was trying out various names. It was Joe when we got here and Joe when he left."

"Last name?"

"He hadn't picked one yet. Didn't need to." She stood up and stretched her back. Hank was worried she meant to terminate their conversation, but she didn't leave. She just leaned both hands against the back of the chair.

"Why'd you leave Pasadena?" he asked.

Dana looked away, still leaning on the chair. She seemed to shrug, but Hank couldn't really tell. It was impossible to read a person with no personality. "No reason," she said in a soft voice.

Hank didn't say anything, hoping she would speak in the void. He still heard the television in the next room. Otherwise, there were no other sounds of life.

"We just needed, *wanted*, to get away," Dana said eventually. "I'd heard about the Christian Colony from some friends at church. Pastor Glen sounded cool. I wanted to see what it was all about."

"Was Hank in your church?"

Dana looked back at Hank and then moved around the chair and sat again. "No way. He didn't believe in God. At least, I don't think so. No, he was freaked out about something that had happened. He wouldn't tell me what it was, but he'd been acting all weird-like just before graduation. When he heard me talking about the Christian Colony, he suggested we hitchhike to check it out."

Hank frowned. "If he didn't believe in God, why would he suggest coming up here?"

This time her shrug was obvious. "Fuck if I know," she said. Then she put a hand to her mouth and looked around, as if she were a little girl who'd done something bad. "Sorry. We're not supposed to swear."

"Were you two lovers?" Hank asked.

She looked around again, as if she were about to disclose a big secret. She shook her head and smiled slyly. "Nah. I think he wanted to be, but he was too shy. He was really good-looking, and I was a lot prettier then. He loved my big tits." She looked down at herself, as if to indicate what she was talking about.

"But he just left without telling you why?"

The smile faded, and she turned from the shy girl back to the aging, lifeless woman. "I'm not really sure. Maybe it was because I told him he didn't belong here if he didn't believe in God. I told him he needed to be more like Pastor Glen." Dana moved toward Hank, as if to tell a secret. "Pastor Glen was really handsome then." She leaned back. "He's kind of let himself go in the past couple of years."

Hank tried hard not to laugh out loud. God, he wished Norm were here. "Are you married to Pastor Glen?" he asked, not caring so much as fascinated.

"Oh, no," she said. "He's God's son, Jesus's brother. He's not allowed to bind himself to any one woman. He was told that by God himself."

"Okay. Back to Hank for a minute. Can you remember any of his close friends in Pasadena? Who he hung out with? Who he might have contacted?"

Dana's lower lip moved out and down, as if pouting, although it was obviously one of her mannerisms while thinking extra hard. After a moment, she said, "Let's see, maybe Kurt Valentine. He was kind of the leader of a group of kids who were pretty much the 'in-crowd.'" She made air quotes with her hands. "Not that Hank was part of the in-crowd. He just wanted to be. Then there was Sammy Stone and Elliot Rogers." She picked at her nose. "Those are the only ones I can remember. I don't even know why I remember those names. I don't really recall anything about Sammy and Elliot. They were just followers. It was a long time ago. I'm not sure how close they were to Hank, though."

Hank nodded, committing the names to memory. "Can you think of any place Hank would have gone from here? Any place he talked about? Wanted to visit?"

Dana did the lower-lip thing again. She shook her head. "No, I don't think. . .wait. We spent a day in San Francisco on the way up here. He loved it there. He liked that there were so many different Asians. Maybe he went back down there."

"Anywhere else?"

She shook her head no.

"Did you ever go back or call home?"

"Nope. No reason to. My fam—"

The side door opened, and Pastor Glen walked in. The television noise grew louder for a moment and then faded again with the closing door. "We all done here?" He had a big smile on his face. It was a used-car salesman's smile.

Dana looked up at him as he approached. Hank watched her eyes. They were like the subservient, dependent eyes of a pet dog.

"Yes, I think so," she said. Her tone was light and almost merry. She rose, kissed Pastor Glen on the cheek, waved to Hank, and was gone.

Hank stood. He wasn't sure he'd asked everything he wanted to, but obviously, that was the end of his interview with Dana Clark.

"Let me walk you out," Pastor Glen said. The two men left the room and moved through the beautiful church and out the front door.

As Hank stepped onto the dilapidated porch, he turned to Pastor Glen. "So, Pastor, what did you decide?"

There was a look of confusion on the old man's face. "What do you mean? Decide about what?"

"The fate of the world?" said Hank. "You gonna let us live, or what?"

Whatever good humor was left in Pastor Glen's face faded away. He turned his captivating eyes to Hank's.

They stared at each other for several moments.

Then Pastor Glen broke eye contact and slapped Hank on the left shoulder. "This isn't for public consumption," he said, moving Hank down the steps toward the van. "But I convinced my Father, God, to give mankind another fifty years. If we haven't stopped destroying the planet ourselves by that time, God will finish us off. No more messing around. In the meantime, I've convinced him to slaughter as many Muslims as possible. Jesus made a deal with Muhammad way back when, which is why the Muslims consider Jesus one of their prophets. But the way God sees it, Muhammad broke his word and reneged on the deal."

They had reached the driver's door of the van. Hank looked hard at Pastor Glen, trying to decide if he was putting him on or if this was his reality. He saw nothing in Pastor Glen's face other than filth and seriousness. Hank finally nodded slightly and put his hand out to shake. "Well, thanks for your time, Pastor. And thank Dana for me."

With that, he climbed into the van, waited for Norm to move from the back to the passenger seat, and then drove away from the Christian Colony. In the rearview mirror, through the dust kicked up by the van, Hank could see Pastor Glen standing in the dirt courtyard watching them go.

Chapter 14

The huge redwood trees surrounded the campground like silent sentinels. Hank stared into the campfire, occasionally sipping from a glass of Malbec, which sat on the small folding table between his and Norm's camp chairs. The only other light came from a low-amp spotlight attached to the van. They had just finished a dinner of hamburgers, grilled to perfection by Norm.

Hank had filled Norm in on the events at the Christian Colony, and over the course of their meal, they'd kicked around thoughts and ideas.

"It doesn't make sense to me that the kid would take off and leave everything behind just to maybe get laid by a big-titted chick," Norm said. "I mean, shit, he was just about to head off to Berkeley for college. He was a good-looking kid. He'd have chicks up the wazoo."

"Agreed," Hank said. "And this Dana seemed like a real air-head—which I suppose is okay if all you're looking to do is get laid. But to run away with her? No, there was more to it than the whiff of sex. According to her, they weren't doing it anyway. She said he'd been freaked about something. We need to find out what that was."

A gust of wind rustled the branches of the monolithic trees. The fire did a short-lived, herky-jerky dance and then settled back down.

Norm shivered. "I'm going to grab a coat. Want anything?"

"Nah, I'm okay for now. Thanks." Hank continued to stare into the fire as he heard Norm make his old-man-getting-up noise.

Then he heard a crack, like a branch breaking. The fire and the spotlight cast strange, moving shadows. He heard Norm rummaging around inside the van. Then he heard a noise that sounded like it was at the perimeter of the campground, just at the edge of the trees. Without really thinking about it, he reached down for the old-fashioned hardwood billy club he'd brought on the trip. He'd been given it by a great-uncle who'd been a Chicago policeman in the forties. He'd never had to use it, but he kept it near his bed as protection against burglars, and he figured it would be a comforting thing to have on hand while camping.

The wind gusted again. Trees creaked and groaned. Hank was about to let go of the billy club when he felt the presence of someone to his right. He turned his head just as a young man wearing dirty coveralls stepped into the light of the fire. He stopped about two feet away from Hank's right arm, which was hanging down toward the ground, the billy club still in his hand.

The man was holding a pistol. Hank looked up into his face. He was young, maybe eighteen or nineteen. He had a full, scruffy beard and long hair. His face and hair looked as dirty as his coveralls. In Hank's irreverent brain, he heard the opening banjo riffs from *Deliverance*.

Hank caught movement behind the man. So there were two of them—at least. He wondered if the other man was armed. He didn't hear any sound coming from the van.

"Evening," Hank said. "Everything okay?" He nodded toward the gun.

The second man came into view then. He didn't have anything in his hands. He looked like he could be the first man's younger brother.

"We don't like that you bothered Sister Dana," said the young man holding the gun. "She was real upset after you left."

Hank kept his voice even. "Sorry to hear that. She seemed fine while she was talking to me."

"Well, she wasn't. And Pastor Glen don't like anyone coming around who doesn't intend to worship with him." The man's voice sounded young, maybe even a little scared. He was fidgety, in constant pointless motion. Hank wondered if he was on drugs. More likely it was his first rodeo of intimidation.

"Okay. Please give both Dana and Pastor Glen my apology. Now please get the hell out of my campground."

The man's gun hand shook slightly. It had been pointing down, but now it began to move up so that it would be pointing at Hank. He saw the anger take over the man's face—childish, hurt-looking anger.

Without waiting to determine the man's intentions, Hank brought the billy club straight up into the man's wrist. He heard the bones break as the gun dropped to the ground. Then he swung the club laterally, directly into the assailant's left kneecap. It made an awful sound, like wood on wood.

Hank rose from his chair as the man fell to the ground and then turned his attention to the brother—or whoever he was.

The kid seemed frozen, but the older man was screaming. "Get him. Kill that motherfucker! Fuck you, old man. You're gonna fucking die now."

The younger kid looked down at his companion writhing in pain and saw the gun lying on the ground. Hank could see the indecision in the kid's eyes, could see the kid wondering how stupid he needed to be to save face with Pastor Glen. Just as it looked as if the kid was going to make a move for the gun, Hank heard Norm's voice behind him.

"I wouldn't do that if I were you," Norm said. He was standing in the side door of the van.

Hank and the two intruders looked toward him. Norm was holding a gun.

Hank chuckled to himself and then turned back to the two men. The older one was still writhing around on the ground, moaning. *At least he's stopped calling me old man,* thought Hank.

That was pretty insensitive. He bent down and picked up the gun. It was an older Beretta that looked like it hadn't been cleaned in some time. But there was a full clip, and the safety was off. Hank disassembled the gun in a matter of seconds and then threw the individual parts off into the darkness of the forest.

"You carrying a weapon?" he asked the younger man.

The kid shook his head. He seemed too scared to speak.

Hank walked to him and did a quick pat-down anyway. Then he turned to Norm, who had climbed down from the van, still holding the gun. "Gimme that thing."

Norm smiled and handed it over. "Camping's always scared me," he said. "I thought it might come in handy."

Hank grunted and looked back at the two intruders. The one on the ground was crying. The young one was standing still. He looked like a child waiting to be spanked—which, thought Hank, was probably how he'd been raised by the Jesus-loving preacher.

"Now tell me why the fuck you little shits are here," Hank said.

The younger one looked down at the older one, saw he wasn't going to answer, and looked back at Hank. "Pastor Glen said to make sure you'd never come around again. He said you were evil men who meant to harm us all, that you were interfering with God's will." The kid paused, looked down again. "That's all we know."

Hank thought about it. "Who are you?"

"We're brothers," said the kid. "I'm James. That's Joshua."

"Is Pastor Glen your father?"

The kid nodded yes.

"Who's your mother?" Hank asked.

"Dana."

"Then why'd your brother call her Sister Dana?"

The kid shrugged. The talking had relaxed him a little. "All the womenfolk are called Sister."

"What's Sister Dana or Pastor Glen got to be afraid of?" Hank asked. "Why are they afraid of me?"

The boy shrugged again. He looked down at the ground. "Don't know. All we know is what I told you."

Hank looked at Norm, who raised an eyebrow and tilted his head slightly.

"All right," Hank said after a moment. "Drag your sorry-ass brother out of here and get on home."

James walked over to Joshua and bent over to help him up.

Joshua was moaning, crying, and swearing. "You broke my fucking wrist, you old cocksucker," he said, his voice tight with pain and anger.

"C'mon, man," James said. He pulled his brother up by his good arm, and Hank and Norm watched in silence as the two slowly made their way back into the woods. A few minutes later, the sounds of their retreat faded into silence.

Norm said, "I thought they weren't supposed to swear."

Hank handed the gun back to Norm and then picked up his wine and drank it down in one gulp. He kicked some dirt on the dwindling fire and began folding up his chair. "Let's get out of here."

They had the fire out and the van packed in a matter of minutes. When they were settled in the front seats, just as Hank started the engine, Norm said, "Now can we get a dog?"

Chapter 15

Six hundred miles to the south, Mai cuddled against Eva's substantial backside. She smelled the familiar scent of her friend and lover and caressed her smooth skin, running her hand over the great curve of a hip and then up the side of her back. Eva gave a small sound of pleasure, almost a purr.

That morning, Mai had opened the sliding door for the first time since Hank and Norm had come over. Eva had been sitting at her kitchen counter, reading a book.

"What you reading?" Mai asked, trying to sound casual.

Eva set the book down. "*Adrift*, by Mike Mann. I think it's his fifth book. It's really quite beautiful." She paused a moment. "Nice to see you."

Mai smiled a wan smile. She had needed time alone, time to think things through. It was a good word, *adrift*. It was how she felt. She was much more out of sorts than she'd expected from seeing Hank again after all these years. She'd expected to feel nothing, and was surprised to have felt drawn to him, even attracted to him, despite his rough exterior.

Eva had pouted a bit, but Mai let it be known, as subtly as possible, that she didn't find Eva's neediness appealing. Eva was smart enough to pull back. Their deal was to give each other space whenever it was needed, no questions asked.

Eva's breathing changed, and Mai could tell her old friend was asleep. She rolled onto her back and stared at the ceiling. What was she doing? Did she really think Hank could find Hank Jr. after all these years? Did she really want to meet her son, who had become a man, and confront the truth about why he had left her?

Mai rubbed her eyes, breathed deeply, and then let the air out slowly. Of course there was the one possibility she refused to consider, which was that Hank Jr. was dead. She shivered slightly and pulled the comforter up to her neck. Something inside her, some deep-rooted maternal gene or instinct or whatever, assured her she would know if her son were dead.

Now that she'd met Hank again, had seen even in his old age his self-assuredness, she knew this was a good plan. If anyone could find out what had happened to Hank Jr., it was his father. No matter how much it was going to hurt—and she had no doubt that it would hurt, that it would really, really hurt—she was determined to find out why her boy had rejected her, hell, had dismissed her, as if she didn't exist.

Mai closed her eyes, willing sleep to come. She saw Hank's face. She thought the beard suited him. She'd never kissed a man with a beard before. She wondered what it would be like.

Chapter 16

"If you don't shut that fucking dog up, I'm going to toss him out of this moving van," Hank growled.

"You need to start calling him by the name we agreed on, which wasn't 'Fucking Dog,'" Norm replied.

"Okay, shut the fuck up, Stoner!" Hank hollered.

"Pull into that rest stop ahead," Norm said. "I think he needs to take a dump."

They were traveling along Highway 80 in eastern Nevada. Just before Stoner had begun barking, they'd been debating whether to sleep in the van near the Great Salt Lake or head into Salt Lake City for a four- or five-star hotel experience. Hank pointed out that now, whenever they stayed in hotels, they'd need pet-friendly accommodations.

Hank pulled into the rest stop and parked near some picnic tables.

Norm called out to Stoner. It was too soon for the West Highland white terrier, also known as a "Westie," to know his name, but he must have picked up on the tone in Norm's voice, as he stopped barking and bounded into the front of the van, presenting himself to be leashed.

"I'm gonna take a whiz," Hank said as Norm and Stoner exited from the passenger side. "I'll leave the van unlocked, so keep an eye on it."

"Aye, aye, Captain."

In Reno, Hank had finally agreed to look into getting a dog, so they'd found an animal shelter near downtown. The shelter volunteer, a cheerfully obese woman, listened as Norm explained they wanted a small dog that did not shed, was intelligent, traveled well, and would be a good watchdog.

"But we're not picky," Hank said sarcastically.

"You're not going to believe this," the woman said, "but the perfect dog for you just came in last night." She lowered her voice, conspiratorially. "To be honest, I was thinking of keeping him myself, but my husband would kill me if I brought another dog home." She opened the cage, and a small, furry white dog approached her outstretched hand, sniffed it, and then allowed her to pick him up.

"I'm not sure if he's a purebred, but these dogs are a pretty big deal. They've got great temperaments, train easily, and should be perfect traveling companions so long as you let them get enough exercise. Someone seems to have done a pretty good job training this guy."

The dog had piercing, dark brown eyes that seemed to latch on to Hank although it was Norm who took the dog from the handler's arms.

"I love him already," Norm said, stroking the dog's short hair.

"That's why you had so many wives," Hank said. But he knew what Norm was saying. The dog was still watching Hank, and Hank couldn't help but feel the dog possessed a strong sense of self-esteem.

Thirty minutes later, after a half-hearted inspection of the other dogs available for rescue, the two men were now two men and a dog. When they let the dog into the van, he sniffed around for a while before stopping in front of a drawer under the closet. He barked twice and looked at Hank.

Both men began laughing. The dog had wasted no time in sniffing out their stash of marijuana.

Chapter 17

Norm took over the driving duties after the rest stop, and Hank took a seat in the comfortable leather chair at the dining nook. He opened his laptop computer, which automatically joined the van's built-in Wi-Fi. Checking his email, he saw he had something from Gene Rodham, his former second-in-command at HR Security.

> *Hank—*
> *Great to hear from you, although it's under pretty bizarre circumstances. So you're a daddy. Anyway, I'm glad to help in any way I can. Attached is our simulated aging illustration of the kid. I've always found the program to be slightly less effective for mixed ethnicities. But I think it's reasonable that a good-looking kid would turn into a good-looking man. Which means I don't see much of you in him. Ha ha. We'll do a search of our databases using his given name (funny about the last name spelling). But I doubt we'll find anything as he's obviously using an alias. Take care and happy hunting.*
>
> *—Gene*

The night before, during their stay in Reno, Hank had called his former protégé and filled him in on the situation involving Mai and their son. Under Hank's founding leadership, HR Security—which had been Hank Reagan Security for the first year of its existence—had grown into a large and powerful security and investigation firm with offices in twenty states. Five years ago, at Hank's suggestion, Gene Rodham and a small group of investors bought Hank out for a tidy sum of $16 million. It had been a good deal all around.

Now Hank opened the attachment and stared at a photo-quality rendering of a good-looking, forty-something man with slightly Asian eyes and chiseled features. His *son*. He said the word to himself, but the reality was that it was still just an abstraction. It was still just a story his ex-lover had told him and which he'd taken at face value. He didn't really doubt it—it was just that he hadn't yet accepted the reality of it, like Norm at first refusing to believe his beautiful trophy wife was banging the tennis pro.

Hank stared at the rendering, searching the features for similarities to his own. *Maybe the nose*, he thought. *Or the strong chin.* Or, more likely, he was reading more into the rendering than was really there.

After he'd printed out three copies on the compact Canon color printer, Hank brought up the Google search results he'd saved on Kurt Valentine, one of the three names Dana Clark had given him as having been close friends of Hank Jr. Dana had said Valentine was the leader, so Hank decided to start with him. The search results were sparse.

According to what he'd read, the Valentine family had been über-rich, old-money Pasadena. Kurt had grown up in the family mansion on Orange Grove Boulevard. Hank's check of Google Earth showed that Kurt's residence could not possibly have been in the same school district as Hank Jr.'s. Valentine should have gone to either Blair or John Muir High School, and Hank Jr. had gone to Pasadena High. Yet Valentine's Facebook page clearly showed his high school as having been Pasadena High School—PHS.

In any event, there wasn't much about Valentine on Google. He had taken over his dad's publishing empire, but from what

Hank could see, was president in name only. He lived in Aspen, Colorado, with his wife, Randi, and their two children. He'd served one term as head of the local Republican Party. His current Facebook page was rife with right-wing postings. Some were outright racist.

Could this really have been a close friend of my son? Hank wondered.

Hank had learned from his days as an investigator that confronting a potential witness in person rather than by phone almost always produced more results. It was even better if the person didn't know Hank was coming. This theory was, of course, proven over and over again by the intrepid reporters from *60 Minutes* appearing on the doorsteps of malfeasors week after week. Caught unawares, they almost universally incriminated themselves.

So Hank and Norm decided a nice drive to Aspen was in order. Hank hadn't been there since he'd stopped skiing a dozen years ago. Norm had never been there, although one of his wives had taken her divorce settlement and set up house in Aspen for as long as it took to net another rich husband.

Hank sighed and looked out the window. The sky was blue and endless, the terrain brown and endless. He was about to unbuckle his seat belt and move up front with Norm when Stoner jumped onto his lap, briefly startling him. Without thinking about it, he began scratching Stoner's chin while the dog looked up into his face. After a few moments, Hank gave Stoner's torso a good hard rub and then leaned down toward the dog's ear. "Don't tell Norm," he said. "He gets jealous."

*   *   *

Norm pulled off Highway 80 at West Wendover, just short of the Utah border, and announced they needed some provisions. It looked as if the purpose of West Wendover, Nevada, was to provide last-chance or first-chance gambling opportunities, depending on one's direction of travel.

Norm found a grocery store near the Peppermill Casino and parked. "Why don't you take Stoner for a walk while I do some quick shopping?" He grabbed two cloth shopping bags and climbed out of the van.

Hank walked Stoner away from the casino. In the warm and pleasant early-summer afternoon, they crossed Wendover Boulevard and headed toward what looked like a park. As they crossed a parking lot and came upon the West Wendover Tourism and Convention Bureau, Hank smiled to himself. "What do you think of West Wendover as a convention spot?" he asked Stoner, who did not reply, probably because he was too interested in the stand of trees just ahead. Hank let himself be led to a couple of trees before Stoner made his selection and commenced to pee.

Once Stoner had relieved himself, the two made their way to the park, which was bordered by two tennis courts, both of which were empty. The only person Hank saw was an elderly black man rummaging through a trash can next to the tennis courts.

As Hank and Stoner approached him, the man stood upright and closed the lid on the trash can. Hank saw that the man was indeed old—older even than Hank. He had sparse tufts of white hair on the sides and back of his skull and a dark, heavily lined face. The whites of his eyes had red veins running through them. He wore a brown work shirt and heavy blue work pants. His shoes were old black wing tips, dress shoes incongruous with the rest of his attire. He smiled at Hank and then glanced down at Stoner.

"Hey there," he said. "Good-looking dog you got there." His voice was cultured and smooth.

"Thanks." Hank put his hand out to shake. "I'm Hank."

The old man's smile broadened as he took Hank's hand. "Conrad," he said.

"Look," Hank said, "I don't mean to intrude, but I'd be happy to buy you a meal if you'd like."

Conrad appeared confused for a moment but then looked at the trash can he'd been going through and chuckled. He ran a hand over his balding head. "Mighty nice of you, Mister, but I'm probably the richest man in this shit-hole of a town."

It was Hank's turn to look confused. Was this old man demented? He was trying to think of a diplomatic response when Conrad motioned to a bench adjacent to the tennis court's fence.

"Mind if I take a load off? I turn eighty-five next month, and I'm starting to feel it." He chuckled again. It was a deep, throaty, good-natured sound. Without waiting for a reply, he sat. Then he patted the bench next to him.

Hank sat. Stoner began investigating the limited area his leash would allow.

"I can see why you thought I was a bum," Conrad said. "I look like one, and you saw me going through the garbage. I don't have anything else to do with my days, so that's kind of become a hobby for me. I pretend it's an anthropological exercise, but frankly, around here, it's not all that interesting." He paused for a beat.

"I was tossing out a paper coffee cup one day a couple years back and noticed a lotto ticket lying on top of the garbage. On a whim, I checked it out, and it turned out to be worth three thousand bucks." The old man grinned. "So I cashed it in and donated the money to an Oakland charity I support, and I've been going through the garbage ever since. That was my one and only worthwhile discovery."

"So you live here? Sounds like you don't like it much."

Conrad grunted. "Hate it."

"If you're rich, why don't you move?"

Conrad looked away for a moment. The good-natured look he'd shown Hank transformed into something else, something Hank couldn't read.

"This is probably going to sound crazy to you," Conrad said, "but I'm not really here willingly. I'm here 'cause my wife died in a car accident here." He pointed toward the highway. "Just a couple miles from here on the highway." He paused, and his melodious voice went low. "I killed her. The accident was my fault. It had been a long day of driving, and we wanted to make it to Salt Lake City. I nodded off for a second or two and crossed the center line. The semi I hit had swerved to avoid us, but the passenger side of our car was hit by the truck's big bumper and we flipped over. Gloria was killed instantly, and I walked away without a scratch. We'd been married over fifty years." He shook his head from side to side. "Can you imagine? Fifty glorious years, and I killed her."

Conrad stopped talking, and Hank didn't say anything for a time. They both watched Stoner nose around the corner poles of the tennis court.

Hank broke the silence. "I was married to my wife for thirty-five years when she died of cancer." He patted the old man's arm. "So I know a little bit about what you're going through. I'm sorry for your loss. But that doesn't explain why you're here. When did this happen?"

"Almost five years ago."

Hank cocked his head so he could stare at Conrad. "Did you say five years ago?"

Conrad nodded and stretched his legs straight out. "Seems crazy, doesn't it? The night of the day she died, I was a mess. I couldn't stop crying. I thought of killing myself. Of course, I couldn't go anywhere then. I'd totaled the car and killed my wife, and the police were still investigating the accident even though I'd told them over and over it was all my fault. Luckily the driver of the truck I'd run into was fine. Just some cuts and bruises.

"So I took a room at that casino hotel." He pointed to the Peppermill. "I cried and prayed and wondered what I should do. The obvious choice was to join her. To kill myself. But I woke up in the middle of the night, and I heard Gloria talking to me. She said she was near. She said she loved me and forgave me and that she wanted me to stay near her, but not to come to her yet." Conrad blinked, as if holding back tears.

"I was awake, Hank. It wasn't a dream. My eyes were open, and I could hear her voice as if she was lying in bed next to me."

Conrad turned his red eyes to Hank. "Crazy, like I said. But I didn't care about anyone or anything else in the world. She was my world. I decided that night to stay here, to be near her." He stood, grunting heavily. "Got to stand now. I tighten up when I sit too long." He put his hands on his low back and stretched. "Been living in that casino ever since."

Hank noticed the look of sly humor he had first seen.

"I'm beginning to wonder whether I've stayed long enough. I don't feel Gloria's presence anymore—haven't for a while now. The people here look right through me, like I don't exist. They see an old black man by himself and have no use for me. Even after five years of living in one of the penthouse suites, the management barely tolerates me. I can see it in their eyes. They look surprised every month when I make another payment." Conrad gave Hank another one of his chuckles.

Hank heard more than just humor in it. It sounded to him as if Conrad's throaty chuckles were actually an editorial comment on whatever he'd been saying. "Where're you from?" Hank asked.

"Oakland. I own about a five-block-square piece of downtown Oakland." Conrad grinned. "Plus various and sundry real estate spread around the rest of the Bay Area. Like I said, I'm rich. But I don't have anybody to be rich with, and that's a goddamn bitch."

"No children? Grandchildren?"

Conrad shook his head. "We had two kids. One died in his teens in a drive-by shooting while he was walking to school. The other died of a heart attack when he was sixty-two. He didn't have any kids."

Hank felt Stoner pulling at the leash. The dog had become bored with the confined area and wanted to explore.

Hank stood. He put a hand on Conrad's shoulder. "I wish I could invite you to come along with my buddy Norm and Stoner and me," he said. He was surprised at how much he meant what he was saying. "We're on a driving trip of sorts. But we have a van with only limited space."

Conrad laughed now, a good solid laugh that made his face look younger. Hank saw then that he'd been a handsome man. He could feel Conrad's sense of schizophrenia. He still felt it himself. There were days—nights, mostly—when the weight of Becka's death felt like his insides were turning to cement, so that even though he was still living, existing, he was on the brink of being just as dead.

But then there were the times, more now every day, when he felt okay, pleased to be alive. He still refused to allow himself to acknowledge happiness although deep down there were times when he knew he was, in fact, experiencing just that. He felt guilty when he thought he might actually be happy at a particular moment, just as he'd felt guilty when he thought of himself with Mai.

Yet here was Conrad—a man who had completely given in to his wife's death. He'd let it, accentuated by guilt, take control of his life, such as it was. Conrad didn't even know why he was still living in a casino hotel in the middle of nowhere. He had tried and convicted himself and had created this jail of mindless boredom: his personal death farm.

"Get out, Conrad," Hank told him. "Go home. Gloria wouldn't want you living like this." He patted Conrad's shoulder again. "I gotta go. It's been an honor to meet you."

Conrad nodded. "Thanks, Hank. It's been good meeting you, too. Maybe you're just what I needed." He looked around at the empty park. "Frankly, I haven't had a conversation of any substance with anyone of any substance for a long, long time. It felt good." He chuckled, still nodding his head.

Chapter 18

Norm, back in the driver's seat, was silent for a long time after Hank finished telling him about Conrad. They were coming up on the salt flats when he finally spoke. "No matter what happens in our search, I think we owe Mai a debt of gratitude for getting our asses out of Sunrise and back into the land of the living." He gestured at the wide open, deserted, and desolate space ahead and grinned. "Even though there isn't actually anything living in sight at the moment."

Sitting in the passenger seat with Stoner on his lap, Hank was unconsciously scratching under the dog's jowls. "What got me was the contradiction. On the one hand, Conrad's obviously smart and, assuming he was telling the truth, rich as hell. Yet on the other hand, he let his life be hijacked by a nighttime voice of the wife he'd just killed. I mean, he had to know in his intellect that whatever he heard was his own guilt talking to him, that it was absurd to believe his wife spoke to him from the hereafter to instruct him to stay near the scene of her death."

They drove in silence while the miles passed and the mountains in the distance appeared and grew, like the time-lapsed baby bump of a pregnant woman.

"He's old," Norm said. "We're old. Our families are gone. We've evolved from being the masters of the universe to being old men who are barely tolerated pending our demise. Conrad's not only old; he's black. Double whammy without family. He heard what he wanted to hear and accepted the nugget of purpose it gave his life."

Hank grunted ambiguously. He stopped scratching Stoner, who promptly looked up at him and then nudged Hank's hand with his nose. Hank ignored him. "Yeah, I think you're probably right, but it scares me."

When Hank didn't continue, Norm asked, "What does?"

"Being meaningless."

Chapter 19

Hank had never been to Aspen in the summer. It was a different world from the Aspen he knew—greener, for one thing. It was also crowded. The sidewalks were full of people wearing shorts, T-shirts, and tank tops. *Summer dress isn't quite as stylish as winter dress*, he thought.

Outdoor patios at restaurants were packed with patrons having late lunches. The ski runs on Aspen Mountain were sloping, verdant pastures. The gondola was running—available to mountain bikers, hikers, and sightseers.

They hadn't thought to make a hotel reservation. They'd spent a loud night in an RV park south of Salt Lake City, with a group traveling together in four large RVs partying well into the night. Stoner had barked until he got too tired or too bored and then curled up at the foot of Norm's bed.

Both men were awake and grumpy at five-thirty the next morning. Of course, the revelers were all sound asleep.

"Let's get out of here before any of those asshats wake up, and I say something I shouldn't," Hank said.

So they'd hit the road early and were in Aspen by midafternoon.

"Want me to go online and see if I can find something?" Norm asked.

"Nah. We're here, so let's just try a couple places." Hank made a U-turn on Main Street and pulled up to the Jerome Hotel.

"I'll run in and see if they have any rooms," Norm said. A few minutes later, he climbed back into the van. "All full. The desk clerk said to try Little Nell. You know where that is?"

Hank nodded and pulled into traffic. "At the foot of the mountain. I know it's pet friendly, but it'll be expensive."

Twenty minutes later, they were installed in a beautifully appointed mountainside room with two double beds. Norm had negotiated the assistant manager down to $700 a night, including parking.

"Can we stay longer than a night?" he asked Hank. "Huh? Please, Daddy, can we?"

Hank ignored him and pulled out the Aspen phone book. The Valentines were listed. He put the address into Google Maps and brought up directions. Straight across town, up Red Mountain, to Placer Lane. "Shall we go see if we can catch this guy at home? Then we can wander around town."

*   *   *

Kurt Valentine's house wasn't particularly large by Aspen standards, but it was big by most others. This wasn't just one-percent-ville; it was more like point-five-percent-ville. The house's two stories had lots of large windows facing town and Aspen Mountain. A four-foot-high river-rock base surrounded the structure. Above the river rock, the house was faux log cabin. A black Escalade was parked in the driveway.

An Eastern-European-looking maid opened the door.

"Hi," Hank said. "Is Kurt Valentine home?"

The maid's accent confirmed her origins. "May I tell him who's asking?"

"Sure, but he won't know who we are. Tell him we have some questions about an old high school chum of his."

The maid gave Hank a quizzical look and then turned and disappeared into the house, closing the door behind her. A full minute later, Hank was just about to knock again when it opened to reveal a tall, athletic-looking man with blond hair and tanned skin. Hank recognized Valentine from the online photos he'd seen.

"Can I help you?" His voice sounded friendly enough.

"We hope so," Hank said. "We're trying to find a man you went to high school with in Pasadena. We understand you were one of his buddies. Do you remember Hank Raygun?"

Valentine's face changed, the friendliness gone. "Hank wasn't a buddy of mine. Who told you that?" His tone was aggressive.

"A woman by the name of Dana Clark," Hank said. "She and Hank ran away together, and his mother hasn't heard from him since."

Valentine made a harsh-sounding laugh. "Dana? She was the class whore. Where is she now? I wouldn't believe a thing she says."

"Okay," Hank said. "But can we come in and talk for a little bit? Maybe you know something that's important but don't even realize it. I mean, whether he was a buddy or not, you did know Hank, didn't you?"

Valentine looked over his shoulder, back into the house. "You staying in town?"

Hank nodded. "Little Nell."

Valentine looked at his watch. "There's a bar there called Chair 9. It should be open now, but it'll be quiet. I'll meet you there in thirty minutes." With that, he closed the door.

Hank looked at Norm and shrugged. "Well, that was weird."

Norm smiled. "At least we can get a drink."

*   *   *

Chair 9 was indeed quiet. Two couples sat at private tables, and one man sat at the bar, talking to the lone male bartender. Hank and Norm settled into comfortable leather chairs at a table. Stoner curled up at Norm's feet. They sat there, ignored by the bartender, for a full three minutes before Norm said, "Fuck this." He groaned as he got up. "Tito's?" he asked Hank, who nodded. Norm ambled over to the bar and interrupted the bartender's conversation.

Valentine walked in at the same time, spotted Hank, and walked over to him.

The twenty-something bartender interrupted Norm's attempt at ordering. "Hi, Mr. Valentine! I'll be right over!" he called out. He turned his attention back to Norm. "You with Mr. Valentine?"

"Yeah," Norm said. "So you coming over, or do I order here?"

"I'll come over."

After the men had ordered, Oktoberfest beer for Norm and Valentine and a Tito's vodka for Hank, Valentine leaned forward in his seat and addressed Hank. "Look, sorry if I was a little rude earlier, but you kind of took me by surprise. I haven't thought of Hank or Dana or pretty much any of my high school friends in years."

"No worries," Hank said. "But if I may ask, what was your relationship with Hank if you weren't buddies?"

Valentine sipped his beer, set it down, and then ran a hand over his short blond hair. "Are you guys detectives hired by his mother or what?"

"Close enough," Hank said. "She asked us to try to find him. She hasn't seen or heard from him since he ran away right after graduation."

Valentine seemed to consider that for a moment and then nodded, as if to himself. He looked at Norm, then back at Hank. Hank was sure Valentine was about to comment on their age, but he didn't.

"I knew him throughout high school. He was a nice enough kid, but he wanted to be in our clique and kind of made a pest of himself. When I first met him, I thought he was a Mexican or something. You know how a lot of the Mexicans have Indian blood. His eyes and his high cheekbones looked Indian to me. Plus, our school was full of spics. Then someone told me he was part Vietnamese."

"Why didn't your clique want him?" Norm asked.

Valentine tilted his head. "We were all white guys. Surfer types mostly, or at least we all looked the part. We didn't want anyone different." He saw Hank and Norm staring at him and reconsidered his words. "We weren't racist or anything. We just preferred our own kind. God knows there were enough blacks and Mexicans and Asians to hang with each other. They didn't need to hang with us. Probably wouldn't have wanted to, anyway."

"But Hank did," Hank said.

Valentine did the head tilt thing again, this time in conjunction with a one-shoulder shrug. "Yeah. I don't know, maybe his Oriental buddies didn't like him."

"He had *Oriental* buddies?" Hank asked, emphasizing the word "Oriental," but there was no indication Valentine had picked up on the sarcasm.

"Fuck if I know," Valentine said. "But those people usually stick together. That's why we thought it was weird he wanted to hang around us."

There was a long moment of silence.

Hank asked, "So if you didn't want him to hang with you guys, did you just tell him so?"

Valentine picked up his beer and took another sip. "More or less. We mostly just ignored him. One of the guys in our group, sort of on the fringe really, became friends with Hank. They'd hang out together after school and on weekends, I think. I lived kind of far away from school, so I mostly cut out right away."

"Yeah, I was going to ask you about that," Hank said. "From what I could tell, you lived on Orange Grove Boulevard, which wouldn't have been in the Pasadena High district. How'd you end up there?"

Valentine grinned. "I got into trouble my first week at Muir High. Kind of a fight with a bunch of the black guys who got in my face. They beat the shit out of me after I lost my cool once and called them 'niggers.' My parents arranged for me to be transferred." He paused, and his grin faded. "From a school with a bunch of blacks to one with a bunch of spics."

What a pleasant man, Hank thought.

"Your family was rich," Norm said. "Why didn't they put you in a nice white private school?"

Valentine looked hard at Norm, as if trying to figure out if Norm was calling him a racist. But Norm's voice had been calm and agreeable, almost as if he were commiserating with Valentine. "They tried to get me into Polytechnic, which is over by Cal Tech, but I didn't do so well on their entrance exam, so I ended up at PHS."

"Anyway," Hank said, "what about Dana Clark? You called her a whore. What's her story?"

"Dana was pretty hot. She had really big tits for a high-schooler. So the boys were all over her. Her parents were white trash, and Dana wasn't discriminating about who she'd go out with. She even went out with some of the black football players. She got a reputation. Some of my friends banged her, but I didn't. I was afraid of what I'd catch."

"Do you know how she ended up running away with Hank?" Norm asked.

Valentine raised his right hand chest high, palm up. "Don't know. I remember seeing Hank with her around the last week in school. I asked Monty, our buddy who'd become friends with Hank, if they were doing each other, but Monty claimed he didn't know."

"Do you remember Monty's last name?" Hank asked. Dana hadn't mentioned a Monty.

"Monty Washburn. I haven't talked to him in years. Last I heard, he was a financial adviser of some kind in San Diego."

"Any idea why Dana would list you as one of Hank's buddies?" Hank asked.

"No idea. I'm surprised she even knew my name."

"She told us Hank was freaked out about something, which may have been why he ran away," Hank said. "Any ideas?"

Even in the dim light of the bar, Hank saw that something seemed to change in Valentine's face. It was slight, and it didn't last long, but Hank had the feeling the question had struck some kind of nerve.

"Nope. No idea," Valentine said. He glanced at his watch. "Look, I have to get to a field hockey game. My youngest girl is on the Aspen High team."

"Can you give me the names of any other kids who really might have been close to Hank?"

Valentine stood, then bent over, picked up his beer, and drained it. "Nope. That's about it. Maybe Monty can give you more. Sorry I can't be more helpful." He put out his hand to shake.

Hank and Norm stood and shook, saying good-bye. They sat down and watched him wave to the bartender on the way out.

Neither man said anything for some time. The ambient noise in the room had picked up slightly as a few more drinkers came in from the sunshine.

The bartender appeared at their side, attentive now that he thought they were friends with Valentine. "Get you gentlemen anything else?"

Hank shook his head no.

The bartender put down a brown leather folio. "Here's the check. No rush. If you decide you want something more, just give me a shout."

"So, what do you think?" Norm asked once the bartender had gone.

"You mean about the racist prick we just interviewed?"

Norm snorted. "Yeah, him. You notice he never even asked for our names?"

"Couldn't be bothered, I guess." Hank took a last sip of vodka. "I can't figure out why Dana would have sent us to this schmuck."

"Unless he knew Hank Jr. a lot better than he's letting on," Norm said.

Hank nodded. "Yeah, but would he virtually admit to being a racist rather than admit to having known Hank Jr.? Did you catch his change of expression when I asked about Hank Jr. being freaked out about something?"

Norm shook his head. "Didn't notice." He stuck some bills in the folio and got up. Stoner watched him and got up as well, stretching as he did so. "Let's walk around a bit. I want to see enough of Aspen to say I've been here."

"To say to whom you've been here?"

Norm sighed. "Good point."

Chapter 20

Mai didn't often think about her life in Vietnam. Even if she tried to think only about the good things, her year with Hank, cooking with her parents, it all ended in tragedy and heartbreak. But when she made a large pot of pho in her own kitchen, the comforting smells of onion, ginger, cinnamon, and anise would waft throughout the condo, and she would find herself transported back to the kitchens of Saigon or to her little apartment where she had cooked for Hank.

Now, with Eva off on a business trip and the connecting door to her condo closed, the glorious smells from Mai's kitchen seemed to follow her from room to room, and they made her smile. She thought about Hank and the long, hot lovemaking sessions while a pot of pho simmered on her tiny stovetop. Most of the time Hank put on a show of being happy-go-lucky, always ready with a humorous quip or a sarcastically cynical response to the latest American radio propaganda about how the South was winning the war. But after making love, while still lying in her single bed, when the street noise reasserted itself and the smells from the pho made his stomach growl, Hank would often become serious, almost morbidly so.

He would talk about their love and what would happen to them when the war ended, which he foresaw long before most people thought it possible that the all-powerful United States of America would allow itself to be on the losing end of a civil war. Mai felt his strong arms around her as she watched him talk, and despite the words meant to reassure her that they would find a way to be together, she could see the sadness in his eyes, and she could sense the inevitability of their separation. She would let him believe she believed what he was saying, and when he finally stopped talking and she could see he was on the verge of being overwhelmed by his own delusions, she would disentangle her body from his and walk naked to the kitchen to dish up two bowls of pho.

Now Mai sat on her soft beige leather couch and closed her eyes, breathing in the smells. She could see the young couple, both naked, sitting up on the small bed, leaning against the wall, slurping the noodles and broth. It was never long before the old Hank was back, telling a joke, or—one of his favorites—hanging a noodle out of his nostril while reciting an important piece of news he'd heard that morning on Armed Forces Radio. They would dissolve into laughter, and more often than not, the bowls would be put on the floor and they would make love again.

Mai sighed and reached for the remote control, but before she turned on the television, the phone rang. It was the landline, which she hardly ever used. She debated not getting up to answer it, thinking it was probably a solicitation of some kind, but she'd never been able to ignore a ringing phone. "Hello?"

"Is this, uh, Tran Yuan Mai?" The voice was male, an adult. He pronounced "Yuan" as "You Ann" and there was a hesitancy in his speech.

"Yes," she said, though her name was Tran Xuan Mai. "Who's this?"

"That's not important. What's important is that you tell those old men looking for Hank to give it up. Hank died a long time ago."

Mai felt her chest go tight. She wanted to ask how and when, and who was this person on the phone, but she was having a hard time swallowing.

"I'm sorry to break it to you, ma'am. Someone should have told you a long time ago. But that's all there is to it. He's dead and gone, and those old fools you sent looking aren't doing anybody a favor."

Mai willed herself to speak. "Who are you? How . . ."

The man hung up.

Chapter 21

Hank and Norm were camping at a deserted RV park near Tres Piedras, New Mexico. The view across the high desert, filled with sagebrush all the way to the Sangre de Cristo Mountains that towered above the town of Taos, was nothing short of spectacular. As the sun set, for a few minutes the mountains turned purple.

As darkness fell, Norm set up the hibachi to cook some steaks while Hank made a campfire and set up the picnic table and chairs. With cocktails of Tito's vodka, tonic, and lime, they sat in the camp chairs and smoked a joint while they waited for the briquettes to come to an even glow. The stars began to appear. There were no sounds other than the occasional popping of the campfire. They said nothing, simply passing the joint back and forth.

Both men jumped in surprise when Hank's cellphone broke the bucolic reverie. It was Mai calling.

"Hey, Mai, what's up?"

Mai's voice sounded frantic. "I got a call from someone, a man, who asked for me by name. He wouldn't tell me his name. He told me Hank was dead and that we should stop looking for him." She stopped talking and took deep, gulping breaths.

"That doesn't make any sense, Mai. We've only talked to two people so far, neither of whom gave any indication that Junior had died. Both played dumb as to why he disappeared though it sounds like something strange might have happened right around graduation that caused him to freak. But that's just conjecture so far. We really don't have much to go on."

Mai said nothing for a moment. Hank could hear her sobs. He wanted to reach out and take her in his arms and comfort her. But what could he say to assure her that her son was still alive? He corrected himself. That *their* son was still alive.

Mai spoke again, clearly with great effort. "If he's alive, why would someone call me to say he's dead? That doesn't make any sense either. What kind of animal would do such a thing?"

Hank closed his eyes. He felt the warmth of the fire on his face. "We're heading to San Diego to try to track down another high school friend, but we'll swing by Pasadena on the way. We're in New Mexico now, so it'll be a couple days."

"I'll be okay, I guess," Mai said. "It was such a shock. It's the first time in over twenty years that I've heard anything from anyone who knew Hank. It'd be good if you could stop by here on your way to San Diego."

"Okay, I'll check in with you tomorrow. Try to relax. It doesn't make sense to me. In fact, it seems just the opposite. If he were really dead, whoever called you wouldn't be trying to scare us off the investigation."

"You don't think those guys you're tracking down killed him, do you? The ones who were supposed to be his friends?"

"That's a possibility, but I doubt it. Junior disappeared from the church camp. That was *after* he was last seen by his high school buddies—at least as far as we know. If one or more of them had killed him, they would've had to know where he'd gone after he left Dana. How would any of them have known that?"

Mai was silent, but when she finally spoke, it was in a soft-sounding voice, yet Hank heard a sense of resolve. "You're right. Besides, he can't be dead. I'd have known it. I'd have felt it if he'd died. He has to be alive. But he could be in trouble. That guy called for a reason, Hank. We need to find him." Her voice trailed off.

"We'll be there as soon as we can. In the meantime, try not to think about it. As I said, it doesn't make any sense. He's alive, and we're going to find him."

After he hung up, Hank filled Norm in on the conversation.

"Interesting," Norm said, plating their steaks and salad. "I guess it's safe to assume the caller wasn't that prick from Aspen. If it were him, why wouldn't he just tell us Junior was dead? And since it was a man, it wasn't Dana. But one or both of them had to have called someone to report on our investigation. Why?"

Hank didn't answer. Instead, he grunted in acknowledgement and dug into his food.

The night was cool and comfortable. The sky looked like a blanket covered in spilled glitter, the Milky Way a slash of white. Somewhere off in the darkness, a coyote gave a short, high-pitched howl. Stoner, lying under Hank's chair, growled.

When the two men were done eating, Hank cleared the dishes and poured them each two fingers of single-malt scotch. They sat in silence, staring into the fire, sipping their drinks.

Suddenly, Stoner stood and snarled. The dog looked out into the blackness and emitted a long, low growl. Hank picked up his billy club. He saw movement from Norm and assumed he was reaching for his pistol.

Stoner began to bark.

Hank thought he heard something. Then he saw a white garment of some kind. "Who's there?"

A woman came into view. She was old, her gray hair wild. She wore a long white nightgown and was barefoot. She stepped into the light of the fire and laughed.

No, thought Hank, *not a laugh so much as a cackle.*

"What have we here?" The old woman's voice was raspy, as if she weren't used to talking, but her tone was friendly. "A couple gentlemen callers?"

"Just passing through," Hank said. "Who're you?"

As the woman moved closer, Hank could see that her cotton nightgown was worn and dirty, and her feet were black with dirt. Her wild hair was matted, her long face wrinkled and creased. But she wore a huge smile that showed off her yellowed teeth.

"I own this place," she said. "You owe me twenty bucks for the night."

Norm stood. "Would you like a seat?"

The woman nodded, still smiling. "I wouldn't mind." She walked to Norm's chair and lowered her small body into it. "I knew you was gentlemen."

Norm pulled another camp chair from the van and set it up so that the woman was sitting between them, making a half circle around the fire.

"Sorry about not paying you," Hank said. "We didn't see any kind of office or anything. We thought the place was deserted." He pulled a twenty-dollar bill from his pocket and handed it to the woman.

She took the bill and stuck it in a small pocket in her nightgown. Then she pointed off into the darkness. "My place is just over there, at the tree line. Not much, but it's home. Don't blame you for thinking this place was deserted. It pretty much is. When Shorty died—that was my husband—I had the land cleared and put up that sign you might have seen coming in. Falling down now. But this ain't no place for any kind of an RV park. Just wishful thinking on my part, I guess. You got anything to drink?"

"Scotch?" Norm offered.

The woman smiled. "Hell, yeah." She watched Norm as he went to the van to get a glass. Then she looked down at Stoner. "What's his name?"

"The dog?" Hank replied.

She nodded.

"Stoner."

The woman cackled, which then dissolved into a cough. "My kind of dog."

Norm poured some scotch into the glass. "I'm Norm, and that's Hank," he said as he handed the drink to the woman.

"I'm Gilda." She took a sip of the scotch and gave an appreciative hum.

"When did your husband pass away?" Norm asked.

"Thirty years ago," Gilda said in a matter-of-fact tone. She put the glass on the small side table and reached into another pocket in her nightgown. "You boys fancy a hit of some fine weed?" She pulled out a small pipe and tinfoil packet. Without waiting for an answer, she opened the packet and pinched a large bud, which she then placed in the bowl of the pipe. "Got a light?"

Norm chuckled and handed her a lighter.

She lit the pipe, took a big hit, and passed it to Hank.

"How come you're walking around in your nightgown?" Hank asked after he'd taken a hit and passed the pipe to Norm.

Gilda looked down at herself as if she hadn't realized what she was wearing. "Oh, hell, I pretty much live in this thing. Why? You think it's too revealing?" She grinned and punched Hank on the arm. "You dirty old man."

Hank smiled. Gilda was awful to look at, but he forced himself to study her. The fire flickered on her face, making it difficult to tell her age, but his best guess put her at about eighty.

"You trying to guess my age?" she asked, looking straight at Hank.

"I'm sorry," he said. "But yeah, I guess I was. Is that rude of me?"

"Shit, do I care? I'm ninety-two." She paused. "But I don't think I look a day over eighty-seven, do you?" She cackled some more before accepting the pipe from Norm and took another long drag.

"This is some pretty good shit," Norm said, leaning back in his chair and staring up at the countless stars.

"Thanks," Gilda said. "I grow it myself."

"Stoner!" Hank said. The dog was licking Gilda's dirty foot.

Gilda giggled. "Oh, leave him be. I haven't been licked since Shorty and I did a threesome with Popeye, the forest ranger. Let's see . . ." She rubbed her chin thoughtfully. "That was thirty-two years ago."

Hank said nothing, trying to get the image of Gilda in a threesome out of his mind.

"They called him Popeye 'cause he had the biggest forearms you ever saw. But boy, did he have a little dick. Certainly the littlest I've ever seen." She held up her forefinger and thumb on her right hand, about two inches apart.

"Oh, man," Norm said. "Too much information."

Gilda snorted. "The man may have had a tiny dick, but boy could he lick. Made me sing."

"Make it stop, Daddy," Norm said.

Hank was trying to figure out how to get rid of this crazy woman when she suddenly reached out and grabbed both his and Norm's hands. Hank could feel her jagged nails and rough callouses dig into the palm of his hand. Her grip was stronger than he would have thought.

"What . . . ?"

"Hush," Gilda said.

The hush was so harsh and authoritative that both men were silenced, letting their hands be held as the campfire cast a surreal yellowish hue.

After about two minutes of silence, Gilda said, "He's alive."

Hank felt his stomach lurch. "Who's alive?"

"The person you're looking for." She turned her head toward Norm. After half a minute, she did the same to Hank. "He's related to you, isn't he?" she said to Hank.

Hank made a grunting sound. His head was spinning. How could this gross old woman know anything about what they were doing?

Gilda let go of Hank's hand and turned back to Norm, still holding his hand. "I like you. You're like a honey badger—you don't give a shit. You just go along, taking whatever life throws at you, don't you?" She didn't wait for an answer but turned back to Hank. "I'm sorry for your loss. Your wife, yes?" Gilda's voice and entire demeanor had changed since she'd taken their hands. The lascivious, somewhat mocking tone had been replaced by a more throaty, kind-sounding voice.

Hank nodded dumbly. "How do you know these things?"

"I see things, feel things." She patted her matted hair as if she were a young ingenue making sure her hairdo was in place. "That's why I live alone out here," she continued. "I get overwhelmed when I'm around too many people."

Hank thought for a moment. "Can you tell me more about the person we're looking for?"

Gilda shook her head. "Nope. You've never met him, have you?"

"No."

"So I can't pick anything up through you." She snorted and jerked her thumb back toward Norm. "And all I get from that guy is that he's pretty damn horny for such an old man. Makes me wish I'd put on some makeup before coming over." She cackled and went back to her old persona. "Well, gotta get back to nothing. Thanks for patronizing the Tres Piedras RV Park and Campground."

Gilda chuckled to herself as she stood and walked past the fire into the darkness. Hank and Norm watched her leave.

But a moment later she reappeared, stopping at the edge of the ambient light, looking more ghostly than ever. "By the way," she said, her tone serious again. "Watch out for the Mexicans." Then she disappeared again.

Hank and Norm sat in stoned silence for a good ten minutes. Hank stared up at the stars. Norm stared into the fire. The mournful wail of a nearby coyote brought them back to reality.

"Was that woman real or has our weed suddenly gotten better?" Norm asked.

"I think she was real."

"Hank," Norm said in a loud whisper, nodding toward the chair between them. On it lay a small pipe and a large marijuana bud.

Chapter 22

Hank and Norm didn't talk about Gilda again until they were on the road the next morning.

"That was particularly potent marijuana," Norm said, sitting in the passenger seat sipping coffee.

Hank snorted. "Whatever happened to 'That was some good shit, man'?"

"Your Cheech impression sucks," Norm said. "So, do you think she's really psychic, or clairvoyant, or whatever you call it?"

"Who knows? But you gotta admit it was pretty damned weird she knew we were looking for someone related to me."

"And that we were wondering if he were dead or alive," Norm said. "And what was that shit about Mexicans?"

Hank grunted. "I reckon she was just fucking with us at that point." He'd never believed in psychics, even though he'd known some police forces to actually employ them in cases that were otherwise going nowhere. But there was no way Gilda could have known what they were doing, and a lucky guess seemed even more unlikely. He thought about Gilda being unable to "read" anything more because he'd never met Junior and had nothing to impart. *Would she be able to tell more from Mai?* he wondered.

The thought of trying to convince Mai to go to New Mexico to meet an unkempt old woman who may or may not be a psychic made Hank smile. "You know, she could have been lurking in the dark and overheard my conversation with Mai. From that, she'd have known we were talking about someone who might be dead."

Norm grunted.

The miles rolled by.

"You ever do a threesome?" Norm asked. "Maybe we should've done a threesome with Gilda."

Hank choked, and the van swerved. "What the fuck, Norm? You're grossing me out here."

"You ever do a threesome?"

Hank kept his eyes on the road and shook his head. "Only in my fantasies. But I don't think Gilda factored into any of those."

"Bet she was hot when she was younger and doing her husband and Popeye."

"You are one sick puppy," Hank said. "Now do me a huge favor and shut the fuck up about Gilda. You're going to give me nightmares."

Norm was silent a moment. "Fine. You've got Mai to dream about. Who've I got? Or can I dream about Mai, too?"

"How about what's-her-name at the death farm, Tiffany?"

"No Mai?" Norm asked, his tone petulant.

"No Mai."

Norm pointed to a sign they were passing. "I thought we were going to stop at Ojo Caliente for the hot springs."

"Mai's kind of freaked out," Hank said. "I feel like we need to get to her as soon as possible. We can stop near Flagstaff tonight and then get to Pasadena tomorrow."

They drove past small forests of juniper trees and rugged, flesh-colored hills that reminded Hank of the folds in discarded linen napkins. "Georgia O'Keeffe country," he said.

Norm grunted again. "I'll bet *she* stopped at the hot springs."

Hank laughed. "If you stop pouting, I'll buy you an ice cream at lunch."

Stoner barked once.

"You too, Stoner," Hank said.

*   *   *

It was still early when Hank and Norm got to Flagstaff, so they decided to go on to Kingman, Arizona. It would make the drive to Pasadena more manageable.

"It would've been more fun setting up camp in the Coconino Forest at Flagstaff," Hank said as they pulled off the highway in Kingman, onto Andy Devine Boulevard. "But we'll have to settle for this RV park tonight." He pulled into a half-full RV camp and stopped at the office.

As they climbed out of the van with Stoner, they noticed a small crowd gathered around a mobile home at the edge of the park and decided to investigate. When they got close enough, they saw that a work crew appeared to be tearing off one side of the trailer.

Norm approached a middle-age man with a graying ponytail and an enormous potbelly and asked, "What's going on?"

The man turned to Norm. "Old Luke died in bed last night," he said, as if that explained everything. He turned back to the action.

Norm looked at Hank, who shrugged. Then he addressed the ponytailed man again. "They're tearing apart the trailer because the owner died?"

Ponytail looked back at Norm. "Old Luke weighed over four hundred pounds." He spoke in a patient tone, as if he were explaining the obvious. "He hasn't left his trailer in over a year. He's too big for the coroner's office to get through the door, so they have to take the side of the trailer off to get him out."

At that moment, the workers pulled an entire panel from the trailer, exposing the inside and releasing an invisible cloud of noxious odor, the predominant smell of which was shit. The crowd of onlookers gagged as one. Most covered their noses and moved back, as did Hank and Norm.

A whale of a man was lying naked on a bed against the opposite wall. It looked to Hank like there was a line of bedpans beside the bed. Beer cans were strewn about the room. There was a haphazard stack of frozen dinner trays mixed in with the bedpans.

"Jesus." Hank pulled on Norm's shirtsleeve. "Let's get out of here."

They turned to head back to the van and almost bumped into a large-breasted woman with shorn gray hair. It looked as if she had cut it herself, as the lines were choppy and uneven. She wore a stained and faded flower-patterned smock, which hid everything except the enormity of her breasts. She appeared to be in her sixties.

"You boys with that van over there?" Her voice was cheerful and she smiled broadly. "Need a spot for the night?"

"What's up with that guy, Luke, over there?" Norm asked.

The woman continued to smile. She looked over at the trailer for a moment and then back at Hank and Norm. "Oh, that's just my husband. He died last night. Good-bye and good riddance, I say. The old fart got so big he couldn't even get out of bed. I moved into the office a couple months ago."

Norm looked back over his shoulder. The crowd had edged farther away from the trailer. Two men wearing masks were climbing into the room where the big man lay dead. He turned back to the woman. "Who's been taking care of him since you moved out?"

The woman shrugged, still smiling. "Me, mostly. When I had the time. Sometimes I got the kid who lives in that trailer back there"—she jerked her head toward a rundown trailer on the opposite side of the park—"to help out. So, you need a spot for the night or not?"

Hank spoke up before Norm could answer. "No, thanks. We just stopped by to see if you knew of a quiet campground nearby. We figured RV people would be most likely to know."

The smile eased off, and the woman scratched her head. "You going east or west on 40? Or you heading to Vegas?"

"West on 40," Hank said.

"Can't really say I recall anything that way," she said. She absently scratched under one of her breasts, causing both to jiggle and bounce. "But we'd be happy to accommodate you here."

"Oh no," Norm said. "We'll make do. Thanks for everything." He pulled on Stoner's leash and headed for the van. "C'mon, Stoner."

"Let's get a hotel," Hank said as they drove out of the RV park.

Norm replied, "I don't remember reading about any of this kind of shit in *Travels with Charley*."

Chapter 23

Hank had been feeling weird the whole day driving to Los Angeles. It was an edgy kind of nervousness that he felt in his gut, the kind where you don't know what's going to happen next. Norm had been uncharacteristically quiet, and Stoner seemed to have picked up the strange vibes, spending most of the trip curled up in the back of the van.

By the time they got on the 210 Freeway heading into Pasadena, Hank admitted to himself that he was looking forward to seeing Mai again. He wasn't sure what that meant, but considering she'd been pretty much all he'd thought about during the long drive, it wasn't something he could just ignore. But what did not ignoring it mean? And what was "it?" Was he falling in love with this woman again?

He'd been with Becka for so long, he'd forgotten what it was like to have these strange feelings of . . . of what? Was he sexually attracted to her? Of course. She was still beautiful. Was he emotionally attracted to her? That was the confusing part. He liked the short time they'd spent together. She was smart and funny and seemed to "get him" in the same way Becka had.

Becka. Therein lay the rub. He couldn't seem to think about Mai in any kind of romantic way without a flood of guilt pouring into him. Which, he knew, was stupid. Becka no longer existed. He did. Mai did. He knew Becka would not begrudge him a chance to fall in love again with the only other woman he'd ever loved. A woman who, despite having had his child, had stayed away so she wouldn't interfere with his and Becka's relationship.

By the time he exited the freeway, Hank had worked himself into an anxious mess. In his mind, he knew there was no way Mai would be interested in her old, broken-down ex-lover.

Would she?

They followed North Pasadena Avenue to East Colorado Boulevard and turned left, passing through Old Pasadena where historic buildings now housed upscale stores and restaurants: sushi bars, Mexican restaurants, even an Argentinian steakhouse. As they approached the edge of Old Town, the historic buildings were interspersed with boxy sixties- and seventies-era office buildings. Hank turned right on Fair Oaks and then into the alley of Mai's condo.

Mai answered the door wearing a beautiful silky, scarlet caftan. Her hair was pinned up. She gave Norm a hug and a peck on his cheek.

The hug she gave Hank seemed to him to last just a little longer. The kiss, on the lips, felt soft, and to Hank's confused mind, seemed to linger. He felt his face burn slightly and hoped he wasn't blushing.

Mai wiggled her nose and smiled. "I've never kissed a man with a beard before. It tickles." She ushered them into her living room and offered them coffee.

Hank and Norm sat in side-by-side leather library chairs and watched Mai walk to the kitchen. After a moment, Hank could sense Norm's gaze on him. He looked at Norm, who had something akin to a shit-eating grin on his face.

"What?"

"What grade are you in?" Norm asked.

"Fuck you."

Norm nodded toward Stoner, who had followed Mai into the kitchen and was licking her leg. "Bet you wish you were Stoner about now."

Hank was about to reply when Mai returned with a tray in her hands. "Thanks for stopping by," she said, pouring the coffee.

"I know that call was upsetting," Hank said. "But hopefully you agree it doesn't make any sense. If Junior were dead, you'd have heard about it before now."

Mai nodded though Hank could see from her expression she wasn't totally convinced.

"Besides," Norm said, "we met a psychic in New Mexico who said Hank Jr. was still alive."

Hank groaned.

Mai looked confused.

Hank spoke before she could ask anything. "We were camping in New Mexico, and this weird old lady came into camp, pretty much out of nowhere, and offered us some dope. She was totally off the wall, saying all sorts of weird shit, but then, out of nowhere, she said whoever I was looking for was still alive. She could feel it was someone related to me, but because I'd never met Junior, she couldn't tell me anything more."

Hank stopped talking. He and Norm hadn't discussed whether they would or would not tell Mai about Gilda. He shrugged and tried a smile. It was hard for him to tell what Mai was thinking.

"Do you believe her?" Mai asked.

Hank shrugged again. "I already believed Junior's still alive, so yes, I guess I do."

"I do," Norm said. "There's no way she could've known we were looking for someone, or that we were concerned whether that person was still alive. Totally weird."

"My good friend Eva believes in that kind of thing," Mai said. "She's even gone to a couple of séances. But I've never been able to buy into it. Your encounter with that woman seems too strange not to be real, but if she couldn't read anything more because you'd never met Hank Jr., how could she *feel* he was still alive?"

Norm coughed.

Hank nodded. "Well, it doesn't really matter. I think Junior's alive, and the fact that an old witch thinks so too can't hurt."

Mai finally smiled and shook her head. "Whatever. So what's the plan now?"

Hank had already given her a brief account of their meeting with Kurt Valentine in Aspen, but now he went over it again, ending with their intention to try to find Monty Washburn in the San Diego area. "Norm's already compiled a list of possibilities. He's not on Facebook, which would have allowed us to confirm which Monty Washburn went to Pasadena High. We'll probably find him by the time we get to San Diego."

Mai nodded. "What's up with these people so far? I mean, that girl Hank ran off with, Dana Clark, claims she didn't know why he went with her or where he went after. You said that Kurt fellow claimed to barely know Hank. If so, why did Dana give you his name? It all seems so bizarre to me."

"My working theory," Hank said, "is that something happened to Junior during that last week of school that caused him to run away. I don't know if these people know anything more than they claim or if they're sending us off on wild goose chases, but I'm pretty confident we'll connect the dots eventually."

"But even if we find out why Junior left," Norm said, "that doesn't mean we'll necessarily know where to look for him."

They grew quiet. Stoner rose from the kitchen floor and walked over to Mai. He looked up at her and tilted his head slightly. Norm started to call him off, but Mai patted her lap and the dog jumped up, nestling into the softness of her belly.

Hank let his gaze linger on Mai for a moment while she was distracted by Stoner. "Do you have Junior's yearbooks? Particularly the one from his senior year?"

"Sure. He left everything. Want them?"

"I should have asked for them before. Stupid of me. Yes, if we can borrow them for a while, we may be able to find out who he was closest to. Hopefully he has some autographs from friends."

Mai nodded. "He does. I remember in his junior year, he was really proud of how many people—both students and teachers—

he got to sign his yearbook. I don't remember any conversation about his senior yearbook, but I do have it." She gently pushed Stoner off and went into another room.

Norm crossed his legs and sat back in his high-backed chair. "It's seven-thirty. We gonna get dinner, or are we fasting?"

Mai came back into the room with three yearbooks and handed them to Hank.

"You two must be hungry," Mai said. "I didn't make anything 'cause I wasn't sure what time you'd be rolling in. But one of Eva's Mexican restaurants is only half a block away. I assume you're staying the night, so if you want to take a few minutes to get your stuff and clean up, you can pick your bedroom. The two guest rooms are identical."

"I'm game," Norm said. "Give me ten minutes."

"You going to join us?" Hank asked.

Mai looked down at the caftan she was wearing and smiled. "Just as soon as I change into something more appropriate."

*   *   *

Twenty minutes later, they walked into La Casa Ochoa. The hostess greeted Mai in Spanish, and the two had a short, rapid-fire conversation before Mai introduced Hank and Norm. "This is Teresita, one of Eva's most valued managers."

Teresita gave them a broad smile and shook each man's hand.

La Casa Ochoa was not a typical Mexican restaurant. Upscale and modern, it had subdued lighting and tables covered with white tablecloths. Instead of the ubiquitous sombreros and sera-pes on the walls, glass cases held Aztec pottery and intricately painted wooden Oaxacan animals.

The restaurant was full, but Teresita took them to a back corner table on which a *Reserved* sign stood.

When she was gone, Hank looked at Mai. "The owner's table, I presume?"

Mai smiled and nodded. "With Eva living so close, they keep this table available for her."

"What's good?" Norm asked.

"The margaritas, for starters," Mai said.

A young waitress appeared at the table, and once again Mai had a short conversation in Spanish before ordering a margarita made with añejo tequila.

Hank and Norm followed suit.

"The steak tampequeña is Eva's signature dish," Mai said. "It's got medallions cut from filet mignon roast, and the chile relleno is a poblano stuffed with cheese from Oaxaca as well as a local goat cheese. It comes with house-made refried beans and the best guacamole you'll ever have."

"Sounds perfect," Hank said.

Norm nodded his assent.

A moment later, the waitress was back and Mai ordered for the three of them. They had a rapid back-and-forth in Spanish, which ended with the waitress laughing and nodding.

Gesturing to the departing waitress, Norm asked, "You making fun of us?"

Mai was about to answer when Hank said, "She told the waitress to make the green sauce on our rellenos extra hot. She said she wants to know what we're made of."

Mai stared at Hank. "You speak Spanish?"

Hank nodded. "And French and Italian, but not much Vietnamese anymore. Becka was an interpreter for the CIA. She taught me most of what I know." He smiled at the look of embarrassment on Mai's face. "Don't worry. I don't know about my sidekick here, but I can take whatever heat you and your coconspirators throw at me."

Norm said, "I'll be fine as long as you don't mind the top of my head sweating."

There was a moment of uncomfortable silence.

"Sorry, guys," Mai finally said. "Was that kind of a bitchy thing to do? I was trying to be funny."

"Kind of," Norm said. "But I forgive you. And at least now I'm forewarned."

Mai looked at Hank, who was smiling.

"Don't worry about it," he said. "I may have been kind of a dick by not telling you I spoke Spanish when you were telling Teresita that I'd been your boyfriend a million years ago."

Mai covered her face with her hands. "Oh, God."

Hank laughed. "And being described as 'the old guy with the beard' isn't the worst I've heard."

Norm choked on a sip of margarita. "Is that what she said?" He turned to Mai. "So I guess you described me as the younger, good-looking guy?"

The three of them laughed and Hank relaxed. The low-level tension had evaporated.

"The only way you'd ever be described as good-looking is if you had hundred-dollar bills hanging out of your pockets," Hank said.

"Hank!" said Mai, slapping his hand. "Norm's very good-looking."

"Yeah, old guy with a beard," Norm replied.

The three said nothing for a few minutes, sipping their margaritas as the sounds of the restaurant washed over them. Mexican ballads played softly on the sound system. It was a comfortable ambiance.

"So, Mai," Hank said. "So far you've given us the PI's report, and we have some additional names from Dana and Kurt Valentine, but you haven't shared any additional names of Junior's friends. Is there anyone we should be talking to? Especially maybe here in Pasadena?"

The question seemed to have taken Mai by surprise. Her face clouded over, and she looked down at her drink for several seconds before meeting Hank's eyes. "I . . . most of Hank's friends were listed in the detective's report." She didn't continue.

"Okay," Hank said. "But was that all of them? Who was Junior's best friend? Who'd he have for sleepovers? That kind of thing I don't see in the report."

Mai sighed heavily. "I'm afraid I wasn't the best parent in the world. It was at a time when my restaurants were really taking off, and I was working sixteen-hour days, seven days a week. Hank worked in the restaurant most afternoons, but I didn't see him much at night. There was a kid named Wesley who I think Hank hung around with for a while, but I don't know his last name. He was a Japanese kid. There was a black kid I saw every once in a while, but I don't know his name."

Mai paused as the waitress set their plates in front of them. Then she stared down at her plate for several beats before looking back up at Hank. "I'm embarrassed at how little I know about Hank, especially in that last year."

This time the silence wasn't comfortable.

After a minute, Norm said, "This looks great."

Mai looked as if she might cry.

"No worries, Mai," Hank said. "We'll figure it out."

She nodded tentatively and picked up her fork. "Thanks," she said in a soft, almost childlike tone.

Hank took a bite of his chile relleno. The green sauce was seriously hot.

Chapter 24

Mai was furious with herself as the three walked back to her condo after dinner. She'd embarrassed herself by acting superior and childish. First, she'd shown off by speaking Spanish with Teresita, and needlessly told her about Hank. Then she showed off her Spanish again with the waitress, and even more embarrassing, had told the girl to make the chile hot. On top of all that, she'd had to admit she knew very little about her son's last year at home.

Norm excused himself to go to bed as soon as they entered the condo. "I'll take the yearbooks with me and see if I can make any connections," he said, kissing Mai on the cheek.

"Nightcap?" Mai asked.

"Why not?" Hank followed her into the kitchen.

"Wine, vodka, or tequila?"

"Vodka's fine. Just a little."

She poured a few fingers of Tito's over ice. The two stood close to each other at the kitchen counter. They clinked glasses without verbalizing a toast and then each took a sip.

Mai put down her glass and looked at Hank. "I'm really sorry about tonight. I acted like . . . ."

Hank put his right hand on her cheek and touched her mouth with his thumb. His touch was soft and gentle. Mai felt a tightening in her chest and she closed her eyes. *This is a man who knows how to comfort a woman*, she thought.

"You don't need to say anything," Hank said softly. "I have a feeling we're both still a little off-balance with each other."

Mai moved toward Hank and put her arms around him. He pulled her into a firm embrace. He smelled good. She detected a subtle, almost grassy cologne mixed with his muskiness from a long day of travel. It turned her on. She moved her head back so she could look at him.

His eyes were as she remembered from forty-something years ago. They were penetrating, kind-looking eyes, which always seemed to be ready to shift into another dimension—amusement, understanding, sadness. She leaned in and kissed him on the lips. A long, slow, sensuous kiss. She felt her nipples harden. She felt Hank's body stir. When they broke off the kiss, she looked into his eyes. "Do you want to . . . ."

He touched her mouth again, shushing her, this time with two fingers. "I want to more than anything." His voice was husky. "But not now. Not tonight. I'm not ready. I'm . . . ."

It was her turn to silence him, which she did by kissing him again. Then she backed off, picked up her drink, and held it up for a toast. "To possibilities."

"To possibilities."

They drank.

Chapter 25

"I found the Wesley kid," Norm said. "He's listed in the yearbook as Wesley Tanabe. There's a strange message from him in Junior's book. It says, 'Don't go—love ya always, Wes.' I wonder what the 'don't go' part refers to. Do you think he knew Junior was getting ready to take off?"

They had just said their good-byes to Mai and were pulling out of her underground garage, with Hank driving. He stopped short of the street. "Were you able to find out where he lives now?"

Norm nodded. "He's on Facebook. He teaches computer coding at some sort of private institute just up Colorado Boulevard. Turn right."

Code Red Coding took up one floor of a four-story modern building on Colorado Boulevard, just past Lake. The reception area was small and stark, and there was no one at the tiny desk. Hank pressed a buzzer, and in seconds a young man with dirty, shoulder-length hair, a tight black T-shirt, and black jeans stuck his head out through a doorway that obviously led to the work areas.

"Help you?" His body was mostly in the back room, as if it were his tortoise shell.

Hank answered, "We're looking for Wesley Tanabe."

"He expecting you?"

"No. We're just in town for the day and need to take a few minutes of his time on a personal matter."

The kid looked from Hank to Norm and back again and held up an index finger. Then his head retracted into the back room and he was gone.

A few minutes later, a wiry Asian man came through the door. He, too, wore jeans and a T-shirt, as well as flip-flops. His black, medium-length hair was streaked with gray. "I'm Wes Tanabe. Can I help you?"

Hank extended a hand to shake. "I'm Hank Reagan. This is Norm Rothstein."

Tanabe shook Hank's hand, then Norm's. "I knew a Hank Raygun in high school. How do you spell your name?"

Smiling, Hank replied, "Not R-A-Y-G-U-N, if that's what you're asking."

"Ah, so you knew him? Do you know where he is?"

"Unfortunately, no. That's why we're here. We're looking up some of his old classmates to try to figure out what happened to him." Hank looked around. "Is there someplace we can talk for a bit?"

Wes looked at his watch. "I have a class starting in twenty minutes, so I can give you some time. Come on back to my office."

The door led to a large room in which two long workbenches held about thirty computer stations, all of which were in use. The black-clad tortoise kid was bending over one of the stations, apparently pointing something out on a student's screen. To the far back of the large room were three small private offices and a huge flat screen. All the walls were glass. Wes led them to the last office. The room was cramped, but there were chairs for Hank and Norm. Wes sat behind his desk.

Norm asked, "You own this business?"

Wes smiled and nodded. "That's the only reason an old man like me is tolerated around here."

"I've heard coding schools are a pretty big business," Norm said. "What is it, thirty or forty grand for a sixteen-week course?"

Wes shrugged good-naturedly. "Something like that. So, what's all this about Hank? I haven't seen him since he disappeared. And who are you guys?"

"I'm his father," Hank said. "Although I just found out about him a week or so ago. His mother tracked me down and asked me to help find him."

Wes looked at Norm.

"And I'm his friend who's retired and has nothing else to do," Norm said.

"Seems like kind of a long time to decide to start looking for the guy," Wes said, scratching the top of his head.

"His mother tried to find him that first year. Then the trail went cold. When she reconnected with me, she asked for my help." Hank paused. "What was that entry you made in Hank's yearbook about? 'Don't go.'"

Wes looked up, as if trying to remember. Or maybe he was trying to decide what to disclose. "Look," he finally said. "Hank had some issues. He was smart. Really smart. He instinctively understood computers. But he had serious issues with self-esteem. He wasn't happy just hanging out with geeks like me. He was always trying to break into the 'cool-guys' group."

"Cool guys like Kurt Valentine?" asked Hank.

"Exactly! Why he thought guys like Valentine were cool was beyond me. As far as I was concerned, Valentine was an ignorant, racist, bigoted prick. But for some reason, Hank was fascinated by Kurt and the rest of them." Wes scratched his head again. "I don't know, maybe it was a mission for him. Like he wanted to find out for himself what made those guys project coolness or whatever.""

"Did you know he was going to take off?" Norm asked. "Is that what your note was about?"

Wes shook his head. "No. The day before graduation, a group of guys, led by Valentine, were planning to go up to Mount Wilson and get crazy. Probably get high. Mess around with whatever chicks went up. I don't know—end of high school shit. It sounded like trouble to me. Somehow, after being shined on by these assholes for our entire senior year, Hank was suddenly invited to go with them. He was stoked. I tried to talk him out of going. That's what that note was all about."

"So he went?" Hank asked.

"As far as I know. I saw him once after that—at graduation, which would've been the day after the trip to Mount Wilson. Everyone's parents were around, so we kind of just hugged each other and said 'see ya,' and that was the last time I ever saw him."

No one said anything for several moments. It was clear to Hank from Wes's voice that he and Junior had been good friends.

"Do you know anyone besides Valentine who was supposed to go up to Mount Wilson?" he asked.

Wes shrugged. "Valentine's usual clique, I guess. Let's see: Monty Washburn, Sammy Stone, Tom Bushman." He paused. "There were probably a couple other guys, but I can't reel them in right now."

Norm asked, "What about girls?"

Wes shook his head. "That, I really don't know about." He looked at his watch, then back at Hank and Norm. "I don't know what happened up there or even if Hank actually went. But I'd focus on that if I were you. He left the day after graduation, and on graduation day itself, he was just kind of walking around like a zombie, like he was going through the motions." He paused again and then stood. "I sure hope he's alive and well. He was pretty much my best friend that last year in school. All of us geeks took a lot of shit from guys like Valentine, but it bothered Hank a lot. I didn't really give a shit. I just wanted to get out and head off to college."

Hank and Norm shook hands with Wes, and Hank handed him a card. "If you think of anything else, please be sure to call," he said.

"If you find him, tell him to come see me," Wes said. "I still think about him."

Chapter 26

"Iknow that name, Tom Bushman, from someplace," Norm said. He and Hank were on the freeway, heading south. "I want to say he was a politician or something. I'm going to get my iPad and Google it." He unbuckled his seat belt and made his way to the back of the van.

A moment later he was back in the passenger seat. Stoner sat in the well between the two front seats, gazing up at Norm with a pathetic look.

"Here he is," Norm said after a few minutes. "He *was* a politician." He paused. "Oh God, I remember him. What a nut job."

"What?" Hank asked.

"He was that congressman from Orange County who was Mr. Family Values. He's the one who said there's no such thing as a Christian homo—that's the word he used. And he's been a strong supporter of these so-called religious freedom laws that allow businesses to refuse goods and services to LGBT people based on religious beliefs. Of course he's against abortion, and he thinks there's already Sharia law in some parts of the United States."

Hank chuckled. "Sounds like pretty standard stuff for a rep from Orange County. He's not in Congress anymore?"

"Don't you remember?" Norm asked. "He's the guy who was caught by one of his interns in his congressional office jerking off to Internet pictures of women in burqas."

"Huh?"

"I told you he was a sick puppy."

106

"But he must've had a pretty good imagination," Hank said. "Where is he now?"

Norm was silent as he stared down at his screen. He grunted a few times, but otherwise said nothing for several minutes. "Can't tell," he finally said. "He resigned from Congress after a tearful apology with his wife standing by his side, but I can't figure out what he's doing now. He seems to be keeping a low profile."

"Was his wife in a burqa?"

Norm laughed.

Stoner barked.

*   *   *

After a dozen calls to people named Washburn in Pasadena, a man who said he was Monty's uncle told Norm that Monty lived in Leucadia, north of San Diego. From that information, it was easy enough to find an address.

The house was a small stucco affair with a shingle roof, located two blocks from the ocean. It looked like it might have been a 1960s beach bungalow, except now it was surrounded by large, multimillion-dollar homes. There were other surviving bungalows in the area, but it was clear their days were numbered.

Hank and Norm pulled into the short driveway and parked behind a red Nissan Rogue with surf racks on the roof. A middle-age man with bleached blond hair and a gray goatee answered the door on the first ring. He wore an orange North County Surf Shop T-shirt and faded blue swimming trunks that came almost to his knees.

"Hey, there," Hank said. "We're looking for Monty Washburn."

"That's me," said the man. "Who's asking?"

Hank extended a hand. "I'm Hank Reagan, and this is Norm Rothstein."

Washburn's gray eyes squinted at Hank. He took the proffered hand to shake. "Hank Reagan? Is that what you said?"

"Yeah, it is. I think you knew my son, Hank, back in high school. Can we come in?"

Washburn stared at Hank a little longer. Then he turned to Norm and shook his hand before gesturing for them to follow him into the house. "Sorry for the mess. I live alone and don't always keep things so neat." He picked some clothes and a towel off the couch and gestured for the two men to sit. He sat in a cracked leather easy chair facing them, across a coffee table piled high with what appeared to be mostly surfing magazines.

"I didn't know Hank had a father." He sniffed and wiped his nose on his bare arm. "I mean, of course he had a father, but I thought he didn't know who he was."

"He didn't," Hank said. "I just found out about him myself a little over a week ago. His mother tracked me down and asked me to help look for him."

Washburn gave a half nod and then shrugged. "Well, good luck with that, but I sure can't help you. I haven't seen the dude since graduation."

Norm asked, "Were you and Hank friends?"

Washburn's mouth turned down as he shook his head in the negative. "Nah. Barely knew him. He tried to hang around my crew, but nobody really liked him." He paused and looked at Hank. "No offense."

Hank shrugged. "No worries. I don't even know if I'd like him. I've never met him. But Kurt Valentine told us you and Hank were friendly. He said you were the only one of your group who'd hang around with Hank."

Washburn laughed and ran a hand through his unkempt blond hair. "You talked to Kurt? What an asshole. Fucking guy couldn't write a literate sentence if his life depended on it, but now he's CEO of a publishing empire."

"Well," Norm said, "if it makes you feel any better, from what we've learned, he doesn't do anything. He's president in name only. He lives in Aspen, far away from the company's home office."

"Why would that make me feel better?" Washburn asked. "It just means the fuck is living the high life without doing shit to earn it."

"I thought you were buds," Norm said.

Washburn snorted. "We hung together pretty much because I liked most of the other guys in the crew, and Kurt was the self-appointed leader."

"Alpha male?" Hank asked.

"If being the biggest asshole, the most racist, the most sexist, and the biggest criminal in the group means he was the alpha male, then yeah, I guess that's what he was."

"No offense," Hank said, "but we were getting the idea that your whole clique—or crew, or whatever you want to call it— were racists. Kurt specifically said you guys didn't want non-whites in the group."

Washburn shrugged and crossed his legs, revealing leg hair bleached by the sun. He wore no shoes, and Hank could see that the bottom of his foot was dirty and calloused. "True enough," Washburn said. "I don't know that you could actually call most of us racists, but I also couldn't really make a strong argument that we weren't prejudiced. I don't know, is that the same as being racist? But in any event, some of us have mellowed with age."

A small grin on his face, Norm asked, "Like Tom Bushman?"

Washburn laughed out loud. "What a fuckup that guy turned into."

"Speaking of Bushman," Hank said, "do you know where he lives now?"

Washburn frowned. "I'm not sure. Last I heard, he may be in Lake Tahoe or Truckee, or someplace near there. I'm out of the loop, and he went into self-imposed hiding after being caught with his pee-pee in hand."

"Did anyone call you to tell you we might be coming by?" Hank asked.

Washburn frowned again. "Why would they do that?"

"I don't know," Hank said. "Someone's been trying to get us to stop our search, but we don't know who or why."

"Who've you talked to so far—besides Kurt?"

"Besides Kurt, Dana Clark and a friend of Hank's named Wes Tanabe," Hank replied. "That's all."

Washburn rubbed his nose again, this time with his right hand. "I kind of remember Wes Tanabe. Geeky little Asian fuck?"

"That's one way to describe him," Norm said.

Hank asked, "Did you go up to Mount Wilson with Valentine and your crew the day before graduation?"

Washburn's eyes narrowed. "Who told you about that? Kurt?"

"No. Wes Tanabe said he'd heard you guys invited Hank to go up there with you. He tried to talk Hank out of it."

Washburn shrugged theatrically. "I really don't remember. Some of the guys went up there, smoked some dope, drank some beers. You know, end of high school shit. I can't really remember if Hank came with us or not."

Hank watched Washburn closely. His mouth had turned down again, and his eyes were active, moving back and forth between Hank and Norm.

Norm asked, "Who else went up there?"

Washburn shook his head. "Can't remember. I think I got fucked up."

The room was quiet except for the occasional car passing on the street outside.

"Pretty cool spot living so close to the beach," Hank said. "Do you work here in town?"

Washburn appeared to relax with the change of subject. "Nah. I'm not working right now. I was a financial adviser, but I got divorced and thought I'd take some time for myself. I'm pretty much surfing and reading and shit. I'll go back to work soon."

Hank had been looking around the living room as Washburn spoke. It didn't look much like the home of a successful financial adviser. There was a huge bong sitting beside the easy chair. Two highly waxed surfboards leaned against one wall. Other than a large flat-screen TV, the furniture was old and ratty. It looked more like the pad of a twenty-something surf bum than a middle-age financial guy.

"So," Hank said, "getting back to Hank for a minute, are you saying you didn't really know him well?"

"That's right. Hardly knew the guy. He seemed nice enough. I hope you find him."

"What about Dana Clark?" Norm asked. "Did you know her?"

Washburn gave what looked to Hank like a leer. "Sure. Most guys knew Dana. Or at least *of* her. She was pretty much the class whore."

Norm asked, "Were she and Hank an item?"

Washburn made a face, almost like a grimace. "I don't think so. Maybe. I don't know. I heard they ran off together, but that's pretty much all I know."

Hank decided to push a little. "Something happened up on Mount Wilson that day before graduation, didn't it? Something bad. Something involving Hank."

Washburn stared at him. "Why would you say that? We went up. We smoked some dope. Drank some beers. Then we graduated the next day, and everyone went their separate ways. End of story."

"What aren't you telling me, Washburn?" Hank's tone turned hard, accusatory.

"What the fuck, old man? I told you what I know. Or at least remember. Get out of my face and out of my house if you're going to act like an asshole. I've had enough assholes in my life." Washburn stood.

Norm glanced at Hank and then stood as well.

Hank stayed seated. "Your little band of racist shitheads got Hank up there with you so you could fuck with him in some way, didn't you? What'd you do? What caused Hank to run away two days later?" Hank stood now, staring hard at Washburn.

"Get the fuck out," Washburn said. "Now, before I throw your ancient ass out." When Hank made no move, Washburn moved into him, arms out, as if to push him away from the couch toward the front door.

In an instant, Hank grabbed Washburn's right hand, twisting it and the arm so that it forced Washburn into an about-face.

"Ow! What the fuck?" said Washburn. "That hurts. Let go!"

Hank gave a tug up on the arm but then released it before doing any damage. Washburn fell away, stumbling over the coffee table.

Hank moved toward the door. "We're going to find out what happened up on the mountain that day. Whoever helps us first will have the best chance of not getting hurt. Call me if you want to be the first." He flipped a card at Washburn. It hit the man's chest and fell to the floor.

Hank and Norm walked out.

Chapter 27

"What the hell, Hank?" Norm said once they were back in the van. "You went all commando on the dude. Don't you know how old you are? You could strain something."

Hank snorted. His heart was racing as he stared at the road. "I can't believe I just did that. And I also can't believe a son of mine would've wanted to hang around with those assholes."

"Well," Norm said, "he didn't know he was a son of yours, so he didn't know how bitchin' he was supposed to be."

"Fuck you."

Norm said, "You know, you're one of the most articulate men I know."

"May your progeny be stuck in a never-ending orgy of pig copulation. How's that for articulation?"

They rode in silence for a minute, heading back up the coast. Hank breathed deeply, and his pulse steadily slowed.

"Pig copulation?" Norm said after a couple of miles.

"Yeah. They don't get as clingy as sheep. I guess they're not as needy."

Norm grunted and nodded, as if Hank had said something very wise. "So, I never asked you about Mai," he said after a couple more miles. "Did you guys get together after I went to bed?"

Hank didn't answer right away. Traffic was light on the Coast Highway, the ocean a glassy gray-blue. The sky held few clouds, just stray wisps left behind by their celestial family unit.

"Interesting segue," Hank finally said. "Not that it's any of your business, but I just don't think I'm ready for any kind of relationship right now."

"Ready? I don't mean to be a dick, but Becka's gone and you're seventy years old." Norm paused, looked down at Stoner staring up at him with his patented pathetic look, and patted his lap. Stoner immediately jumped up. "I really think Mai likes you, man. Although I don't know why."

"Fuck you."

"Ah, more insightful words from my fellow traveler." Norm looked down at Stoner. "What say you, young canine beast?"

Stoner gave a short yelp and buried his head in Norm's crotch.

Hank drove on. He'd been thinking about Mai whenever he could stop thinking about the move he put on Washburn. He smiled to himself. *Not bad for an old dude*, he thought. But when it came to Mai, Hank's thoughts were as confused as ants at a foodless picnic.

He thought about the old black guy in Nevada. What was his name? Conrad. The guy had let the death of his wife dictate the terms of his next five years. And what were those terms, exactly? Don't do shit except hang out at the Peppermill Casino and pout.

Hank didn't want to be a Conrad. He had a limited time left to exist. But even so, he didn't want to rush into something on impulse. He'd already hurt Mai. He'd abandoned her in Vietnam when she was pregnant. He'd stopped looking for her when he began to fall in love with Becka. There was so much he'd done wrong. The disappearance of Junior was partly his fault. The kid had grown up a half-breed without a father at a time when the country was still healing from its Vietnam wounds.

Hank realized Norm was saying something—something about Mai.

"Whatever you decide to do, just remember that Becka would want you to be happy. And Mai's a big girl who can obviously take care of herself."

Hank nodded. The words were all correct. Now he just had to make everything right in his head.

"So," Norm said, "we gonna spend the night at the death farm since we're down here? Or head up to Pasadena so you and Mai can make eyes at each other some more? Or are we off to find another racist prick Junior wanted to hang out with?"

"I think we can rule out the death farm," Hank said. "You need to pick anything up there? 'Cause otherwise I don't intend to go anywhere near it."

"Nah, I'm good. So, Pasadena or elsewhere? Let's see, Tom Bushman, the burqa fetishist, is up in Lake Tahoe. That's pretty. That's Stoner's and my vote."

Hank chuckled. "You can't just usurp Stoner's vote like that. You're disenfranchising him."

"Stoner," Norm said in an authoritative voice.

The dog looked up at him.

"Tahoe?" Norm asked in a voice full of expectation and excitement, as if he was asking Stoner if he liked licking his own balls.

Stoner barked once, and then put his head down.

"See?" Norm said. "He votes for Tahoe."

"Jesus," Hank mumbled. "Two stooges and a dog set out to solve a twenty-three-year-old mystery. What could go wrong?"

"We may be stooges, but we're old stooges."

"Tahoe it is," Hank said. "Let's go as far as Morro Bay today. We can camp out on the beach tonight."

Chapter 28

Hank and Norm ended up in a small camping area between the highway and the ocean, just down the hill from Hearst Castle. The sun was fading in an anticlimactic sunset marred by the presence of interloping clouds.

The only other camper at the site appeared to be a single man who already had a fire blazing. His rig was a camper attached to the back of a pickup truck. Whenever there was a slight shift in the wind, Hank could hear Bob Marley telling the world every little thing was going to be all right.

Hank and Norm set up their camp chairs, lit a fire, and fired up the hibachi. Salmon steaks were on the menu.

Norm set a pot of salted water on the fire. "You want pasta with garlic and olive oil or something else? I have crushed Marzano tomatoes. I can make a puttanesca."

Hank laughed. He opened a bottle of red wine. "You must have been really shitty in bed. You've got a shitload of money, and you can cook. Why would all those wives leave you?" When Norm didn't answer the non-question, Hank said, "Just olive oil and garlic is fine."

Hank glanced over at the campsite next to theirs. Through the fading light he saw a man stacking wood for a fire. "Hey," he said to Norm. "I could use a break from the Hank and Norm show. Why don't we see if that guy over there would like some company?"

"Sure."

Hank made his way over to the neighboring campsite and introduced himself to a lanky, long-haired man. He couldn't make out much of the man's features in the dusk, but he appeared to be in his forties, maybe early fifties. He was barefoot, in baggy shorts and a tight-fitting T-shirt.

"Bob," the man said, extending his hand. "Bob Schlitzman."

"Care for a glass of wine or a little pasta?" Hank asked.

"Thanks, I'd like that," Bob replied, following Hank back.

"This is Norm Rothstein," Hank said, pointing to Norm. "My personal chef and valet."

Norm wiped his hands on his apron and shook hands. "Have a seat, Bob. We have wine." Norm pointed to his chair.

Bob sat and Stoner sniffed his feet.

"Where you from, Bob?" Hank pulled a wine glass from the picnic basket at his side and poured.

"Jackson, Mississippi," Bob said. "How 'bout you guys?"

"We both live in Southern California, more or less," Norm said. "You traveling by yourself?"

Bob accepted the glass from Hank and took a sip. "Umm. Nice. Yeah, I'm taking a year off to travel the country. On my own."

"Your wife or significant other doesn't mind you taking off for a year?" Norm asked. "Or are you between at the moment?"

Hank couldn't see Bob's expression, but a small cough and an adjustment to Bob's body language got his attention.

"I lost my wife this past year," Bob said. His voice cracked. "She was murdered."

"Jesus," Hank said. "Murdered? How? By whom?"

Bob looked at Hank and then at Norm. "You guys pro-lifers, by any chance?"

"Which ones are pro-life?" Norm asked. "The ones who want to make sure the mother has the right to live her life based on what is best for her and her unborn, or the ones who want to force women to have unwanted children and who then don't want to pay anything to take care of them once they're born? I get confused."

Bob chuckled softly, shaking his head. "I guess that answers my question. My wife was a doctor who volunteered her time on weekends working at a women's clinic. Mostly she counseled women, but she performed abortions as well. Some anti-abortion asshole shot her one Saturday morning as she walked from her car to the clinic entrance. She died at the scene."

No one said anything. The fire crackled, and the waves pounded the beach. Every once in a while, they heard a car roar by on Highway 1.

Hank was trying to come up with some sincere-sounding platitudes when Bob spoke again. "Here's the kicker. Melanie—that's my wife—had saved the killer's daughter a year earlier. The little girl's mother had brought her into the ER. She'd been choking on something, and by the time she got to the ER, she was hypoxic. She wasn't getting any air. And Melanie saved the girl, because that's what she does. . .did."

"Fuck me," Hank said. "Did Melanie's killer know he was offing the doc who'd saved his daughter?"

Bob shook his head. "I don't think these ignorant pieces of shit think. In their black-and-white world, they see the abortion doctors as murderers, period."

"What'd he say, or do, once he found out who he'd killed?" Norm asked.

Bob laughed bitterly. "Went to fucking prison."

The men sat in silence.

Hank thought about Becka and Mai, and about old Conrad. *We each handle our grief in our own way. The problem is that grieving itself is akin to not existing. It's essentially a self-indulgent pity fest. Too many people allow themselves to become immersed in empty grief while day after day of precious existence is put on hold or even forgotten. That was Conrad. That would have been me if Mai hadn't come along. I would've been back at the death farm, ticking off the days, and the rounds of golf, till I died. Bob had set off on an adventure of exploration, but he sure seemed to have a lot of shit to work through. Anyone who, within a few minutes of meeting someone, ponied up the fact that his wife was murdered, had issues.*

"What about you guys?" Bob asked, pulling Hank out of his reverie. "No offense, but you look a little old to be wandering the world trying to find yourselves."

"It's never too late to find yourself," Hank said. "But the fact of the matter is that we're looking for my son. I didn't know I even had a son until recently, and his mother hasn't seen him for twenty-something years."

Norm asked, "You didn't happen to run into him on your trip, did you?"

Bob looked confused.

"He's kidding," Hank said.

Bob laughed. "I thought it must be a joke, but then I didn't think it was cool to joke about another guy's missing son, so . . . ."

"We can joke about it because we don't know anything about him," Hank said. "He could be a real asshole, for all we know."

Norm added, "And judging from the high school chums we talked to, he may very well have been."

"Jeez," Bob said. "So you're saying you didn't know you even had a kid. And this kid ran away from his mother? When?"

"On the day after his high school graduation," Norm said. "We're trying to find out what happened. Then maybe we'll be able to find him."

Bob asked, "And the mother has no idea why he left?"

"Not a clue," Hank said.

"None of the guys you've found so far know anything?"

"Oh, we think they know a lot more than they're telling us," Hank said. "But so far, no one's giving us much to go on."

Bob finished his wine and stood. "Well, thanks for the wine. I'd better get back to my burnt chicken." He turned to leave, but then turned back. "Try to find out if he had a girlfriend or any friends who were girls. They'd know a lot more about your son than the guy friends. Even if they don't know exactly what happened, just their intuition alone will be worthwhile. Trust me on that."

"What do you do for a living, Bob?"

"I was a child psychologist. Now I'm a tired and bitter man in the prime of his life who'd like to round up every single right-wing, hypocritical, pea-brained, gun-toting, poor-hating, religious zealot and force march them into Texas Stadium, where they would be required to listen to Sarah Palin talk until she said something smart." He paused and nodded agreeably. "In other words, life sentences. Thanks again, and good luck with your search."

Chapter 29

Bob Schlitzman was gone from his campsite when Hank stepped out of the van with Stoner on a leash. A dense fog had slunk in like a creepy voyeur sometime in the night. It was cold and wet, and Stoner pulled hard against the leash. Hank figured Stoner wanted to do his doggie dump as fast as possible so he could climb back into bed with Norm, who so far had refused to budge.

The ocean appeared as gray as the world around it. Hank heard a thunderous crash on the beach and then watched a sheet of white water move toward him. The tide and the surf were up, and although it ultimately retreated faster than Iraqi soldiers the first time ISIS invaded Mosul, the water came uncomfortably close to the outskirts of their camp.

Hank let Stoner do his thing, and then they returned to the van. Stoner jumped on Norm, and Hank pulled on Norm's foot until he coughed, cussed, coughed again, farted, and sat up.

"The tide's up and the fog's in," Hank said. "We're getting out of here."

*   *   *

Fifteen minutes later they were on the road, driving almost blind in the fog. Every once in a while, a car would come up on their rear, obviously anxious to get around them, but none, except for one, was crazy enough to attempt a blind pass on a two-lane winding road. The one exception was a bright-red Camry, which spent less than three seconds on their tail before making a Hail Mary pass on the left. Hank braked hard just in case he was driving into a head-on collision, but providence, or whatever, was with the Camry and its driver.

Other drivers had various ways to convey their impatience. Some would start flashing their lights, some would tailgate so close that Hank could barely see them through his side mirrors, and some would veer in and out of the left lane as if they would miraculously be able to see more than thirty or forty feet ahead. Some actually had the balls to honk.

The prevalence of "good guys with guns" who had co-identities as "assholes with guns" had caused Hank to curtail his habit of using his middle finger to convey his good wishes toward those with whom he shared the road. In all cases, after a few moments of fun during which he would categorize each driver according to his or her preferred mode of rushing toward death, he would eventually pull over as far to the right as he could and signal with his arm that it was okay to pass.

Hank breathed a big sigh of relief when the fog finally lifted and sunlight filled the van's cab.

Stoner raised his head, squinted into the sun, and then re-buried his head in Norm's crotch.

"We can be at Pebble Beach in a couple hours if you want to stop," Hank said. "Maybe it would be a good place for some brunch."

Norm, who had been mostly quiet all morning, grunted, "Sounds good."

Hank glanced over at his friend. "You okay, buddy? You're awfully quiet and reserved this fine day."

Norm sighed. "I've been thinking about that Bob dude all night. I mean, can you imagine? Two doctors with their lives ahead of them, trying to do good, and some motherfucker kills the very woman who had saved his daughter. And all in the name of religion." He paused. "I tell you, if there were a Christian version of Sharia law, these assholes would be all for it. And they don't even understand the irony of that."

"It surely does make a person wonder. But forget about Bob for now and enjoy these amazing views. I'm glad the fog lifted so we can enjoy this."

"You're right," Norm said. "Between the beauty of Highway 1 and Stoner nuzzling my dick, what've I got to complain about?"

"That's what I'm talking about."

*　　*　　*

Lunch overlooking the eighteenth hole at Pebble Beach, arguably one of the most famous and beautiful holes in all of golf, seemed to be the final icing on the cheering-up-Norm cake. Considering the cost to stay and play at Pebble, the average net worth of the patrons was probably in the multiple millions.

Nonetheless, thought Hank, multimillionaires figured out how to make themselves unhappy every bit as easily as the poorest of the poor. Here at Pebble, however, even the usually bored, demanding, and blasé one-percenters actually seemed excited to be there.

"Insular," said Hank aloud.

"What?" Norm asked. He'd been staring out the picture windows at the latest group of golfers hitting their approach shots to the eighteenth green. The ocean beyond the green of the fairway was a deep blue, with the sky working hard to compete. Large strands of burnt-umber seaweed floated on the water.

"Look around you," Hank said. "Except for that table of Japanese tourists over there, how many minorities have you seen since we got here?"

Norm looked around, a bemused expression on his face. "I saw a black guy on the putting green outside. And a number of Asian golfers." He paused. "I assume you're not including the help 'cause there's a bunch of Hispanics on the wait staff."

"My point," Hank said, "is that once people hit a certain age and achieve a certain level of financial status, we as a society tend to segregate ourselves into comfortable little like-minded groups. We're no exception. Look at the death farm. Other than Leo and his wife, there aren't any other blacks in the entire complex."

Norm nodded. "True, but it's not all the fault of the one-per-centers. Many immigrants have felt, and still feel, more comfortable around their own people, which is why we have Chinatowns, and Little Saigons, and Little Koreas. The Irish and the Italians did the same thing in their day."

Hank grunted an acknowledgement. "I know, and I'm not making a judgment. I'm making an observation. We fell into the same trap—shutting ourselves away in a wealthy retirement enclave."

A waiter set a perfect-looking hamburger in front of Norm and an equally beautiful mahi-mahi sandwich in front of Hank.

After the waiter had gone, Norm said, "I was just coming out of my blues, and now you're bumming me out again."

"Sorry. It's just that I was thinking about Junior. Do you suppose he's hiding out in some version of Little Saigon somewhere? What could possibly have happened, either on Mount Wilson or in his own mind, to cause him to leave everything behind? And where would he be now? Insulated like we are—and like the people around us are? Living in some micro-geopolitical enclave, looking out at the rest of the country through the lens of that enclave?"

"Jesus, dude! You went there just because all these rich, mostly white people are hanging with other rich, mostly white people? Enjoy your sandwich and the view, and then let's go find some fucking diversity for you."

Hank laughed and took a bite of his sandwich. He reckoned the mahi-mahi he was ingesting would have preferred to hang out with its own kind.

*   *   *

"Let's stay in San Francisco tonight," Hank said once he and Norm got back on the road. "We can try to find out where the other two guys whose names we have live. It's not very efficient driving up and down the coast."

"No, but it's fun."

Hank smiled. "True that."

"Also, remember how you told me Dana Clark said Junior loved San Francisco? Maybe we should circulate some of the age-adjusted pictures of Junior among the Vietnamese community in the city. Like you suggested, maybe he tried to go back to his roots or something. You know, blend in."

Hank thought about it. He'd been feeling kind of embarrassed about his lack of detecting skills, but it was pretty hard to find someone who went completely off the grid. One thing they had going for them, however, was that Junior was half Vietnamese and half Caucasian. Hank didn't necessarily expect other Caucasians to be able to tell the difference between Junior and a full Vietnamese. If anyone were likely to regard Junior as someone who stood out, it would be other Vietnamese.

"Good idea," he said. "In fact, I'm going to call my old firm. We used to have a Vietnamese guy who worked for us in San Francisco. He was really tied in to the community. I don't know why I didn't think of him sooner. If he's still around, I can ask him to get the photos out. I suspect we'd be viewed with suspicion if we stood on a street corner in the Vietnamese part of town asking if anyone had seen Junior."

"Cool," Norm said. "And why don't you also ask him to look into any police reports from that day in the Mount Wilson area. Maybe there was an arrest, or an accident, or a missing person or something."

"Will do."

Norm leaned over and picked up his laptop. "And I'll try to find us a pet-friendly hotel."

*   *   *

After a call to Gene Rodman, former second-in-command at HR Security, Hank was able to contact Tommy Phan, the managing director at the San Francisco office. Hank recalled that Tommy Phan's birth name was Phan Quang Chu. But for some reason, Americans 1) seemed to be unable to pronounce most Asian names, and in particular Vietnamese names, and 2) couldn't grasp the concept that the family name always came first, followed by a middle name, and then the given name. Phan Quang Chu simply got tired of people calling him Phan instead of Chu, so he changed his name to a good American first name while keeping his family name.

After working through the niceties—or not so niceties, which included Tommy asking about Becka, and Hank having to tell him she no longer existed—Hank explained the situation and told Tommy about their mission to find Junior.

Tommy seemed to get a real kick out of Mai's spelling of Hank's surname. Hank resisted his initial urge to defend Mai's spelling faux pas. Then, after realizing there was nothing to defend, he wondered about his instinctive reaction. Was it some version of a male's natural response to protect his woman? Was Mai his woman? Hadn't evolution rid American males of their ego-driven conviction that they were all derivatives of the proverbial "white knight"? As if Mai needed defending in any way. Hank eventually concluded that his reaction said more about his evolving feelings toward Mai than about the greater concept of male evolution.

Tommy agreed to meet them as soon as they got into town.

*   *   *

In the waning hours of a cloudless, fogless San Francisco day, Hank and Norm checked into the old Saint Francis Hotel on Union Square and headed to the bar to meet Tommy Phan.

Tommy had worked his way up the HR Security ladder during Hank's time at the helm. And although the two men hadn't had a great deal of contact over the years, in the course of preliminary small talk, Tommy told Norm that he felt he owed his career to Hank and his policy of diversity and inclusion.

Hank joked, "But I didn't tell Tommy to change his name."

"No, because you actually called me Chu, but that just confused people all the more." He laughed. "I remember one guy at our annual get-together took me aside and asked why the boss wouldn't call me Phan when he used first names for everyone else."

"Anyway," Hank said, handing Tommy a stack of the time-aged renderings of Junior, "here's the picture. Whatever you can do to get this out to the community would be great."

Tommy set the photos to his side and took a sip of beer. The room was dark and empty except for one man hunched over the bar and the bartender, who was polishing glasses.

"Not a problem," Tommy said. "Little Saigon is actually little. It's in the Tenderloin, pretty much just around the corner and down the street from here. Most of the Vietnamese community is in the San Jose area." He scratched his head. "Hell, I think there are close to a couple hundred thousand living there now."

"Hmm. You have any connections down there?" Hank asked.
"Sure."

"Did anything turn up in the Mount Wilson area from around the time?" Norm asked. "Any police reports that could tell us something?"

"Nothing," Tommy replied. "Hank, do you know anything at all about your son's abilities, hobbies, likes, dislikes—stuff like that?"

Hank shook his head slightly. "Not really." He paused a moment. "His friend we spoke with in Pasadena said Junior was good with computers."

"Okay," Tommy said. "If he ultimately got into the computer industry, San Jose would be a natural. I'll call some contacts in San Jose and see if we can get these photos spread around. Obviously a long shot, but what the hell. We have to start somewhere."

Chapter 30

Tom Bushman, the burqa-loving self-diddler, lived in a large house directly on Lake Tahoe, near Incline Village. A Hispanic maid in a white uniform opened the door.

"*Buenas tardes, señora,*" Hank said. Good afternoon, madam. "*Es Señor Bushman en casa?*" Is Mr. Bushman at home?

Her face was brown and heavily wrinkled, her eyes tired. Hank figured she probably had one hell of a commute every day.

"*Sí,*" the maid nodded. "*Quiénes son ustedes? Qué quiere usted?*" Who are you? What do you want?

Hank switched to English. "My name is Hank Reagan. Mr. Bushman went to high school with my son, and I'd like to talk to him about that." He paused. "*Entiendes?*" Do you understand?

The maid nodded. "I understand. Please wait."

She closed the door and slid the deadbolt into place.

"Trusting people," Hank said.

"I guess he doesn't want anyone interrupting him when he's jerking off," Norm whispered.

A few moments later, the lock unlatched and the maid opened the door, motioning for them to follow her. They walked through an entryway and into a huge modern living room. The view of the lake dominated everything, like a bully demanding to be the center of attention.

Hank and Norm were still taking in the view when the infamous whack-off artist entered the room and dismissed the maid.

"I'm Tom Bushman," the man said. "Which one of you is Hank's father?" Bushman was a big man. Hank figured him for at least six feet three. He had a barrel chest, a thick neck, and dirty-brown hair cut military short. His face was oddly pink. He peered at Hank with gray-looking eyes, which may have been green in the sunlight.

"That's me," Hank said, extending his hand. "And this is my friend Norm."

Bushman shook Hank's hand and then turned to Norm. "You a Jew?" he asked, extending his hand to shake.

"What is it with you guys?" Norm asked. "All of a sudden everyone wants to know if I'm a Jew."

Bushman shrugged his indifference. "What do you mean by everyone?"

Norm replied, "All Hank's high school chums."

Bushman motioned for the men to sit. The furniture was arranged so that the bully lake would get the attention it demanded.

"We've been interviewing a number of your classmates to try to find out what happened to Hank," Hank said. "Apparently your old clique didn't like blacks, Hispanics, or Jews."

Bushman chuckled. "Yeah, well, that was then. It wouldn't surprise me that some of the guys are still racist and otherwise all-around bigots. But I got over all that nonsense in college. When I ran for Congress, my demographics were strong among the minorities."

"Then why'd you ask if I'm a Jew?"

"Just wondering. You know, when I was in Congress, I did a lot for Israel. I was one of their strongest supporters."

Hank saw Norm's face cloud over and decided to jump in. "So, Congressman Bushman, do you—"

"Call me Tom," Bushman said. "Those days are long gone and best forgotten."

Which led Hank to wonder why he'd brought it up. "Okay, Tom. Do you remember my son?"

"Sure I do. But as far as I recall, there was no father in Hank's life. Where'd you come from?"

"I didn't even know I had a son until Hank's mother reached out to me a couple weeks ago and asked me to help find him. We'd had a relationship in Vietnam, where I was stationed, but when Saigon fell, we were separated. I didn't know she was pregnant."

Bushman rubbed his chin and then crossed his legs. He had a look that Hank could only describe as wary. Or maybe, thought Hank, he was thinking about jerking off to Vietnamese women in their traditional garb.

"Okay. So what do you want to know? It's not like we were best friends or anything. Hank wanted to hang out with our crowd. Some of the kids were okay with it; some weren't."

"Like Kurt Valentine?" Hank asked.

Bushman chuckled. "You met Kurt? Yeah, he was kind of our leader. He hated pretty much anyone who wasn't white and at least fairly rich. He also wasn't all that smart. But then, to lead a bunch of high school kids, all you needed was to act macho and bossy and not give a shit what the teachers or administrators thought about you. That was Kurt. I hear he's pretending to run his father's publishing business now."

Norm added, "Pretending being the operative word."

"Do you know anything about why Hank ran away the day after graduation?" Hank asked.

Bushman shook his head. "Nah. I heard about it, of course, but I had no idea why he split like that."

"Did you go up to Mount Wilson with the rest of your crew the day before graduation?"

Bushman squinted at Hank, as if trying to figure out if there were an accusation there. Then he nodded slightly. "Yeah. A bunch of us went up. Just to hang out and drink some beer and smoke some pot."

"We heard you guys invited Hank to go up."

Like a child trying to figure out if he were in trouble, Bushman gave another small nod. "Yeah. Kurt invited him. Hank jumped at the chance."

"Why would Kurt invite Hank?" Norm asked.

Bushman shrugged. "Not sure. He didn't talk to me about it first."

"Let's cut to the chase, Tom," Hank said. His voice took on a hard edge. "What happened on Mount Wilson that day? What happened to cause Hank to run away?"

Bushman let out a big sigh. He stood and walked over to the picture window. There were whitecaps on the vast lake. No one said anything until Bushman finally turned from the window and, still standing, answered Hank. "I've already lost my reputation and career. I'm pretty much persona non grata among my old acquaintances, which is why I live here, in quiet, comfortable exile." Bushman walked back to his chair and sat. "I'm a lawyer, although not practicing. So I understand the ramifications of what I can and cannot tell you." He went quiet again.

Hank and Norm waited him out.

"I'd love to tell you everything," Bushman said. "But I can't."

Hank leaned forward. "Tom, there's a mother in Pasadena who hasn't seen or heard from her son in over twenty-three years. The fact that he just left with no explanation has torn her up inside. She wonders if it was something she did or didn't do. Was she that bad of a mother? Help us out here. Tell us what you can, and don't tell us what you don't feel comfortable telling."

Bushman made a harrumphing sound. "Easier said than done. Let's put it this way. There were crimes involved. We all agreed never to discuss what happened—with anyone. Most of us went our separate ways anyway. Hank disappeared. My guess is he couldn't live with his guilt and didn't want to face his mother."

The room fell silent.

After about a full minute, Hank spoke up. "Wouldn't the statute of limitations be up on most every crime that may have been committed twenty-three years ago?"

Bushman rose. "Sorry. I've said too much already. I sincerely do wish I could tell you everything, but I simply can't." He began walking toward the entry hall. "Let me see you out."

Hank tried to ask more questions, but Bushman had said all he was going to say.

Chapter 31

Eva Ochoa smelled slightly of green chile, but that suited Mai just fine. It was a familiar and comforting smell, and she let Eva cuddle into a spoon. Eva's arms wrapped around her like a horny boa constrictor, pulling her close.

The two women hadn't made love since Mai had connected with Hank, and Mai felt a little guilty about that. She could see Eva was working hard not to show she was hurting, and there were certainly times when Mai thought a little pussy licking might be a nice gesture. But it just didn't feel right. She hadn't known she had such a Victorian sense of morality until she realized she had somehow decided it would be cheating on Eva to make love to Hank and vice versa. So even though she hadn't made love to Hank yet, she'd decided a time-out with Eva would be the right thing to do. Whether not making love with your lesbian lover so as not to cheat on a man you haven't had sex with for forty-plus years constituted Victorian morality was not something Mai was inclined to debate with herself.

So she cuddled and made out a little bit and tried not to think about Hank's arms around her instead of Eva's.

Hank had called earlier in the evening to tell her about Bushman's revelation that something criminal had happened on Mount Wilson the day before graduation, and his confirmation that Hank Jr. had been there. But Bushman had refused to offer up details. What was telling to Hank and Norm was that Bushman, who was a lawyer, knew the statute of limitations would have expired on everything—except the unspoken crime of murder.

Had someone died that afternoon on Mount Wilson? If so, Mai hadn't heard about it. But what else could it be? Hank said Bushman seemed to want to open up, but wouldn't, or couldn't.

The thought of young Hank being involved in something criminal the day before his graduation sent a chill of fear through Mai. Why hadn't he come to her? Had he run out of fear of being arrested? If so, why hadn't the other kids run?

Hank's working theory was that the other guys had pushed Hank Jr. into doing something criminal, and although they all might have legal culpability, they probably put the fear of God into Hank Jr., telling him he'd be the one to go down. Meanwhile, the rest of the assholes were all buddies and believed they could trust each other's vow of silence.

Mai acknowledged it seemed a good working theory. But if it were true, and those *pinche cabróns* went ahead and lived their lives while her son was forced to give up his life, it was a horrifying scenario—especially if the crime Bushman referred to was as serious as murder. If that were the case, what was the most she could hope for? That Hank would find Junior, but he still wouldn't be able to come home? That there might have been extenuating circumstances so that he had a defense to whatever he was running from?

Mai felt a shiver pass through her. Eva must have felt it too as she pulled Mai further into her embrace. Mai sighed and breathed in Eva's chile scent and let her mind empty itself in anticipation of sleep.

Chapter 32

Pleasantly stoned, Hank and Norm sat on some big rocks on the bank of Lake Tahoe, staring at the lights of the South Shore casinos. An occasional boat with running lights would pass by, creating a momentary, if unfulfilling, diversion. The wind had settled down and the lake was glassy, as if a water Zamboni had wiped away all the whitecaps.

Stoner slept at Norm's feet, but he was having some kind of dream; he emitted a kind of low growl, and his whole body twitched. Maybe, thought Hank, looking down at him, it wasn't a growl, but a doggie moan. Maybe Stoner was having a doggie sex dream.

Norm asked, "Where we headed next?"

"Dunno," Hank said. "We have two more names. Sammy Stone and Elliot Rogers. Think they're worth talking to?"

"Can't hurt. Where are they?"

Hank laughed. "You're the one who looked them up."

"Yeah, but I'm too stoned to remember."

"Stone is in Carefree, Arizona. He's a golf pro at a club there. The other guy, Elliot Rogers, lives in Huntington Beach, so he's convenient."

"Let's go to Carefree," Norm said. "Please, Daddy, please, can we?"

Hank snorted and then coughed. "Too bad we didn't find him earlier. We were pretty close when we went through Flagstaff."

Stoner suddenly sat up and barked. Looking toward the van and the dwindling fire, he barked again.

Hank and Norm stood up, both grunting. They looked at each other for a moment and then walked toward the van.

A man was bent over with his head inside the vehicle's sliding door.

Hank spotted a solid-looking stick, which he bent down and picked up.

"Looking for something?" he asked as he moved in closer.

The man jerked up and turned around. He was young, maybe in his early twenties. His dark hair fell to his shoulders. He had a stubble of a beard. Besides hiking shoes, he wore dirty khaki pants and a short-sleeved brown shirt that looked like one of those wrinkleproof and waterproof backcountry jobs. "Oh, hey, I was just looking to see if there was anyone around." His voice was high, almost squeaky.

"Well, question answered," Norm said. "Here we are."

The kid squinted through the flickering light at Hank and Norm. "I'm camping just over there," he said, gesturing into the darkness of the tall pine trees. "I thought I smelled marijuana, but I must have been wrong."

"Why?" Hank asked.

"Why what?"

"Why must you have been wrong about smelling marijuana?"

"Well, I don't know. It's just that you guys look pretty old. I don't imagine you're sitting around doing drugs."

Hank laughed. "Kid, we were smoking dope before your mother lost her virginity."

Now Norm laughed. "Yeah. We were smoking dope before your father had his first boner."

Stoner barked.

The kid looked amused. His eyes moved from Hank to Norm and back to Hank again, and he gave a tentative-sounding laugh, a stick-your-toe-in-the-water kind of test laugh.

"Let's sit," Hank said. He pulled out another camp chair and set it up so that the kid would be between him and Norm. "We can have a couple of nightcap tokes."

Hank pulled out his stash and began filling a pipe.

The kid introduced himself as Ash Adams. "I work in the boot section of Tahoe Sports during the winter, fitting ski boots. In the summer, I'm mostly a guide. You gents need any guiding?"

"Can you guide me to some sweet fifty-year-old pussy?" Norm asked. "It's been so long since I've gotten laid, I'll need direction."

Hank shook his head in a What're you going to do with him? way and then took a long pull on the pipe. He passed it to Ash, who took a pull and handed it to Norm.

"Careful, Norm," Hank said. "You sound like you're still stoned."

"Nuh-uh." Norm proceeded to take a long pull.

"So," Ash said, "what're you guys up to? Just traveling the country?"

It was probably the dope, but for whatever reason, Hank proceeded to tell Ash the story of Mai and Hank Jr. and their search and their working theory that something involving a crime had occurred on Mount Wilson the day before graduation.

It took a little while for Hank to tell the story, so each man had had another toke by the time he was done. Now well and truly stoned, they stared into the fire, mesmerized by man's greatest invention.

"Sex," Ash said, after a long period of silence.

"What?" Norm asked.

Ash let out a kind of chortle. "Sex. You know, the good fun stuff you old guys don't do anymore?"

"Very funny," Hank said. "What about sex?"

"These guys just graduated from high school, yes? What were you guys thinking about constantly at that age?"

"Sex," Hank and Norm said in unison.

Stoner barked in apparent agreement.

"I'll bet whatever happened on Mount Wilson had something to do with sex."

The campground was quiet as Hank and Norm pondered Ash's statement.

"So you're thinking maybe the guys took some girls up the mountain with them?" Hank said.

Ash shrugged. "I'm not saying anything except it wasn't so long ago that I graduated from high school and I don't think I'd have gone off to celebrate without some babes on hand."

"But if something happened on Mount Wilson that caused Junior to run, it had to be something criminal," Norm said.

"Whatever." Ash shrugged again, as if he were done contributing ideas.

There was another period of silence before Hank said, "But the statute of limitations is long past for anything criminal except murder, and I can't see that. That would have been big news. Anything else, Junior could have come home without fear of prosecution."

Ash laughed, and Hank saw residual smoke blow out the kid's nostrils. "Dude. What's he gonna do, walk into his mom's house and say, 'Hi, Mom, I'm home. Sorry I left for twenty years, but I was involved in some criminal shit the day before graduation, and I had to go into hiding until the statute of limitations ran out'?"

"He's got a point," Norm said, looking at Hank.

Hank nodded. "It's a good point."

"Or maybe he got butt-fucked by those racist dicks, and he couldn't face his mom. Or . . ."

"Okay, okay, we get the picture," Hank interrupted Ash. "Jeez, this is my kid you're talking about."

"Oh, sorry," Ash said. "Just exploring the potentials."

An uncomfortable silence ensued during which Ash scratched at his crotch, Norm started to nod off, and Hank stared into the fire, thinking about the various scenarios that could have driven Junior into hiding.

Ash finally got up. "Well, thanks for the hits. Good luck on your search." He walked away, through the flickering light and into the darkness.

Chapter 33

The next morning, coffee cup in hand, Hank strolled around the area, which was not a formal campsite, just an opening in the woods next to the lake.

"I can't find any sign of Ash or even of a recent campsite," he told Norm back at the van. "There aren't any houses or other buildings within at least two miles of here."

"As far as you know," Norm said, "he could live in a small cabin in the woods on the other side of the highway."

"I suppose. In any event, let's pack up and get breakfast in town. It's about a twelve-hour drive, so we might want to stay somewhere tonight."

*   *   *

Breakfast took longer than expected, as Norm had some bowel issues he needed to deal with before hitting the road.

Ah, the pleasures of old-man travels, Hank thought.

"What do you think about what Ash said last night?" Norm asked as Hank navigated the winding turns of Kingsbury Grade.

"Actually, it makes sense," Hank said. "I mean, even if whatever happened was no longer subject to prosecution, that doesn't mean Junior would want to come home."

"That kind of makes sense to me, too. We're talking about young bucks who thought they owned the world and would get away with anything. Maybe they got Junior up there to force him to participate in something and humiliate him."

"Hmm. Maybe we should be heading back up to talk to Dana," Hank said. "Every one of those assholes made a point of calling her the class whore. And she ran away as well."

Norm scratched Stoner behind his ears. "Great. We can have another nice chat with those pleasant boys who grew out of Pastor Glen's sperm."

"I still want to talk to the other two guys first. We might be able to bluff or bully one of them into talking."

"Worth a try, I guess. But if the statute of limitations on whatever they did really has run out, why wouldn't Bushman talk to us? He said he wanted to."

"I've been thinking about that," Hank said. "I don't know the answer, but one possibility is that his protestations of wanting to tell us everything was all an act. Maybe he still has strong ties to one or more of his old clan and is sticking to the oath of silence. Remember, word spread quickly that we were investigating Junior's whereabouts, and someone called Mai to try to intimidate her."

*   *   *

Over the course of the day, the scenery changed as fast as diapers on a baby with diarrhea—from woodlands, to farmland, to desert, to scrubland. Despite Norm's entreaties, Hank declined to detour to either the Grand Canyon or Las Vegas.

"Okay, but just don't make me stay in Kingman again," said a dejected Norm.

Hank laughed. "Fine."

So the Mercedes Sprinter blew through Kingman with nary a second glance. For a while, they considered going all the way to Carefree or maybe Scottsdale. Maybe it was the mind-numbing boredom of the scrubland along Highway 93, or maybe it was just because they were old, but Hank finally admitted he was too tired to go any farther. He asked Norm if he wanted to drive.

"Let's stop as soon as we spot a decent place," Norm said. "I'm tired, too." He consulted a map on his iPad. "There's a place called Wikieup not far ahead. It has an RV park. I don't fancy camping out in this open wilderness."

"Okay," Hank said. "I agree. I'm getting tired of weirdos coming out of the dark."

Located on the outskirts of the desperate-looking little town of Wikieup, behind a country store and gas station, the park currently housed three big-rig RVs. Hank and Norm paid, gassed up, and picked a parking spot as far from the other RVs as possible. The warm summer evening was still light enough to set out the camp chairs, mix a cocktail, and unwind from the long day on the road.

As the pink sky faded into gray, a beat-up green pickup truck turned into the park and drove directly to the Sprinter.

"Jesus," Norm muttered.

The pickup stopped, and a thirty-something man wearing well-worn coveralls with no shirt stepped out of the cab. His face was grossly pockmarked, and his teeth were crooked and yellowed.

"Hey, guys," he said, grinning. "Y'all want to buy some guns? I got a shitload to sell." He removed a faded red Diamondbacks ball cap from his head and gestured toward the bed of his truck.

"Guns?" Hank asked, knowing it was a stupid thing to say even as it was emerging from his mouth.

"Yeah, guns. I got about ten AR-15s, if you're interested. Also a bunch of handguns, mostly Berettas. After Obama got elected, I started buying as many guns as I could afford. Like everyone else, I just knew that Kenyan fucker was going to mess with our Second Amendment rights." The gun man chortled and ran a dirty-looking hand across his closely shaved head. "But the pussy didn't do a damn thing. Typical liberal piece of shit. Now I'm stuck with all these guns. I only need a few for myself."

Hank looked at Norm, who was staring at the gun man as if he were part of some kind of impromptu skit. When Hank looked back at the gun man, he had turned his back and was reaching into the bed of his truck. He pulled out an AR-15, the automatic weapon of choice for American mass shooters.

"Thanks for the offer," Hank said, keeping his voice as polite as possible. "But we don't need any more guns. We're fully supplied. Good luck to you."

The man caressed the AR-15. "You sure? No one's gonna fuck with you when you got this beauty by your side."

"Quite sure," Hank said.

The gun man's face showed disappointment. He stood there, right hand still gently stroking the barrel of the gun. Then, after a few beats, during which Hank realized he'd been holding his breath, the gun man shrugged, tossed the weapon carelessly into his truck, and walked around to the driver's side. "Well, you fellas take care, then." He climbed into the truck and drove across the RV park toward the other rigs.

After a moment, Norm asked, "What the fuck?"

"At least it was still light when he showed up. Welcome to gun country, U.S.A." Hank got up. "Let's go in and make some dinner."

Chapter 34

Sammy Stone was the head pro at a prestigious golf resort in Carefree, Arizona. Norm booked two rooms at the resort for them as they drove. At just under $300 a night for each room, it was expensive for the middle of summer, but as Hank said, "It'll be nice to fart in peace for a change."

Summer in southern Arizona is not prime season, and the resort's occupancy was clearly down. Even the golf course, as they drove toward reception, looked empty. Norm pointed out what looked like a bobcat sitting atop one of the numerous smooth boulders that dotted the landscape. Some of the big rocks looked to Hank as if they'd been precariously perched on top of other rocks. Disney himself couldn't have done a better job of landscaping.

The two men dumped their overnight bags in their respective rooms and promptly headed to the pro shop to see if Stone was available. He was.

The pro's office was neat and uncluttered. Photos of Stone and other golfers adorned one wall. Against another wall stood a credenza that held a number of trophies. Several golf bags with "Sammy Stone" written on the front stood side by side. Only one bag held clubs.

A handsome man with blond hair and a killer tan, Stone wore a resort-logo pink golf shirt and white pants. His light green eyes looked friendly.

Hank went through the introductions and background story in much the same way he'd done with Bushman. As he did so, Stone's expression mutated from friendly to serious, but not necessarily hostile, which Hank took as a good sign.

"Yeah, sure, I remember Hank. We all made fun of the way his name was spelled, like he was Flash Gordon or something. He didn't much like being made fun of, but he still came around. Glutton for punishment, if you ask me, which you didn't." Stone leaned back in his chair and picked up a glass golf ball paperweight, which he proceeded to toss from one hand to the other.

"We're interested in the day before graduation when you all went up to Mount Wilson," Hank said. "Hank went with you, yes?"

Stone nodded. "Yeah. That was Kurt's idea. Kurt Valentine. I'm not sure what he intended, but knowing Kurt, the invite wasn't out of the goodness of his heart. The guy was a real jerk."

"How come you ran with that crowd?" Norm asked. "You seem like a nice normal guy."

Stone laughed. "You mean I don't seem like a racist asshole?"

Norm smiled. "Yeah, something like that."

"They were more or less considered the 'in-crowd.'" Stone made air quotes. "I put up with their inane shit so I could be cool. I guess that's why Hank wanted to hang around the group, but that was never going to work. Behind his back, Kurt referred to him as 'that half-breed gook.'"

Hank asked, "Who all went up the mountain that day?"

"Hmm. Let's see if I can remember everyone. There was Kurt, of course. Then there was Tom Bushman, Monty Washburn, Elliot Rogers, I think. Billy Campbell, and . . . . No, wait, Billy wasn't there."

Hank noticed a change of some sort come over Stone's face. If forced to put a name to the expression, he would have said *panic*. It was fleeting, but it was definitely there. "Who's Billy Campbell? That's the first time we've heard that name."

Stone waved a hand dismissively, as if batting away a fly. "Just a guy. Kind of peripheral to the group. But I don't think he went up to Mount Wilson that day. There wouldn't have been room for him once Hank was invited."

"So there were six of you?" Hank asked.

Stone nodded. "Yeah, I think so."

"What about girls?" Norm asked. "Wasn't Dana Clark with you?"

Stone's expression changed again. He looked at Norm and then back at Hank, as if trying to figure out what was going on. "Who told you she was there?"

Hank let out a small chuckle. "You just did although we've suspected it for a while."

Stone sighed heavily and put the paperweight back on his desk. "I don't really care anymore," he said in a voice filled with resignation. "Bushman called me yesterday and said you guys were snooping around and to be careful." Stone gave a wan smile and then a small shrug. "I guess I'm too stupid to be careful. Besides, Bushman confirmed there was no possibility of anyone facing criminal charges, so what do I care?"

Hank and Norm glanced at each other and Hank figured Norm was thinking the same thing he was: If there were no possibility of criminal charges, there was no murder.

Stone stood and walked to his office door. "Smiley, hold my calls please," he called to the young man at the pro shop desk. Then he closed the door and returned to his seat, which squeaked loudly as he sat down.

"A bunch of us decided to have one last hurrah before we graduated, so someone got the bright idea of getting a bunch of beer and some dope and driving up to Mount Wilson. Seemed like a good idea at the time. But then Kurt Valentine decided to invite Hank. As I said, probably just to torture the poor kid.

"It was Bushman's idea to bring Dana along. There were too many for one car, so Kurt and I both drove. We found a little deserted picnic area on the edge of a cliff. Pretty cool spot. And we proceeded to get shit-faced. Kurt was ragging Hank pretty good, but Hank was being a good sport about it.

"But then, at one point, Bushman elbowed me and pointed to Dana. She was really fucked up. Her head was lolling around, and her eyes were barely open. That's when things began to get ugly. Bushman and Kurt started undressing Dana. She struggled a little at first but not much. Most of the guys thought it was funny." Stone paused and then said, "I don't know what Hank thought about it. I was too busy looking at Dana's tits.

"Anyway, Bushman decided to have sex with Dana. Right there in front of everyone. Then Kurt went at it. A couple more guys did, too."

"Did you?" Norm asked.

"Nah. I thought it was a cold shit thing to do. But I admit, I didn't do anything to stop it."

"So what did Hank do?" Hank asked. "He did her, too? That why he ran away?"

Stone shook his head. "No. When Bushman tried to get Hank to do her, he refused. But Bushman wouldn't let him off the hook. He started in on him pretty good. Kurt and Billy joined in. Yeah, Billy was there. I lied when I said he wasn't. Sorry about that.

"At one point, Hank was standing over Dana, who was totally out of it by then. She was stark naked. At least three of the guys had raped her already. Billy was holding Hank from behind and then he tried to force him onto Dana." Stone paused again. He picked up the glass golf ball and then put it down. He looked around and spotted a bottle of water on the side of his desk. He took a long gulp, then cleared his throat and continued.

"That's when it happened. Hank reflexively pushed back against Billy, while at the same time elbowing him with his free arm. Billy fell back, tripped, and went over the cliff."

The pro shop office went quiet. Norm was the first to speak.

"So there *was* a murder—or at least a death."

Stone shook his head. "I probably wouldn't be talking to you if there had been. I'm not that stupid. Everyone thought he was dead. He'd fallen a long ways and was just lying there, still as a rock. Everyone was fucked up, and we panicked. Bushman and Valentine immediately blamed Hank, calling him a murderer. The poor kid was crying and shaking."

"But Billy was all right?" Hank asked.

Stone shook his head again. "No way. The others all piled into Bushman's car. They put Dana in naked and threw her clothes in after her. I stayed behind. I was the least fucked up. I said I'd hike down to see about Billy. Then I'd drive my car home.

"The hurried plan was that we'd leave him there, and if and when he was found, the cops would probably think it was a hiking accident." Stone leaned back in his squeaky chair and interlocked his hands on top of his head.

"It was a really stupid plan, but what'd you expect from a bunch of drunk and stoned kids who were scared out of their minds? Billy was wearing street clothes, not hiking clothes. And if he had been hiking, how'd he get there?

"In any event, I scrambled down the hill to where Billy lay and immediately discovered he was still alive. But he wasn't conscious. It took me over an hour, but I finally got him back up the hill and into my back seat. Then I drove him down to the emergency room at Huntington Hospital. I told the doctors, and then his parents, that we'd gone up to have some beers and got a little drunk and Billy tripped and fell off the cliff. I didn't mention anything about the other guys, or Dana."

Stone stopped talking then, but it was clear to Hank that he wasn't finished. Hank had the impression that Stone's telling of the event was cathartic. He'd clearly never discussed it with anyone other than his coconspirators.

"Was he all right?" Norm asked.

Stone didn't answer at first. His face looked sad and suddenly old. The healthy-looking tan didn't look so healthy anymore. "No," he said after a while. "He's a paraplegic."

Hank blew out a lungful of air. "Shit."

"Yeah," Stone said. "Of course, even with Billy crippled, he wasn't about to say he'd been trying to get Hank to gang-rape Dana Clark. I was able to get to him and feed him the simple story of the two of us getting drunk and him falling. I called the rest of the guys that night and filled them in on everything. We all agreed to the story and to never, ever talk about it to anyone outside our group."

"But you didn't call Hank, did you?" Hank's tone had turned hard. "Or Dana, for that matter."

Stone gave a small nod. "Dana wouldn't have mattered. She had no idea what had happened anyway. But you're right. I didn't call Hank." Stone closed his eyes. "It was the most fucked-up thing I've ever done. When Hank disappeared two days later, he left thinking he'd murdered Billy Campbell and that he'd been an aider and abettor in a gang rape. I'll bet he never took the time to find out whether Billy was actually still alive. He just took a dig, thinking he was guilty."

There was another prolonged period of silence.

"Fuck me," Norm said.

"My son may not have killed anyone that day," Hank said, his voice low and hard-edged, "but you guys did. You took his life from him. God knows where he is and what he's been doing." He paused. "Or even if he's still alive."

Norm nodded. "At least Billy was partly at fault for what happened to him. Hank's crime was refusing to gang-rape a helpless girl."

Stone was silent. What was there for him to say? What was there for any of them to say?

Chapter 35

Mai sat in stoic silence through most of Hank's telling of the story, but eventually her eyes filled with tears, and soon she was sobbing. Hank drew her into an embrace and let her cry herself out while he tried not to think about how good it felt to hold his old lover so close.

Eventually, her crying stopped and all that was left was smeared mascara, red eyes, and a runny nose. Being an old man, Hank carried a handkerchief, so he pulled it from his pocket and dabbed at Mai's face. Then, without giving himself time to fall prey to his scrambled thoughts, he kissed her. It took but a microsecond for him to realize she was reciprocating, and the kiss turned into a long, sensuously desperate kiss, which neither seemed to want to end. But, like crying, kisses, too, must end.

It was one thing to start making out on news that their son had witnessed a gang rape and thought he'd killed a man, but Hank knew it was quite another to proceed to sex, to which, he was almost ashamed to admit, he would have been a most willing participant. Instead, the two stared at each other for a long minute before Mai gave him a soft, several-second kiss and then left to go fix her face—not that he thought it needed fixing.

While she was gone, Hank found an open bottle of Chardonnay in the fridge and poured them each a glass. When she returned, he clinked his glass against hers. "To truth."

Mai clinked to the toast but said nothing and sipped her wine. She had wiped her face clean not just of the smeared mascara, but of all makeup, and Hank thought she looked more beautiful than ever.

"So," she said, putting her glass on the kitchen counter where they were both seated, "where do we go from here? Presumably we know why Hank left, but are we any closer to finding him?"

Hank told her about his meeting with Tommy Phan in San Francisco and about their plan to canvass the Vietnamese enclaves in both San Francisco and San Jose with age-adjusted renderings of Junior. "I know it's a long shot, but if Junior was into computers and if he wanted to meld into a Vietnamese community, either place would have been a good bet."

Mai nodded and sighed. "Do you think he'd want to come home even if he knew he wasn't at risk?"

Hank shrugged. "Who knows? If he's really into computers— or even if he's just computer savvy, which most people his age are—I find it hard to believe he wouldn't have checked on whether Billy Campbell had actually died. Assuming he did so, he still didn't come home."

Mai gave a slight nod and then picked up her glass. "Where's Norm?"

"He dropped me off. He's going to visit an old family friend in Long Beach. He'll stay there tonight."

Mai said nothing for a moment. Then she set her glass down, reached her right hand out, and stroked Hank's face. "Take me to bed. Please."

This time Hank didn't hesitate. He stood, pulled Mai up, and kissed her. He let his hands run along the contours of her back. She wore no bra. Slowly, he brought his right hand to her left breast. He was shocked at the intensity of his lust. He was equally shocked at the hardness of his erection. Through her silky blouse, he brushed her nipple, and she moaned softly. Then she took his hand and he followed her to the bedroom.

Their lovemaking was slow and passionate. It had been a long time for Hank, and he suspected he wouldn't last long once he felt himself slip into her silky wetness, so he kissed his way down to the place he once knew so well and licked her into orgasm. It hadn't been so long since Mai had been well licked, but nonetheless she, too, came quickly.

But it had been a long time since she'd felt the hardness of a man inside her, and when Hank entered her, she had another, almost immediate orgasm, which in turn caused Hank, despite his resolve to last more than a couple of minutes, to explode.

PART TWO

Chapter 36

Joseph heard the sheets rustle as Katrina rolled onto her back. She made a small noise—a moan, or maybe a groan—but in any event, he could see she was still sleeping.

The sheet now covered only a part of her left leg, and in the ambient light from the neon sign of the nightclub across the street he saw that she was still covered in a fine sheen of perspiration from their recent lovemaking—like a light dew on a perfectly manicured lawn. Her skin looked golden, the curves of her body maddeningly enticing. Her rosewood-colored nipples made him think of pieces of candy waiting to be sucked.

He took a last drag of his cigarette and tossed the butt into a glass of water on his bedside table. It was a no-smoking hotel, but he didn't care. Joseph hated authority. He resented the government telling him what he could and could not do. As far as he was concerned, the country's laws should be listed on no more than two pages of a yellow legal pad: Don't kill people unless it's absolutely necessary; Don't steal shit you don't need; Don't be a fucking racist; Don't rape people. Just the basics.

He lit another cigarette and looked at Katrina again. Her mouth was slightly open, and he saw a small amount of drool making its way over her luscious lower lip. He took a deep drag of his smoke and thought about the fight they'd had just before she rolled over and went to sleep. *Well, it wasn't really a fight*, he thought. It was more like him just being his usual insensitive self.

No, he thought, *it wasn't even that.* It was that he couldn't, or wouldn't, properly explain himself. She wanted more out of the relationship than he was willing to give.

"I have too many demons," he'd said, realizing as the words came out how clichéd and lame they sounded. *Ah, the old "it's me, not you" bullshit.*

Their sex had been good—as good as it gets as far as Joseph was concerned. The spring Miami night was warm, and the breeze coming through the window was sensuous and calming. They had both been sweating; he could smell the muskiness of their bodies.

He'd tried to describe to Katrina the scars he had from losing his father when he was nine. His skin was black, like his father's, even though his mother was as white and blond as a fairy-tale princess. But how do you explain racism to someone who's never experienced it? Words, just words. They can't begin to describe the degradation, the humiliation, the evisceration of one's self-esteem.

*   *   *

Danny Lee, aka Mike Mann, fka John Huong, fka William Kim, fka Hank Raygun, and various other "formerly known as" names, stopped typing and leaned back in his chair, the old springs protesting. He read what he'd just written and made a couple of changes. But when he had finished, he sighed. He highlighted the new passages and hit the delete button. It was shit writing, he decided, although he did kind of like the "tits as candy waiting to be sucked" part.

He rubbed his face with his hands and vigorously scratched his head. He knew what was happening. He wished he could "select all" in his brain and then hit the delete button. He looked around the sparsely furnished studio apartment—his home. It held a double bed, a beat-up pine chest of drawers, a small refrigerator next to a sink, a counter on which sat a small microwave oven, and the table at which he now sat facing his computer. There were three doors in the room. One led to a small closet, one led to the bathroom, and one led to the world outside—a world that both horrified and fascinated him.

He stood, but he didn't move away from the table. He breathed in and then let out a long, audible exhale. He could tell when the depression was coming on. There was no denying it. There was no running from it. It came with the regularity of imperfect clockwork, every twelve to thirteen months. With the depression starting now, Danny knew he would soon begin having suicidal thoughts. That was all part of what he referred to as his "suicidal cycle." Knowing how it worked helped. Knowing he would come out of it sometime within the next two weeks would become his hourly mantra against doing himself in.

He'd only actually tried to kill himself once. That was at year six, before he'd fully grasped the cycle. Luckily for him, he'd never fired a gun before and didn't realize the safety was on when he tried to pull the trigger. But just the fact that he'd tried to shoot himself hit him like a kick to the nuts, and he'd dropped the gun and cried himself into a depressive stupor. The next day, he went to a pawn shop and sold the gun.

Danny moved away from the table. For years he'd wondered why his writing wasn't better during his depressive states. Didn't some of the most famous writers in literature suffer from severe depression? It irritated him that he probably wouldn't write a sentence worth a shit for the next few weeks. He was behind schedule on his new book, and his agent was pressing him because the publisher was pressing the agent. He figured the $325,000 advance he'd been paid gave them some bitching rights.

Mike Mann had become a famous, and famously reclusive, novelist. No one had ever seen a photograph of him. After his third book had come out, and had won various literary prizes, he'd agreed to do an NPR interview with Terry Gross—by phone.

His bio was sparse: *Mike Mann grew up in California and now lives wherever his whim takes him. He is a confirmed bachelor who is fond of saying his only love is writing.*

Naturally, as his fame grew and his reclusiveness became legendary, the speculation surrounding him became epic. One tabloid claimed he was the illegitimate son of Barack Obama, which explained the recurring theme of growing up without a father in a racially charged society. A Yale professor claimed Mann had been a student of his. His name had been different, but the writing style was recognizable to the professor, who said he wouldn't disclose his student's identity out of respect.

Danny walked to the sink and drew a glass of water. He heard a truck idling outside. A moment later, he heard the hydraulic arms of a garbage truck lift the large green waste bin that stood in the alley next to his building, and then the clangs and thuds of the load of trash falling into the truck. Then the truck's gear ground, and he heard it move away.

He looked around the room, his gaze coming to rest on his computer. The now-empty page of the Word document he'd just erased taunted him, a literate schoolyard bully daring him to sit back down and start writing. But he knew he couldn't. Whatever words he forced onto the screen would be rubbish—trite rubbish. Depression-driven drivel. He walked to the laptop computer and closed the lid, as if telling the computer to shut the fuck up.

"Shut the fuck up," he added for good measure.

Then he grabbed his old, ratty pea coat and headed for the front door. But he stopped on the threshold and looked back. After a slight hesitation, he walked back and sat down in front of the computer. He raised the lid and woke it up. He clicked away from the Word program. On his Yahoo home page, he typed in "Facebook," and the address defaulted to his author's Facebook page. There was nothing personal on it other than a listing of his books, stories, and awards, and the same truncated bio that graced all his works. He didn't bother checking new visitors or comments and instead typed in "Tran Xuan Mai" in the search bar.

A moment later, he was looking at his mother's Facebook page. There was an updated profile picture of her. She changed her picture every year, and this was the first time he'd seen this particular photo. It had been eight months since he'd last checked her page. She looked as beautiful as ever.

"Mommy." The word seemed to escape from his lips like a prisoner squeezing out of a storm drain to freedom.

There were no "friends" listed. The only postings she had ever made in the nine years since he had discovered her page were short pleas for him to contact her. The last one was posted only three days ago.

> *Hank, I have been in contact with your father.*
> *We know what happened on Mount Wilson. You have*
> *nothing to fear. Please come home.*

Danny/Hank stared at the message. He read it over three times. His father? What the fuck? She'd found the asshole who'd abandoned her all those years ago? She'd always claimed he'd done no such thing, that his father had been a soldier killed in action. But young Hank had never bought into that narrative. The American soldier had fucked her and then run away with the rest of the Americans. He'd left a young, pregnant girl to fend for herself as the Vietcong marched into Saigon. Danny/Hank had convinced himself that was the *real* story.

Chapter 37

Contrary to what the clique of assholes thought at the time, Hank Raygun didn't go to Mount Wilson because he wanted to be one of them. He went because he'd been writing a series of short stories about growing up in America as a mixed-breed Asian. Some of the stories were poignant and optimistic. Others, such as the one he'd been working on about Kurt Valentine and his crew, were brutal portraits of rich, young racists who bullied everyone who was not part of their clique. The drinking and pot-smoking party on the mountain was to be part of the story's dénouement, the irony of a celebration of separation by kids who depended on the whole of their group to define them.

Hank hadn't known that Dana Clark—or any girls, for that matter—would be there. She'd come up in the car with Sammy Stone. Hank knew Dana from school, and he'd been toying with the idea of writing a piece about her—or about girls like her. She was pretty, but she wasn't smart enough to realize that using her looks to get guys to like her was never going to turn out well. Like so many kids at that age, she was desperate to belong. It seemed to Hank that the clique to which she sought to belong was mostly irrelevant—it was the belonging that mattered.

He'd struck up a number of conversations with Dana in the weeks leading up to graduation. At first she'd largely ignored him, as if she knew Hank couldn't do anything for her social standing. But then, one day a week or so before graduation, she started talking about a friend of hers having found this "really awesome" preacher in Northern California who "really related" to kids their age. She was thinking of heading up there after graduation.

So he was surprised to see Dana on Mount Wilson. She seemed stoned on more than just pot when she got there. She was acting goofy and loose, as if she'd taken some downers, maybe Quaaludes, but she dove right in to the booze. Hank had never seen anyone pass out so fast. That was when Tom Bushman decided to take her clothes off. In a matter of moments, Dana Clark was lying completely naked on dirt and small stones and pine needles. Even on her back, her breasts were huge, which, of course, drew the most comments from the drunk and stoned teens.

But it was her face that drew Hank's attention. In her unconscious state, she was no longer the wannabe seductress trying too hard to fit in. She looked like a child, an innocent, vulnerable child who did not deserve what was about to happen to her.

"Hey, guys, this isn't cool," Hank said. He tried to be casual about it, but when Bushman pulled down his pants, poured some beer onto Dana's vagina and began to rape her, Hank's cool was gone. He made a move toward Bushman, thinking he would pull him off, but someone grabbed his arms from behind. He wasn't sure who it was.

After Bushman, Valentine had his way with the unconscious girl.

Hank got one arm loose. He looked behind and saw it was Billy Campbell who'd been holding him. Billy's eyes were open wide. His mouth was a thin line. He looked scared.

But then he heard Bushman shout, "Billy! Don't let the fucker go! He's got to be part of this."

Billy roughly grabbed Hanks' arms again.

Washburn and then Rogers took their turns with Dana, and Hank stopped struggling. He closed his eyes and heard their barbaric grunts.

After a few minutes, Hank heard laughter—tentative, almost forced laughter, a false bravado, as if the boys had just realized the enormity of the evil they had committed.

He opened his eyes and saw Rogers zipping up his pants. Bushman slapped Rogers on the back and then turned to Hank.

Bushman's face was flushed and wet with sweat. His eyes were blazing.

"C'mon, man. What are you, a pussy? Take your turn, Raygun, although your little Asian dick will probably get lost in that cave. It'll probably be the last chance you'll get to fuck a white girl with tits like that."

Hank turned his head away from Dana and from Bushman's goading. But when Valentine went to grab Hank and pull him down onto Dana, Hank lashed out. He felt the hands holding his arms loosen and then release.

Then he heard a scream, and in that moment, in that split second, Hank's life changed forever.

*　　*　　*

Now Danny/Hank stared at the picture of his beautiful mother. He read the comment from her one more time. He had a father—a father who wasn't dead and who apparently wanted to be in his life.

Danny/Hank remembered a Christmas when he was about seven years old. His mother had found an old glass globe of a holiday scene. When she turned the globe upside down, it snowed on Santa. Hank thought it was wonderful, and when Mai handed him the globe, he tilted it up and down, up and down, over and over. As he did so, he pretended to be a television weatherman, making up stories to go with each snowfall.

"Well, Steve, it looks like a huge storm coming in. Santa's going to have a hard time delivering presents this year."

Or, "This could be the biggest snowfall of the year. It looks like Santa's getting a little tired of waiting for his reindeer to show up."

Then, just as he'd begun to once again exert his god-like power to stop the snow, he dropped the globe, and it shattered on the hard tile floor of their kitchen.

Now, Danny/Hank felt as if he'd just dropped his life's globe.

Chapter 38

For a moment, time seemed to stand still for Hank after Billy Campbell went over the cliff. There was his piercing scream, and then a sickening thud. The silence, which seemed to go on forever, probably lasted only a couple of seconds before panic set in.

"You killed him!" Valentine yelled at Hank. "You fucking killed him!" His face was red and spittle flew from his mouth. For a moment, Hank thought Valentine was going to push him off the cliff after Billy.

But then the impulse to flee kicked in. Valentine yelled to Bushman to get Dana into the car. He grabbed Hank and man-handled him into the car beside Dana. Washburn was crying. Valentine said something to Stone, who had his own car.

Despite the flurry of panicked activity, Hank felt as if he were living through a surreal, slow-motion dream. Dana flopped against him, still naked, and drooled onto his shoulder. He noticed a large mole on her upper thigh, like a dollop of brown paint on a white canvas. The skin around her shaved vagina was wet with beer and semen. Small pebbles and pieces of weeds were stuck to various parts of her body. He pulled a long, thin stick from her hair. Then Valentine climbed into the driver's seat and, moments later, the packed car was speeding down the mountain.

"We gotta call the cops," Rogers said. "Tell them Hank pushed Billy off the cliff."

"I didn't push anyone," Hank shot back.

"Shut the fuck up, Raygun," Valentine said, still driving too fast. "You damn well killed Billy." He paused. "But we can't go to the cops. You guys wanna go down for rape? This asshole would rat us out in a heartbeat."

The car grew quiet except for the sobs coming from Washburn.

"Quit fucking crying, Monty," Bushman said. "Help Raygun get Dana dressed."

As Hank and Washburn clumsily dressed Dana, Valentine and Bushman talked about their options. It was clear to Hank that going to the police was not on the table.

By the time Valentine calmed down a little, the brilliant plan was in place: Silence. No one was to ever talk about what happened. No one had seen Billy Campbell on the mountain that day.

Valentine and Bushman took turns stressing to Hank that if anyone talked, they would all admit to being on the mountain with Billy, but that Hank had gotten fucked up on drugs and alcohol and had raped Dana. Then, when Billy tried to stop the rape, Hank pushed him off the cliff.

Hank wouldn't stand a chance—a baby wildebeest separated from the herd.

They dumped Hank out on Colorado Boulevard, along with a few parting threats. He walked the five blocks home in a daze. He didn't know what to do. He'd never been in trouble. He'd never even contemplated doing something that might get him into trouble. He'd inherited his immigrant mother's fear of doing anything to disrespect their adopted country. Now, at the very least, he was an accomplice to rape and homicide. At worst, if the assholes ganged up on him, as they surely would, he was a rapist and a murderer.

*   *   *

Graduation was a nightmare. Hank tried his best to smile for his mother and for Aunt Eva. The guys who'd been on the mountain avoided making eye contact with him. He was surprised that no one seemed to be talking about Billy Campbell. Weren't his parents and friends worried about why he was missing graduation?

Hank had never known fear like he'd felt that day. It was a fear that tightened his throat and cramped his stomach. There were times when he thought his bowels would let loose. Throughout the ceremony, he kept looking around, convinced the police would be coming to arrest him at any minute.

Dana looked even worse than Hank felt. Her eyes were blood-shot and vacuous. Hank had no idea how the guys got her home, or what they did when they got her there.

He pulled her aside after the ceremony. "Do you want to go up and check out that Pastor Glen guy you were talking about?" he asked.

Dana stared at him.

Hank didn't know a lot about sex, but he assumed she must have known she'd had intercourse—and that she'd been too wasted to remember with whom. But she probably didn't realize she'd been gang-raped.

"Seriously?" she asked. "Are you making fun of me?"

"No. Not at all. I'll leave tomorrow, if you want. I want to get away for a while. Experience some shit before I start college."

She stared at him, her vacant eyes turning suspicious. "Were you on Mount Wilson yesterday?"

Hank feigned ignorance. "No, what do you mean? Why would I be on Mount Wilson?"

Dana shrugged. "No reason. I went up there with Sammy and some guys yesterday, but I must have gotten really drunk, or stoned, or something, because I can't remember shit."

Hank heard his mother calling him. "I'm leaving first thing in the morning," he told Dana. "I'm going to hitchhike north. You're welcome to come along if you want." He gave her a time and place to meet if she decided to join him.

She nodded noncommittally.

And so, the unwitting participant in a gang rape and homicide and the unknowing victim of a gang rape left their respective homes the next morning. One left out of fear and shame. The other left in search of spiritual guidance.

Chapter 39

It had taken Hank and Dana five days to hitchhike to Pastor Glen's church. The days of America's innocence were gone, replaced by a generally unspoken yet pervasive sense of fear and mistrust. People were buying guns at unprecedented rates. Gated communities were all the rage for the wealthy, and even for the almost wealthy. Workplace violence was on the rise. Mentally unstable people with guns were becoming the norm. Less than a month following Hank and Dana's trip north from Pasadena, a man would walk into a law firm at 101 California Street in San Francisco and open fire, killing eight and wounding six—a precursor of the NRA-inspired madness to come.

Pastor Glen's church had been a beautiful refuge in the forest of Northern California. Young people, some as young as fourteen, had flocked to the church, presumably seeking some kind of sanctuary from the growing insanity in the world. It was a nineties version of the hippie communes although if the kids had studied their history, a more apt analogy would have been Reverend Jim Jones's Peoples Temple, which ended in the 1978 mass suicide/murder in Guyana.

Hank had seen immediately that the young pastor was building a cult following. The young women were separated from whomever they had come with, and the word was that Pastor Glen had his pick of the proverbial litter.

Dana had offered to sleep with Hank on the trip north, but he had declined. He had, he'd thought, enough guilt going on in his life. Plus, he couldn't get the image out of his head of one after the other of Valentine's group raping her. When they showed up at the enclave and Pastor Glen had whisked her away with hardly a glance toward Hank, he'd actually felt a sense of relief. She was someone else's responsibility now.

*   *   *

They'd come for Hank's money in the middle of the night. He'd been sleeping, fully clothed, on a cot in a dormitory containing about twenty beds, only half of which were occupied. His head rested on his small backpack, which contained one change of clothes, his toiletries, and his writing notebooks. Dana must have told Pastor Glen about his money belt. He had his life savings, just over $2,000, in the belt. Another two hundred bucks was stashed in his shoe.

The two kids were not much older than Hank.

"Pastor Glen says you have to hand over all your money to stay here," a kid with a face full of inflamed pimples said. "We're all a family here, and we share everything."

Hank wiped his eyes, waking up, trying to think. "No. . .I won't be staying."

The second boy, who had a misshapen nose and therefore spoke with a nasal twang, shook his head. "You're here now. You're sleeping in our bed. You ate our food. Hand it over." He put his hand out, palm up.

Hank sat up, putting his feet on the floor. "I'll leave now, then."

"Too late, bro," the broken-nosed boy said. "Too darn late. The good Lord speaks to Pastor Glen, and then Pastor Glen tells us what to do. He told us you need to hand over your cash. Now."

As Hank stood, the pimple boy grabbed at his shirt, feeling for the money belt. Hank pushed him away, but then nose boy moved to Hank's back and grabbed him by the arms, just as Billy Campbell had done on Mount Wilson.

The kid's grip was strong, and it was only a matter of seconds before pimple boy pulled up Hank's shirt and unfastened the money belt. He backed up with it, holding it like a trophy and nodded to nose boy. "You can stay or go," pimple boy said.

Then the two kids turned and walked out of the dormitory.

"How much did you have?" Hank heard a whispered voice from the next bed.

"None of your fucking business," Hank said.

"Well, God bless you, too," the voice said as Hank walked down the row of beds and out into the night.

Chapter 40

Hank Jr., now Danny Lee, could feel his oncoming depression merge with an intense confusion of emotions arising from the news of his father. Like the confluence of two rivers, his brain felt muddled and turbulent, his thoughts jumping around at random. He felt like he wanted to cry, but for what? Because his life's narrative was bullshit? Because he'd abandoned his life and his mother for reasons that weren't real?

Danny was a grown man, a world-famous author hiding behind a pseudonym. Critics and readers had written thousands of words praising his skill and penetrating insight into the psyche of the common man. Yet at his core, Danny felt stunted, as if he'd never properly matured. He'd lived half his life as a virtual hermit—friendless, cut off from his mother, and sometimes so lonely he would wander the streets just to be in the presence of people.

He was often drawn to Golden Gate Park, masochistically searching for a father playing with his son. Danny would sit on a bench and watch, wondering what it would be like to have a father. More often than not, watching a father/son team interact, he would romanticize it. His father would have sat with him after school to help him with his homework. Then the two would have gone to the park, to play ball or throw a Frisbee. Maybe they would have gone hiking on Mount Wilson. During the summer, his parents would have taken him to the beach, where his father would teach him to body surf, and the three would return home reddened from the sun and itchy from the salt water. Happy.

But of course, the dark side of Danny would sometimes conjure up a father who was mean and abusive. Maybe a drunk who would beat Danny's mother, and if Danny was lucky, ignore him altogether.

Like the character in the now-deleted passage he'd been writing, he didn't allow himself to get too immersed in relationships. He'd thought he'd fallen in love with two women over the past twenty years, but in each case he'd broken it off, afraid of commitment, afraid of discovery.

Now, Danny felt the need to get out into the city, maybe walk from his apartment in the Tenderloin to his favorite Mexican restaurant in the Mission District. It was summer, but that often meant a cold San Francisco fog, so he grabbed his beat-up aviator jacket and walked out into the City by the Bay.

* * *

Danny greeted Alberto, the owner of Chaco's Mexican Grill, in the fluent Spanish he'd learned from Aunt Eva and the Mexican kitchen help in her restaurant. Because of his fluency and his half-Asian looks, there were some who thought he was a mestizo, part European and part Indian. He did nothing to dissuade anyone who ventured an opinion as to his origins.

"*Como estas?*" Alberto asked. He looked closely at Danny. "You look out of sorts."

Danny shrugged. "*Todo está bien.* I didn't sleep so well last night, is all."

"*Bueno, Raul quiere que le llame tan pronto como sea posible,*" Alberto said. Raul wants you to call him as soon as possible.

"Did he say why?" Danny asked, still speaking Spanish.

Alberto didn't answer, just said, "Do you want to use the phone in my office?"

"No, thanks. Let me get something to eat, and then I'll call him."

Alberto handed Danny a piece of paper. "Call him at this number." He motioned with his head toward Danny's usual table. He didn't bother handing him a menu.

As he waited for his enchilada-chile relleno combination plate, Danny pondered the call from Raul Martinez. He felt a buzz go up his spine. His clouded brain tried to focus. *This can't be good,* he thought. It was way too soon to be hearing from Raul again.

Danny was thankful the restaurant was filling up. He liked Alberto—he *owed* Alberto—but he didn't need him hanging around talking to him right now. For about the thousandth time, Danny wondered how involved Alberto was with Raul.

*   *   *

Danny, then calling himself John Huong, had met Alberto shortly after he arrived in San Francisco, after Pastor Glen's people had stolen his money. He'd hitchhiked down to the city, carefully guarding his remaining cash. He'd eaten at fast food joints and slept in the cheapest motels he could find, too afraid to sleep outside where the rest of his money could be stolen. He'd never felt so alone in his life.

Once he arrived in San Francisco, he found a room in a rundown hotel on Eddy Street. He registered as John Huong, borrowing the last name from a Vietnamese friend of his mother's. No ID required. He paid cash for a week in advance and then set out looking for work.

He came across Chaco's on the third day of his job search. It had been a weird job interview. Alberto obviously knew that Danny, as John, wasn't Mexican, although he spoke as fluent and as idiomatic a Spanish as any of his Mexican staff. Danny knew his way around a restaurant, specifically a Mexican restaurant, yet he refused to offer any references or specifics as to where he'd worked. Danny's lack of ID was both concerning and confusing.

"I'm used to working with undocumented Mexicans," Alberto said. "But you're not Mexican, and you won't give me much to go on. How do I know you won't steal me blind if I give you a job?"

Danny smiled and shrugged. "I'm only a kid. I just graduated from high school. I ran away from home. I'm not experienced or smart enough to devise a plot to get a job and then rip you off. I just need to make enough money to live on while I figure out my life."

Alberto squinted at Danny, sizing him up. Then he said, "I'll try you out for a week. You'll be a dishwasher, and if necessary, you can bus tables. At the end of the week, if you're doing a good job, we'll try to get you some papers—driver's license, Social Security card. I'll advance the money out of your future salary. Fair enough?"

Danny breathed a sigh of relief and nodded. "*Bueno. Muchas gracias, señor.*"

*   *   *

Two months later, John Huong, now as Danny Lee, was waiting tables, earning decent money. In the mornings and evenings, he spent his time writing.

He'd moved out of the Eddy Street flophouse and rented a modest apartment, still in the Tenderloin but a definite step up. He stayed away from the Vietnamese community; Alberto had warned him that they'd be curious about him, and if anyone came looking, he'd be easily identifiable.

Alberto also put Danny in touch with Raul Martinez, the man who had arranged for the fake IDs. After Danny had been working for Alberto for about six months, Raul was waiting for him at the end of an evening shift. Danny assumed that whatever Raul wanted would have something to do with his fake IDs.

"Come into Alberto's office with me," Raul said. "I have a proposition for you."

Like the life-changing events on Mount Wilson, this proposition would send Danny down an unexpected—and ultimately dangerous—path.

Chapter 41

As it turned out, Raul's proposition for Danny had little to do with fake IDs.

Alberto's office was small, and even with only two people in it, it felt cramped and oppressive. A beat-up executive chair sat on one side of an old pine desk covered with invoices, receipts, and trade magazines, and a scratched, wooden chair sat on the other. On the walls hung the requisite licenses and permits and a poorly framed painting of Puerto Vallarta's Old Town. Boxes of paperwork were stacked against one wall, labeled "Liquor Sales," "Gross Receipts," "Food Invoices," and the like. There were no windows. There were no family photos. Every now and then, a lethargic ceiling fan fluttered a few loose papers.

A small, dark-skinned man with short black hair and a flat nose, Raul had a round face with smooth skin, except for one long scar that ran from his right ear to his chin. Danny would learn over the years that the scar turned purple when Raul got angry. His eyes, though black as coal, were somehow still able to convey an astounding range of emotions, the most prevalent being stone-cold deadness.

Raul took Alberto's chair and motioned with his head toward the armless, wooden chair. Danny sat. He was still young, but he'd been on the run for the better part of a year by then, living in squalor and working alongside hard-edged illegals who'd done their best to break the new kid. But he'd grown up in restaurant kitchens, and while neither Aunt Eva nor his mother had hired undocumented workers, those people were just as rough. Many had drug habits. Many had police records. Very few, of any of the ethnicities, could put together complete sentences without profanity.

Raul spoke English at that meeting though he knew full well Danny spoke Spanish. "So, how you coming along, kid?" he asked.

"Fine, sir."

Raul smiled, showing crooked white teeth. To Danny it had seemed a chilling, calculated smile, not one born of kindness.

"Call me Raul."

Danny nodded tentatively. He knew that none of the Latino workers in the restaurant referred to Raul by his given name. It was Señor Martinez or, at best, Don Raul.

"I hear you spend a lot of your breaks writing in a notebook. You a writer?"

Danny shrugged. "Trying to be."

"What do you write?"

"Stories. Just stuff I make up. I'm hoping it'll become a novel."

Raul said nothing for a moment. "You're not writing anything about us, are you?"

"You mean about the restaurant?" Danny was confused by the question.

Raul nodded. His dark eyes bore into Danny. "Yeah. The restaurant. Alberto. Me."

"No, sir . . . no, Raul. The book I'm trying to write doesn't even take place in San Francisco. It's about a kid who never knew his father and grew up searching for him while becoming a world-famous actor. It takes place in Los Angeles. Uh, Holly-wood, actually." Danny found he was talking fast, sounding de-fensive, though he didn't know why.

Raul fell silent again, still staring at Danny. After a moment, he nodded slightly. "I have a deal for you. You can make a lot of money working a lot less. You won't need to work here anymore. You can spend your time writing your great American novel." He smiled his dazzling-white, crooked-tooth smile again. It re-minded Danny of the snarl of a German shepherd. Even nineteen-year-old Danny knew whatever was about to be proposed would not be legal. He guessed it would have something to do with drugs. He was right.

The proposal was for Danny to become a courier for Raul, a mule. His people would furnish Danny with the best papers money could buy, including a passport that would pass scrutiny in any country in the world. Crossing borders would not be an issue. What he would be carrying across those borders, though, was the proverbial horse of a different color.

Danny's initial inclination had been to reject Raul's offer, which was couched in vague but fairly obvious generalities. In the back of his brain, he heard his mother's voice, scolding and afraid for him. He figured Raul had pegged him as someone on the run and that he'd therefore be relatively safe to approach. Raul assured him he could say no if he wanted. Nothing would change if he declined.

In the end he decided to try it out. The money offered for the first gig was huge compared to what he'd been making. Raul told him he'd do no more than four runs a year, using different routes and names. Except for those trips, Danny would be able to devote all his time to writing.

But the money wasn't really the deciding factor. In his mind at the time, if he was not an actual criminal, he was at least culpable. He'd witnessed a gang rape and had neither stopped it nor reported it. He'd pushed a kid off a cliff. He still believed he'd killed Billy Campbell.

It was 1994 when Danny went to work for what he later learned was the Sinaloa cartel. Under various identities, he smuggled laundered money into Mexico and drugs into the United States. He found he enjoyed the adrenaline rush of the risks he took, and he enjoyed devising new ways to transport the sealed containers he was ordered to pick up. Of course, he knew damned well it was drugs he was smuggling, but not once did he even peek at the contents.

He refused to think about the consequences of putting drugs onto the streets of America. Drugs would make their way to Americans hungry for a high regardless of what he did or didn't do. He repressed any early thoughts of morality so deeply that they eventually became irrelevant.

The writer in him said he was just another deeply flawed character. He was inherently good, yet he had found himself living in a parallel universe of aiding and abetting evil—while not actually being evil himself. In his rare nods to reality, he refused to allow himself to romanticize his actions. He was no dark hero. He was a criminal, pure and simple. He'd come to accept that.

Danny had started as a basic mule, carrying contraband on his body. The risks were enormous, of course, but that was part of the attraction. What did he have to lose? He was alone in the world; he had nothing but his writing. In his darkest moments, he told himself he could just as easily write in jail.

It didn't take long for Danny to become a rising star in Raul's sphere of operations. His creativity as a writer translated well to the real-world challenges of smuggling. As his loads increased beyond what could be carried on his body, his ingenuity resulted in success after success. The financial rewards also increased.

And he kept writing. It had taken two and a half years to complete his first novel, *The Todays of Tomorrow*, and another eight months to finally land an agent. He submitted the manuscript under the name Mike Mann. The agent sold the book to a mid-level publishing house that did very little in the way of publicity, yet somehow, slowly, the novel gained enough traction to eventually be noticed by some top critics. By the time Danny, as Mike Mann, had completed his second novel, *Todays* had won two prestigious awards and had landed on *The New York Times* bestseller list.

Even after he had become a successful author, Danny continued to work for Raul. He knew it was crazy. He knew it was self-destructive. He knew he'd be inwardly cringing if he were reading a novel whose protagonist seemed determined to destroy his own life. But wasn't his life already destroyed? Did he really have anything of substance to lose?

*   *   *

Now, when the food came, Danny found his appetite had vanished. He picked at the enchilada. Even with the processors in his brain misfiring, he knew instinctively that something was wrong. He had worked for the Northern California boss of the Sinaloa drug cartel for the past twenty years. He knew that Raul Martinez would not summon him for social reasons.

Danny had only just returned from a highly successful run on a yacht from Cabo San Lucas to Long Beach. He never knew how much product he was transporting, but he knew when it was a lot, and this trip had been a lot—much more than he'd expected. He'd actually expressed his concern to Guillermo, his contact in Cabo.

Danny instantly pegged Guillermo as a country bumpkin, out of place in the Cabo San Lucas yacht harbor as he lounged on the aft deck of what Danny assumed was a multimillion-dollar cabin cruiser, an Azimut 64. Despite the hot weather, Guillermo wore blue jeans, cowboy boots, and a long-sleeved western-style shirt. He also wore a straw *campesino* hat.

When Danny spotted Guillermo indiscreetly lazing on the yacht to which he had been directed, he walked past the boat and spent half an hour looking for drug-agent tails. But the popular tourist center was simply too crowded to spot any surveillance so, in the end, he climbed aboard and ordered Guillermo into the cabin, out of sight.

The contact stared at Danny for a long moment, his eyes squinting in his young, hard-looking face. "*Quién eres tú para dar órdenes?*" Who are you to give me orders? Guillermo's voice was gravelly and harsh.

By then, Danny was used to dealing with men who thought of themselves as hardened soldiers, men whose power came from violence and the intimation of violence. Yet there was something off about Guillermo. To Danny, his harsh tone sounded forced, like that of an actor not quite ready for prime time.

"I'm the guy who has to sail this load across an international border," Danny answered in Spanish. "I'm the one taking the big risk."

Danny had obtained his captain's license two years prior, and this was to be his third trip by sea, each time on a different vessel. It was a dangerous proposition.

Guillermo kept his gaze on Danny for several more seconds, still scowling, until his face relaxed into a broad smile. "*Sí, es verdad.*" Yes, that's true. He hoisted his short, stocky frame off the divan and walked into the salon.

Danny followed him into the beautifully appointed main cabin, with its wraparound, white-leather couch, burled-wood cabinets, and beige Berber carpet. Everything was spotless except for a series of dirty footprints on the carpet.

It was easy enough for Danny to follow the prints to cabinets that contained piles of wrapped packages. He walked through the boat then, opening cabinets and closets, finding packages stuffed everywhere. "This load seems over the top, don't you think?" he asked Guillermo. "Are we getting a little greedy?"

Guillermo just shrugged and grinned. "If you get caught, you'll do the same amount of time you'd do if you were caught with half the amount. What difference does it make?"

Danny sighed and nodded. It was true. But it was also a hell of a lot easier to find contraband when it was hidden in virtually every nook and cranny of the boat. He didn't argue. He assumed Guillermo was nothing more than a fledgling soldier, and not a particularly bright one at that. He went to the fridge and found it stocked with plenty of food. He pulled out a couple of Modelo Especials and held one up as an offering to Guillermo, who nodded.

"We may as well relax," Danny said. "I think it's best if you wait to leave until the fishing charters are in and the crews are leaving. I'm going to pull out first thing in the morning."

The two sat in the main salon drinking beer and making small talk. Guillermo said he was from a small town on the Sea of Cortez side of the Baja peninsula. Danny had never heard of it. Guillermo also wasn't quite the innocuous soldier Danny had assumed. He turned out to be related to Raul although he didn't say how. He also answered a question Danny had been wondering about for years: How high up in the cartel was Raul? From the way Guillermo spoke of Raul, it appeared he was very high up indeed.

While the "mere soldier" assumption hadn't been quite correct, the "not too bright" assessment held up. Guillermo talked too much, told Danny more about himself than was appropriate for men in their line of work. There'd been no reason for Guillermo to boast about his family's role in the cartel. Or had there?

In the end, Danny could think of no reason for Guillermo's indiscretion other than a young man's ego.

As the sky turned pink and orange and then faded to gray, Danny noted that most of the yachts had returned to the harbor. As the crews finished with their cleanups, they filed off the boats and headed home. It was a good time for Guillermo to leave.

The trip went smoothly. Danny sailed in a large arc, heading far out to sea before turning back toward the coast once he was inside U.S. territory. He'd arranged to arrive at the Los Alamitos harbor in Long Beach in the late afternoon on a Sunday, when the weekend and day sailors were coming back from their day trips. The slip he pulled into was registered to the boat he'd sailed in. There was no apparent interest by immigration or customs agents. Danny had simply tied up, grabbed his backpack, and walked away.

So what, he wondered, did Raul want?

Chapter 42

Danny felt like the gods were conspiring to fuck with his current cycle of depression. First he'd read the Facebook post from his mother. Then he'd gotten a summons from his drug-lord boss. His head was a mess, his thoughts scrambled and random, but he knew he needed to think as clearly as possible when talking with Raul. His life depended on it.

After about three years of working for Raul, Danny's well-constructed bubble of self-delusion burst. He had traveled to Mazatlán as an Asian tourist, carrying $200,000 in one of his two pieces of luggage. He'd been instructed to pass it off to a man posing as a tour guide who would pick him up at the airport. The man would drive him to his high-end hotel, and when Danny got out of the car, he'd simply leave the bag behind.

Danny had never met the man before—didn't know his name and didn't ask. Everything had gone off without a hitch, and he was looking forward to three days in the sun. Hopefully, he'd pick up a woman tourist looking to have some fun.

The next morning at breakfast in the hotel, Danny picked up a courtesy copy of *El Sol de Mazatlán*, the local paper. A large photo of the man who'd picked him up at the airport stared at him from the front page. The headline read, *"Mazatlán Ciudadana Encontrado Decapitado."* The decapitated man was identified as Umberto Rodrigues and was known to police as a suspected soldier in the Sinaloa cartel. His head, still oozing goop, had been left on top of a garbage can, discovered by an eleven-year-old girl and her furiously barking dog, only a block inland from Playa Norte beach. The police found the rest of the body, hacked into parts, inside the garbage can.

Danny used his prepaid international cellphone to call Raul's disposable cell. He was only supposed to use it in an emergency.

"I thought maybe I'd be hearing from you today," Raul said, without saying hello.

"What happened?" Danny asked.

"Nothing to concern yourself about. We know you passed the package off to your contact, so you're fine. Apparently he had some money problems and thought he could get away with skimming a few thousand bucks."

Danny went quiet for a few beats. "You guys cut off some dude's head over a few grand?"

Raul laughed—a cruel, vicious-sounding laugh. "Lessons have to be learned and taught, my friend. Now go to the beach and enjoy your little vacation."

At that moment Danny knew he would never be able to walk away from Raul and the cartel.

Back home after Mazatlán, Danny went to Alberto's restaurant for dinner and found him in a pensive mood. He took a seat in Danny's booth without asking first and brought a glass of tequila with him.

"I'm sorry I got you into this business," he said. "I thought I was doing you a favor at the time."

Danny looked around, a habit he'd fallen into long ago. The restaurant was crowded, the noise level high. The usual loop of mariachi music was playing over the restaurant speakers. No one appeared to be paying any attention to the two men.

"Not to worry," Danny said. "I had a pretty good idea what I was getting into, but this last week was a little rough." He looked at Alberto, trying to gauge whether his ex-boss had heard about the beheading.

Alberto took a sip of tequila and gave a small nod, as if reading Danny's mind. "Yes, I know about it." He moved a few inches closer to Danny.

Danny could smell the man's cologne, which he wore to cover the sweat and accumulated kitchen smells from his long workdays. His sour breath smelled of tequila.

"Be careful, Danny. Raul is my friend, but if someone displeases him, he can be more brutal than you can imagine." Alberto paused. When he spoke again, his voice was low. Danny knew he was about to commit a rare indiscretion.

"When we were growing up in Tijuana together, Raul became one of the youngest enforcers in the family," Alberto said. "I personally watched him cut off the fingers of one of our childhood friends who had skimmed about twenty dollars' worth of pesos from a drug sale. While our old friend screamed in pain, Raul roasted the fingers over an open fire in a trash can. Then he ate the meat off the fingers."

Alberto's breath had gone shallow with his gruesome revelation, and Danny wondered if he had ever told this story to anyone else.

"He offered a cooked finger to me," Alberto continued. "He held it out to me, smiling, and said, 'It's finger-lickin' good.'"

Alberto drank the last of his tequila, patted Danny on the shoulder, and returned to his place at the front of the restaurant.

Danny wondered why Alberto felt the need to tell him that story.

*   *   *

Danny recalled that day in Mazatlán as he walked to Walgreens to buy a prepaid cellphone. During the walk, he decided that if there were any good sign, it was that Raul had ordered him to call, not to meet. He walked back to his apartment to make the call.

"Raul."

"Danny! Good to hear from you," Raul said. It was a strange, atypical greeting, as if he were making contact with a long-lost friend.

"You asked me to call," Danny said.

"Ah, *sí*. So I did. You wouldn't happen to know what became of the two hundred pounds of cocaine that was on the boat you sailed into Long Beach, would you?" Raul's voice still sounded cheerful, but Danny could hear the artificiality of it.

Oh, fuck, he thought. He worked to keep his voice calm. "Whatever was on board was still there when I docked. You know I don't ask questions about what I'm moving."

"Yet you suggested to Guillermo that it was too much and that we were getting greedy, did you not?" Raul's voice turned steely, like a third-rate actor performing a cross-examination in a TV legal drama.

Danny took a deep breath. "Yeah, so what? That whole scene was a shitstorm waiting to happen. Guillermo looked ridiculous sitting on the deck of a million-dollar gringo yacht with his straw hat. It screamed setup. I tried to make sure we weren't being surveilled, and when I got on board, I made him go into the cabin. Because it was so weird, I opened a couple of obvious cupboards and saw packages stuffed everywhere. A fucking customs agent wouldn't even have to break a sweat looking for contraband. When I saw that, I assumed all the less obvious places had already been taken, so I mentioned the risk to Guillermo."

Danny stopped talking, hoping he hadn't been rambling, hoping he didn't sound defensive. Edgy, he jumped as a truck honked on the street below.

Raul didn't respond.

Danny finally talked into the silence. "Are you telling me the shit's missing? There's nothing there?"

"*Correcto*," Raul said. "*Tenemos un problema.*" We have a problem.

"Jesus, Raul. You don't really think I'd take that shit, do you? How fucking stupid do you think I am?"

"I don't think you're stupid at all, Danny. In fact, I think you're one of the smartest guys I know."

"So, why are you telling me *we* have a problem? I did my job, like I always do. If someone fucked you on this end, go figure it out, but don't lay it at my feet."

Raul went silent again. Danny worried he'd pushed too hard. His head was killing him. His emotions felt raw. He felt a strange sense of rage, which he knew he needed to rein in.

"Okay," Raul said, speaking slowly as though measuring his words. "Did you see anyone hanging around the harbor when you got there? Anything that looked out of the ordinary?"

Danny sighed heavily. "Shit, Raul. When I get to where I'm going with whatever I'm transporting, I look around for cops or undercover agents and then I get the fuck out of there as fast as I can. No, I didn't see any suspicious guys lurking around the harbor." He paused, thinking.

"Look. Think about it. If there was as much product as I suspect there was, it would take one guy dozens of trips to unload the stuff, and it would take at least a van to hold and transport it. Or it would take a number of guys, which would probably raise suspicions. In any event, it would have to have been a delicate operation, most likely spread out over a period of time to make it seem as normal as possible, right? And remember, I called you within a few minutes of docking, and I was home in San Francisco within four hours."

"Mmm . . . ."

Danny was losing patience. His head was spinning. He wanted to lie down and close his eyes. He felt like his stomach was loaded with rocks. "What the fuck does 'mmm' mean, Raul? What are you doing?"

"I'm trying to find out what the fuck happened to thirty fucking million dollars' worth of cocaine."

There was something about this whole conversation, other than the obvious, that felt off to Danny. Raul still sounded like an actor reading his lines.

"I get that," Danny said. "But you're wasting your time talking to me while whoever took the shit is getting away."

"Don't worry about me," Raul said. "We've got people on it. I'm not wasting my time, and I sure hope I'm not wasting yours."

Danny didn't answer. He had a terrible sense of dread. He felt a drop of sweat fall from his right armpit.

"Who did you tell about this run, Danny?" Raul finally asked. His voice was low, menacing.

Oh, shit, thought Danny. *Here it comes.* Raul would have to find some sort of scapegoat if he didn't find the goods. He knew Raul was high up in the cartel, but he didn't know how high. He had his family connections. But thirty million dollars was a lot of money, even for these guys. He figured Raul would be going through some serious shit from the bosses above him. He'd need to deliver a body if he couldn't deliver the drugs.

Danny knew he'd lasted as a courier much longer than anyone would have expected. Yes, he'd been brilliant and successful, but when push came to shove, he knew Raul wouldn't hesitate to sacrifice him to save himself. "No one. I never tell anyone. No one but you, me, and Alberto knows I work for you. Why?"

"Because the guy who was supposed to pick the load up the morning after you docked claims he was sitting in his car in the harbor lot when you docked. He claims he saw you meet and exchange words with a guy after you left the boat. He thought nothing of it at the time, just another boater saying hello, but when he came back the next morning, the stuff was gone."

"Well," Danny said, "your guy's a lying piece of shit. I didn't meet or talk to anyone. Sounds to me like you got your man."

Danny heard Raul sigh through the phone. "He's my relative. It wasn't him."

Neither man spoke for several seconds. Danny felt like vomiting.

Finally, Raul said, "Don't go anywhere, Danny. We need to sort this out."

He hung up, leaving Danny in a cold sweat.

Chapter 43

Danny sat very still. A door down the hall slammed, and a few moments later he heard the elevator doors open and close. The ceiling fan over his computer table hummed—an irritating low hum he'd never noticed before. His head felt like it was in a vise. He smiled a grim smile. It was interesting how un-suicidal he was feeling all of a sudden.

He opened the computer cover and waited a few beats for the screen to come to life. It was still on Facebook. His mother's picture and her note about his father stared up at him. He couldn't help reading her entry one more time.

"Fuck me," he muttered. Then he got up, grabbed his jacket, and walked out of the apartment. Outside, the fog had settled in. It closed in on him, and his skin, wet from sweat, felt cold. He walked three blocks to a Vietnamese deli that had his favorite vegetarian banh mi sandwiches. He'd lost his appetite at Chaco's and had only picked at his food. His stomach had been in a knot ever since Alberto had told him to call Raul, and now he felt hungry.

Nathan, the owner of the deli and a second-generation Vietnamese American, knew Danny by sight, although not by name, and Danny was surprised when he wasn't greeted by Nathan's usual big smile. It was late afternoon, and the small restaurant was empty except for one skinny white kid who looked like a student, sitting at a Formica-topped table, eating a sandwich and staring at his computer. Incongruous Motown music played over the small restaurant's speakers.

Nathan reached under the counter and pulled out a piece of paper. He placed it on the counter in front of Danny. "Is this you?"

Danny looked down at the flier, which showed a photographic likeness of a man who looked almost exactly like him. He picked up the paper for a closer look. He knew it couldn't be a photo of him as he hadn't had a picture of himself taken since he'd left home. Yet it *was* him. He realized it wasn't an actual photograph, but a Photoshopped picture from his senior year in high school. Whoever did the work on the photo had done an amazing job of aging an eighteen-year-old Hank Raygun to a forty-year-old Danny Lee.

Danny looked from the picture to Nathan. "Where'd you get this?" His voice trembled slightly.

Nathan shrugged. "Some guy's going around the neighborhood asking if anyone knows this guy." He pointed to the photo. "Look on the back."

Danny turned the paper over and read the message, printed in large capital letters:

THIS MAN'S FAMILY IS TRYING DESPERATELY TO FIND HIM. IF YOU KNOW HIM OR KNOW WHERE HE IS, PLEASE CALL.

An 800 number was included.

Holy shit, thought Danny. *Can this day get any better?*

"Can I have this?" he asked Nathan. "I think I know who it is."

Nathan scrunched up his face, looking hard at Danny. "This isn't you?"

Danny shook his head and asked for his usual sandwich.

Nathan watched him a moment longer before nodding and going to work.

Danny took the wrapped banh mi and walked back to his apartment. Obviously his mother and long-lost father were pulling out all the stops to try to find him, but what fucked-up timing. He knew how the cartel worked. He knew the days of keeping family out of a cartel's dirty business was long gone. If Raul decided

Danny was guilty or was going to be set up as guilty, and Raul connected Danny to his mother, she could be in serious danger.

When he got home, he sat in front of his computer and ate his sandwich, trying to think, trying to quiet the deluge of thoughts clamoring for attention. He felt as if his nerves were on fire. Every unexpected sound caused him to flinch. If the elevator opened on his floor, his body would tense, the fear a palpable heaviness that rendered him immobile until the moment of potential danger passed. When he could get his brain to actually function, he reasoned he probably had a day or two before Raul would decide to take action. Danny assumed he was now under surveillance.

When he finished the sandwich, he turned to his mother's Facebook page and began typing.

Mother, I love you and miss you, and I'm so sorry for all the grief and sorrow I've caused. Obviously, I'm shocked to hear about my father. I would like to make contact, but I'm in some trouble right now and I need you to have whoever is distributing my picture stop immediately. He (or they) should try to retrieve all existing leaflets. I do not want certain people to make a connection between me and you. That is critical. I've already brought too much sadness and disappointment on you. If we are going to reconnect, I want to make sure you are safe. Is my father intelligent and competent? If so, have him e-mail me at the following address, and we can arrange a time to talk by phone.

Danny knew it was a risk communicating over Facebook, but so far he didn't think anyone knew who he really was. He'd have his mother take down her page as soon as possible. He assumed the campaign to find him was being led by his father. The idea of distributing an age-adjusted photo was fairly brilliant. When

Danny had first read the post by his mother about his father, he'd immediately assumed the old man was feeble, maybe dying, and wanted to assuage some kind of guilt before he died. Now, however, Danny was reassessing.

He hit the enter button to send the post and then stood up, looking around the room. He stood still for a full minute, and then sat back down. A profound change had just come over him. He thought about it. The symptoms of his oncoming depression seemed to be abating—halted midstream by the danger to himself and to his family. The knot in his stomach lessened. His head was clearing. He felt like he did on a big smuggling assignment—focused and alive.

In spite of everything, Danny smiled. He had just reconnected with his mother—well, sort of. He had made the first move toward connecting with his father. It was a bad time to do so, but there wasn't anything he could do about that. His father had somehow learned what had happened on Mount Wilson that fateful day. His parents knew he hadn't killed anyone and hadn't participated in a gang rape.

Yet now . . . he envisioned his meeting with his mother. *I've got good news and bad news. The good news is that I'm a celebrated novelist. The bad news is that for the past twenty-two years, I've been working for the most notorious drug cartel on the planet.*

"Fuck me," he said out loud. But he was still smiling. He realized that however this turned out, he was finally going to be free of the cartel. "Death is a kind of freedom, isn't it?"

Danny sat still for several minutes, his mind wandering. Not only would he be free of the cartel, but there was a good possibility that he would be free of the cycle of depression and suicidal ideation.

He opened the bottom drawer of his dresser, took out a shoebox, and pulled out a bundle of passports held together by a rubber band. Tucked into the first page of each passport was an accompanying driver's license, and in two cases, a birth certificate.

There were five passports in total. Two of the identities had been provided to him by Raul. He set those aside. The other three were identities he had acquired on his own—his insurance policy for a scenario he was pretty sure was about to unfold. One set of IDs was for Mike Mann. The other two were Asian names. There was no ID for Hank Raygun. That had been lost with his money at Pastor Glen's. He'd decided long ago that was just as well.

Next he pulled out a bundle of money, $5,000. Rubber-banded to the stack were three debit cards, each of which matched a set of IDs. He knew there was over $3 million in the Mike Mann account. He had paid taxes on that money. The other two accounts had fairly small balances, basic living-expense money. The millions he had made from working for Raul were safely ensconced in a couple of offshore accounts.

Danny went to his closet and pulled out a small black canvas backpack. He put the money and the three sets of identification papers in two separate pockets. In a third, he put the two sets of IDs that had been furnished by Raul. They might still come in handy. He filled the large pocket of the backpack with some clothes and a fully loaded toiletry kit. If anyone came looking for him, there would still be clothes and toiletries in the apartment. Hopefully, whoever came would assume he'd be returning, which might buy him some time.

He pulled out a stack of notebooks from the top drawer of the dresser and wedged those into the backpack as well. He'd stopped writing in longhand long ago, but these notebooks included the ones he'd left home with twenty-three years ago. He put the backpack on the floor near the front door.

The last item he retrieved from the cardboard box was a thumb drive. He took it to the computer and sat down. There was already a thumb drive stuck into the side of the two-year-old Dell. He ran his backup program so the thumb drive would have everything on the computer. Then he pulled that drive out, plugged in the one he'd just pulled from the box, and waited for it to load. It contained the final drafts of all of his completed novels and dozens of short stories. He ran the backup program so this thumb drive would also have everything from the Dell. Then he erased all of his writings from the laptop and deleted his browser history.

When he was done, the computer contained only innocuous apps and programs. No one who was looking to kill him would take the time—or have the expertise—to look beyond emptied trash. He sat back in the chair and looked around the apartment. His gaze settled on the small bookcase, filled with a few dozen hardback books: *For Whom the Bell Tolls* by Ernest Hemingway, *The Grapes of Wrath* and a collection of short stories by John Steinbeck, *Catch-22* by Joseph Heller, *Jitterbug Perfume* by Tom Robbins, and most of Kurt Vonnegut's novels. There were also the first editions of Mike Mann's books, each one signed by his agent.

Danny pulled the Mann volumes from the shelf. He doubted that a cartel hit man would open any of the books, but eventually the landlord would enter the abandoned apartment. Anyone who found the signed copies might deduce that the tenant Danny Lee was the famous author Mike Mann.

Danny pulled a lightweight knapsack from the closet and piled the Mike Mann books into it. Then, from the dresser, he retrieved the plaques and certificates of awards he'd received for his writing. He tossed those in the knapsack as well. If he made it to the morning, he would take those and one of his thumb drives to the bank and put them in a safe deposit box.

*   *   *

Having survived till the morning, albeit on edge and jumpy, flinching at every sound outside his apartment, Danny put his books and awards in a safe deposit box at Bank of America. Then he walked to Chaco's for lunch. Until he figured out what to do, he'd try to act as normal as possible. Perhaps Alberto would have some news. Perhaps Raul had found whoever hijacked his load. Perhaps Raul would decide Danny was too valuable to throw away.

The sun was bright, but a stiff breeze was blowing in from the bay. Dust and stray litter were caught up in small bursts of dust devils. It felt good to walk into the calm interior of Chaco's.

Alberto was at the host station as usual, but his eyes widened in obvious surprise when he saw Danny.

"*Que pasa?*" Danny asked. What's happening?

The lines in Alberto's already deeply lined face became trenches. His eyes darted around the room. His voice was low, and he spoke in rapid-fire Spanish. "You need to run, Danny. They'll be coming for you today or tonight. I can't stop them now."

Danny could hear the urgency in the voice he'd come to know so well.

"Let me get you some tacos to go so it will look like you were just picking up lunch." Without waiting for a reply from Danny, he turned and walked toward the kitchen.

A part of Danny knew that running was the only realistic scenario, yet he still felt a blow to his gut. He also realized with a pang of sadness that he wouldn't see his old boss/friend again. His self-imposed solitude had been hard—painful at times, and just plain empty at other times. He hadn't allowed himself long-term lovers or friends, so the simple familiarity of Alberto and the crew at the restaurant had, in Danny's mind, acted as some kind of replacement, a living plug in the hole of his emptiness.

Alberto must have grabbed something off the line, an order meant for someone else, because he was back with a to-go bag inside of two minutes. He handed it to Danny and whispered, "Just give me a couple bucks to make it look good. And then go, Danny. Go soon and go far." He looked Danny in the eyes for the first time. "*Vaya con dios. Lo siento mucho.*" Go with God. I'm very sorry.

PART THREE

Chapter 44

Hank opened his eyes when he heard Mai exclaim and then call his name. He'd been luxuriating in her bed, enjoying the crisp, clean sheets with the lingering smells of sex and Mai's delicate perfume. The sun poured into the bedroom through sheer curtains, and he could view Mai's silhouette as she sat at a small desk across the room.

"What is it?" Hank asked, sitting up.

Instead of answering, Mai got up and carried her laptop to the bed. She sat down with her back against the headboard, legs stretched out in front of her. She wore a clinging blue silk nightgown.

Hank tore his eyes from her body and took the proffered computer.

As Mai passed Hank the laptop, she quickly explained how she'd kept a Facebook page going, hoping against hope that Hank Jr. would care enough to look her up. "He's answered," she said breathlessly. "He's alive, but he's in some kind of trouble."

Hank read the post from Hank Jr. twice, and then handed the computer back to Mai. "Do you think it's just a ruse to get us to withdraw the fliers and stop looking for him?"

Mai shook her head, a vehement "no-way" kind of shake. "No. He wouldn't want you to call him if that were the case. He needs help."

Hank nodded. There was no point in conjecture at this point. He needed to make contact with his son and find out what was going on. He patted Mai's leg and said he'd take a quick shower, dress, and then send the requested e-mail.

She opened her mouth as if to say something, but then gave him a tight smile and a slight nod.

Hank could see her excitement, but he needed a moment to confront his own emotions. He would soon be talking with a son he didn't even know he had until recently, a son who was now a grown man and who was apparently in some kind of trouble. "I'll e-mail from my laptop when we go downstairs," he explained. "If he's really in trouble and doesn't want anyone to know who you are, I think it'd be better to send it from my computer."

Ten minutes later, Hank sent Hank Jr. an e-mail.

Hank (or whatever you call yourself now), I am Hank Reagan, your father. We have a lot to talk about, and I know you have a lot of questions, but for now, let's deal with whatever trouble you're in. Give me a number to call. I assume it will be a safe number. I'd recommend using a prepaid cellphone. I'll be standing by and will call as soon as I get a number from you. If you can't take a call immediately, then give me the number and tell me when to call.

Hank looked at Mai, who'd been making coffee. "All we can do now is wait," he said.

Mai nodded. Her eyes glistened with tears.

Chapter 45

Danny heard the beep of his iPhone indicating he'd received an e-mail. It was such a rare occurrence that he actually jerked in surprise. The iPhone and Gmail accounts were both registered to a fake name for which he had no identification. He paid his phone bill in person at the Verizon store. He'd never used the phone or the Gmail to communicate with Raul or Alberto. He had a secondary mail account named mmann@gmail.com, which was routed through the account bearing the fake name. He used the mmann account to communicate with his agent and editor.

He pulled his rented Malibu to the side of the road and took the phone from his pocket. He opened the e-mail and saw the note from his father. He had to smile at the advice regarding a prepaid phone. *If he only knew.*

He pulled one of the three prepaid cellphones he'd purchased out of his backpack and checked the phone number. Then he e-mailed his father with the number and a note to call at noon. A moment later, he was back on Highway 101, heading south.

Yesterday afternoon, when he left Alberto, he had gone back to his apartment and found everything as he'd left it. The bag from Chaco's contained three chicken tacos, and Danny wolfed them down while doing one last check around. Then he grabbed his backpack and took the stairs to the ground floor.

When he got to the small lobby, he turned immediately to the right and headed down a short, dank hallway to the rear door, which opened onto an alley where large garbage containers lined the side of the building. Danny figured Raul wouldn't have devoted more than one guy to keep tabs on him while he decided Danny's fate. He also thought it would never occur to Raul that Alberto would warn Danny to run. It had been a dangerous and brave and foolish thing to do.

Once away from his building, Danny had walked to the Enterprise office on Van Ness and rented a bright red Altima, using one of Raul's IDs. Then he'd driven north. He made it to Healdsburg, where he checked into a Best Western, using the same ID he'd used to rent the car. He'd chosen Healdsburg for two reasons: One, he was tired, and two, there were relatively few hotels, which would make it easier for Raul's people to find him if they were searching hotel bookings under any of his known fake IDs. He didn't know if Raul would devote that kind of energy and resources to finding him, but Danny knew Raul had a number of law enforcement officers on the payroll, and if he utilized those resources, it wouldn't be hard or long before they located him.

Danny went to the room, set his alarm, and fell into a deep sleep. The alarm went off at 6 a.m., a shrill, piercing noise that caused him to awake in a state of confusion. It took him several seconds to remember where he was and what he was doing. It was surreal and chilling, as if he were a character in one of his own novels.

When he climbed out of bed, he went to the window facing the parking lot and peered through the curtains. It was nearly dawn. He saw nothing unusual. Over the decades, he'd become adept at spotting surveillance and drug agents. He took a quick shower and left the room at 6:16.

From the Best Western, he drove to the Enterprise office on Healdsburg Avenue and left the car—keys on the floor, contract on the seat. The credit card to which the car had been billed was in the same name as the ID from Raul and was linked to a Bank of America account in which there was a little over $2,000. He walked to a convenience store that had an ATM. It only allowed him to withdraw $300 from that account. *Oh well,* he thought. That was the last he would use that particular ID and bank account.

Danny hitchhiked from Healdsburg to Santa Rosa, which was easier than he thought it would be. A lonely trucker wanting company picked him up within minutes on Highway 101. It was still early as they rolled into Santa Rosa, so Danny asked to be let out near the airport. He figured the rental car companies would open earlier at the airport than in town.

Half an hour later, he was back on Highway 101 heading south. His rental was a blue Chevrolet Malibu. He'd used his Derek Kong ID. He would now be Derek Kong for as long as he thought it safe.

His plan, if one could call it that, was misdirection. He'd gone north and used an ID Raul knew he had. He hoped Raul's people would assume he would continue north, possibly to Canada. The trail would turn cold after Healdsburg, but Derek hoped Raul would assume he'd stopped using that ID for safety reasons. At the very least, Derek hoped the ruse would buy him valuable time.

He received the e-mail from his father early that morning, just as he passed San Francisco. He checked his map and decided he wanted to get to Santa Barbara before taking a call from a father he'd never met. That would be right around lunchtime.

Chapter 46

The phone conversation with Hank Jr. had been predictably awkward. Mai had wanted Hank to put the phone on speaker, but Hank refused.

"Let me see if I can arrange a meeting first. I'll take Norm, and we'll meet with Junior if he's willing and see what's going on. If we decide it's safe, we'll all come back here."

Mai had argued a little, but in the end Hank prevailed. Hank Jr., now as Derek Kong, had agreed to meet him at six o'clock that evening at the Pasadena Hilton. He'd given Hank a room number and agreed to allow Norm to be present.

Norm and Stoner had been staying at his friend's house in Long Beach for the past several days. Hank filled him in, and Norm agreed to meet at Mai's at five.

Norm asked, "So the fliers worked?"

"We're not sure. We know Junior's seen them, because he's asked us to have them pulled. But whether that was the driving force behind his contacting Mai, we don't yet know."

"Did you tell Phan to pull the fliers?"

"I called him and told him to have his people retrieve as many as possible. Presumably we'll find out tonight why that's so important."

"Okay, see you soon," Norm said.

*　*　*

The afternoon dragged. Mai went from being excited to being scared to being just plain nervous. Hank gave her a lot of space.

He had his own issues to deal with. Besides, he knew whatever he could say to reassure her that all would be well would simply be empty platitudes.

When Norm showed up just after five, the three huddled around Mai's kitchen counter and talked things through. Stoner nuzzled her feet. Hank instructed Norm that when they reached the hall on Junior's floor, Norm was to pretend he was going to another room or to the ice machine until he was convinced no one was watching Junior's room.

It was hard to plan a strategy when they didn't know who the enemy was.

Mai made them promise to try to convince Junior to meet her later, either at her house or a place of Junior's choosing. It was all cloak-and-dagger stuff based solely on Junior's ambiguous Facebook post. Hank felt faintly ridiculous, but ultimately reasoned that Junior wouldn't be putting them all through these machinations without a valid reason. Or at least he didn't think so. For all he knew, Junior was mentally ill and suffering from paranoid delusions. He'd given up trying to figure out what a valid reason would be.

*   *   *

The man who opened the door to Hank's knock looked almost exactly like the age-enhanced photo Tommy Phan had circulated. Hank Jr., now as Derek Kong, was tall, perhaps a little over six feet, like Hank. His short hair was jet black. He was a handsome man, with strong cheekbones and dark, intelligent-looking eyes. His skin was smooth, the color of sand. He wore a light-blue polo shirt, tight at the sleeves, blue jeans, and soft-looking brown loafers.

The two men, father and son, stared at each other across the threshold for a moment. Then Hank extended his hand and smiled. "Thank God you have your mother's looks."

Derek allowed himself a small smile and shook hands. Then, as if remembering the situation, he leaned out and looked up and down the hallway. Norm's figure was just disappearing into a doorway down the hall—the ice and vending room. Derek pointed his chin in that direction. "That your man?"

Hank nodded. "Yeah. Another guy got off the elevator with us, so Norm will make sure he's going to another room. He'll join us in a minute."

Derek stood aside, and Hank walked into the room, actually a suite. The living room had a couch facing a coffee table, a flat-screen TV, and a small table with two chairs next to a curtained window. An opening without a door led to the bedroom.

"Let's sit down," Derek said.

Hank checked himself from making his usual old-man grunting sound as he lowered himself into the chair.

Derek stared at Hank, as if sizing him up. "How old are you?"

Hank snorted. "Old enough to be your father."

"Funny."

"Sorry," Hank said. "An ill attempt at humor. I just turned seventy."

Derek nodded slightly. "You look pretty good for your age."

"Thanks a lot . . . I guess." Hank let out a breath. "Look . . . ." He stopped. "What do you want me to call you? Your mother and I have been referring to you as Junior for convenience, but I reckon that won't sit so well with you."

Derek wet his lips with his tongue. Hank recognized it as a sign of stress—dry mouth. "Call me Derek, for now. That's the name I'm currently using." He looked like he was about to say more when there was a knock on the door.

"I'll get it." Hank opened the door, and Norm came in carrying a bucket of ice.

"All quiet out there," Norm said. "I found this bucket in the ice room. I thought I'd make it look realistic." He put the bucket down on the coffee table and held out his hand. "Norm Rothstein."

Derek took the proffered hand and shook it. "We'd just gotten to the part where I told Hank to call me Derek . . . at least for now."

Norm nodded in understanding. "Well, at least you didn't ask if I was a Jew."

"What's that supposed to mean?"

"It was a joke," Norm said, "albeit a bad one. It seems like most of your old high school chums we interviewed were focused on my ethnicity." He motioned his head back to the ice bucket. "Is there a mini-fridge? Shall I get us something to drink?" Without waiting for an answer, Norm went exploring.

"I'll explain later," Hank said to Derek. "For now, let's get some of the background out of the way. I'd apologize for not being there while you were growing up, but I didn't know you existed until a couple weeks ago."

Derek blinked. "How'd you find out?"

"Your mother showed up at my condo one evening. I hadn't seen her since the day before I was evacuated from Saigon in 1975." Hank paused and smiled. "The way you're holding your mouth right now reminds me so much of some of your mother's expressions from when I first started courting her."

Derek's eyes narrowed for a beat. "Courting?" There was a cynical tone to his utterance. "Seriously?"

Norm came to the table holding three glasses. "Vodka rocks," he said, setting them on the table. Then he sat down on the couch.

"Seriously, was I courting your mother, or seriously, is courting still a word people use?" Hank asked. There was humor in his voice.

Derek shrugged and picked up the drink. "Both, I guess."

"I fell in love with Mai, almost from the first time I met her. Yes, courting is a word we don't hear much anymore, but it exactly describes my attempts to woo her. Mai was an educated, intelligent, beautiful young woman who'd lost her parents in a terrorist bombing. When I first showed an interest in taking her out, she was dubious, undoubtedly thinking I was just another American looking for an exotic fling. So I had my work cut out for me."

"You were in the military?"

Hank shook his head. "CIA. Mai thought I was a diplomat attached to the American embassy." Hank picked up his drink and took a sip. "Long story short, we fell in love. We were making plans for the future. It was no fling."

Derek let out a small grunt. "But you left her there."

"Yeah, I did. I had no choice. Go back and look at some of the news reports from the time. Saigon fell quickly. The embassy was on the verge of being overrun. The Vietnamese with money and/or power were fighting to get out. I went to Mai's work and gave her money to use to hide or escape. Her employers had been CIA informants." Hank paused again, looking at Derek. "You don't know any of this? What did your mother tell you about me?"

Derek shrugged. "She said my father had been an American who'd been killed in action. That's pretty much it. I didn't really believe the 'killed' part. I thought she'd been abandoned."

For several seconds the only sound in the room came from the hum of the air conditioner.

"I looked for her after I got back to the States," Hank said at last. "Of course, I had no idea she was pregnant. But she'd disappeared. It was a mess trying to find refugees." He paused and looked away for a moment. "Eventually I fell in love with the woman I would later marry. I stopped looking for Mai."

Hank heard the tinkle of ice in Norm's glass. The motor in the small refrigerator clicked on.

"How did Mother find you?" Derek asked.

Hank recounted Mai's explanation that she'd hired a private investigator to search for him once she'd made enough money to do so.

"So she's known who you were and where you were for decades?" Derek asked incredulously.

Hank nodded. "Apparently."

"Why didn't she contact you? Why didn't she tell you about me?"

Hank rubbed his chin. "You're thinking like an American, brash and dogmatic as to right and wrong. That's not the way Mai thought. Or at least it hadn't been back when I knew her. Mai had found me, but she'd also discovered I was married. She didn't want to ruin my life, is one answer. Pride may be another. She didn't want to waltz into our lives as an immigrant with an illegitimate child. I don't frankly know. You'll have to ask her." Hank held up his right hand as if to stop Derek from talking. "But one thing you must know is that it wouldn't have ruined our lives. Both Becka—that was my wife—and I would have accepted you and shared whatever responsibility Mai felt comfortable giving us."

Derek leaned his head back and stared up at the ceiling. "You still married?" he asked, continuing to look up.

"No. Becka died a couple months ago. I think that's why Mai felt comfortable coming to me."

"God."

The room was silent again, this time for a full minute.

Hank asked, "You want to tell us what's going on with you?"

Derek sighed heavily, as if asked to do something distasteful. After a moment, he looked at his father and gave a small nod. "I'm fucked, is what's going on with me. But first, tell me about trying to find me. That's what Mother asked you to do? You and Norm?"

Hank nodded. "She asked me. I asked Norm to help. We've been interviewing most of the guys who'd gone up to Mount Wilson with you that day. That's what Norm was alluding to when he mentioned your high school chums."

"We also had the pleasure of meeting Pastor Glen," Norm said from the couch.

"Really? That fucker's still up north in his church?"

"Still there," Hank said. "Although I suspect he looked a little better back when you encountered him." Before Derek could ask, Hank added, "And Dana is still there. She looks like a dumpy old woman now."

Norm chortled. "A couple of her kids from Pastor Glen tried to roust us at our campground and intimidate us into leaving them alone. We don't know what they thought we intended to do to them."

"Probably just paranoid," Hank said. "Anyway, we eventually got the story about what happened on the mountain. Most of the guys are still covering for each other, but Sammy Stone finally gave us the whole story. You didn't know Billy Campbell hadn't died?"

Derek shook his head. "Not until you told me in our phone call. Once I left, I decided there was no looking back. Those assholes would have put whatever blame there was on me, whether it was for the rape or Billy. It was what it was."

"Okay," Hank said, "so you did a great job disappearing. But obviously now something's wrong. What's up?"

Chapter 47

As Derek told Hank and Norm how he'd been recruited by Raul to smuggle money and drugs, he was impressed by how impassively Hank took it all in. Other than a slight frown—and at one point, a sigh—he listened without comment. Derek didn't try to rationalize what he'd done.

No one spoke for a long minute after Derek finished his story.

It was Norm who broke the silence. "That's some seriously bad fucking luck. I mean, you had to run from something you didn't do, only to have to do it all over again a quarter-century later."

Derek sighed heavily. "Yeah, well, I'm a little more at fault this time around."

"At least it's full circle back to home," Hank said. He gave Derek a penetrating look. "I understand how you got involved in the first place. You were young and on the run and had no money and no identity. And I do understand how you realized you probably couldn't get out of the game without running again or putting your life at risk. But it's been twenty-three years. Is that all you did? Did you have any real job?"

Derek looked away from his father. It was a question he knew would be coming sooner or later, and he'd been debating how to answer. He thought—hoped—it would mitigate their view of him as a criminal, but by the same token, he wasn't yet sure how far he wanted these people in his life. He hadn't made the decision about what to say until that very minute.

"I'm a writer. The money from the smuggling allowed me the free time to write. Eventually I made enough money writing that

I didn't need the dirty money, but as you said, it was something you don't just walk away from."

"What kind of a writer?" Norm asked.

Derek turned to look at him. "Novelist. My pen name is Mike Mann." He could see the shock register on Norm's face.

"Mike Mann, the famous novelist?"

Derek nodded and looked back at his father, who smiled tightly.

"I've heard of you, of course," Hank said, "but I admit I've never read any of your work."

Derek smiled and shrugged good-naturedly.

"I've read all your books," Norm said. "There seems to be a recurring theme about fathers dying or going missing. Am I right?"

Derek shrugged again, still looking at his father, a wry smile playing on his lips. "I guess I'm going to need a new theme."

Chapter 48

Hank tried to talk Mai and Derek out of their reunion that night, but neither would be put off. Mai had ordered takeout from Eva's restaurant so that by the time Hank, Norm, and Derek showed up, a sumptuous Mexican meal was waiting for them.

Stoner had stayed home with Mai and began barking when Mai and Derek fell into each other's arms, both sobbing. Norm picked up the dog and talked to him softly, assuring him that the strange man was not hurting Mai.

Hank and Norm, still with Stoner, headed to the kitchen to open some wine and to give mother and son some time alone.

"What do you think about his story?" Norm asked in a low voice.

There was a soft pop as Hank extracted the cork from a bottle of Malbec. He poured two glasses. "Pretty much what I said earlier. It's a fucked-up mess, but I'm not going to beat him up over getting involved in the first place. It's done. The problem is, these people don't fuck around, and we need to figure out how to deal with it."

Norm grunted and took a sip of the wine. "You don't think he can just stay disappeared?"

"I wouldn't want to take that chance. Those guys have so many people on their payroll that sooner or later someone's bound to recognize him." Hank paused, rubbed his chin. "Besides, those flyers we sent out could prove lethal."

The two men heard Mai stifle some kind of utterance in the next room.

"I presume he just told her about being a drug runner," Norm said.

*   *   *

It was late by the time they ate dinner, but no one seemed inclined to go to bed. The topic of how to deal with Raul and the cartel had been scrupulously avoided during dinner, but now, over more wine, the group moved to the living room and settled in for a serious discussion.

Hank and Derek were on the same side: It wouldn't be enough to simply pretend the threat didn't exist, that the cartel wouldn't discover Derek's current identity. If that happened, it would be more than Derek's life at stake.

Derek had proposed simply disappearing again, but Mai wouldn't hear of it. "You're back now, and this is a family problem to solve." She looked to Hank for support, and he nodded. Something in her tone of voice seemed to concern Stoner, who jumped into her lap. She absently began rubbing his chin.

Norm asked, "So what do we do?"

Hank looked at him. "*You* don't have to do anything. I don't want you in harm's way over our family problem."

Norm shook his head. "Screw you, Hank. You can't ditch me that easily. You guys are the closest to family I have now, and I'm with you all the way."

Hank chuckled and gave a slight nod. "I figured."

"So, seriously, Hank," Mai asked, "what do you think we should do?"

Hank took a sip of wine. "The best I can come up with is we find out who took the drugs and get Junior—er, Derek—off the hook." He turned to Derek. "What do you think?"

Derek blinked, then rubbed the top of his head. There was still a tinge of red in his eyes from crying with his mother. "You mean do what Raul said he couldn't do?"

Hank nodded. "Well, at least we should kick it around. Tonight, why don't you try to remember everything you can about that last transaction. Who you met in Cabo. Who you think was supposed to take delivery. That kind of thing. Tomorrow we can see if there's any sense in trying to formulate a plan."

"Wouldn't it be less dangerous to simply hope they never figure out who Hank Jr. really is?" Mai asked.

"It's Derek," her son reminded her.

"Sorry, Derek. Besides, how in the world are you going to solve a mystery the cartel itself can't solve?"

"Because," Hank said, "if someone ripped off thirty million dollars' worth of cocaine from the Sinaloa cartel, the chances are close to a hundred percent that it was the work of either another cartel or someone in the Sinaloa cartel itself."

Mai sighed and stood. "It's late." She looked at Derek. "Hank and I are sleeping together, in case you're wondering, so there are two open guest rooms. Why don't you both stay here tonight, and we can continue this discussion in the morning when we're fresh."

Derek looked at Hank, who looked somewhat abashed. "I think I'll go back to the hotel tonight. Tomorrow I'll check out and turn the car in. I seriously doubt anyone was able to track me to Pasadena, but if so, it wouldn't hurt to create another dead end. I'll come right here from the rental agency."

"Does this mean we'll have to start calling you by another name already?" Norm asked, smiling. "You know, we're kind of old and have a hard enough time remembering names."

Derek chuckled. "I think it'll be safe to stick with Derek Kong for a while, especially if I don't use any credit cards and keep a low profile." He turned to Hank. "You agree?"

Hank nodded and smiled. "What could be more low-profile than trying to track down members of the Sinaloa drug cartel?"

Chapter 49

Hank held Mai tight against him, or maybe it was the other way around. They were in the spoon position, and every time Hank loosened his hug, Mai pulled him back. With his face buried in her neck, breathing in her citrusy perfume, his left hand cupped her breast through her silky nightgown. He knew she didn't want to make love, but he found himself growing hard anyway.

"What are you thinking?" Hank asked, talking into the cup of her neck.

"You mean besides wondering what's poking me in the back?"

"Yeah, besides that."

"He's handsome, isn't he?"

"He has your looks."

"He has the best of both of us." She paused for a moment. "Our son is a famous writer. He's brilliant. Wait until Eva hears about that. She absolutely loves Mike Mann."

"He's also a drug smuggler who has a contract out on him."

Mai grunted. "He didn't have to run away in the first place. It's all so sad." She paused again. "Do you really think you can help him out of this mess? Really?"

It was Hank's turn to say nothing. He thought about the strange turn his life had taken at seventy years old. In a matter of months, he'd gone from losing his beloved Becka to reuniting with his lover from almost half a century ago, a lover who'd had his child. He'd found the child/son, now a man, and now he had to figure out a way to stop one of the most dangerous criminal enterprises in history from murdering him. *Plus*, he thought, *I'm getting boners with alacrity.*

"I have to try," he said finally. "I have to try, for our son." He paused. "And for us."

* * *

Early the next morning, Mai opened the sliding door and invited Eva over for a breakfast reunion with Derek, who wasn't yet there. Hank gave Mai a cautionary look as she began to fill Eva in on Derek's life and predicament. Mai noticed the look and stopped talking. She turned to Hank.

"Eva and I are sisters. She helped raise Derek. She has a right to know what's going on." Mai's tone made it clear that she would not listen to a counterargument. She turned back to Eva and continued. "But I've saved the best part for last. You'll never guess who Hank Jr. is."

"You mean besides a drug smuggler whose ass is in deep-shit trouble?" Eva's tone was harsh.

Mai ignored the comment. "He's Mike Mann, the writer."

The grim look on Eva's face morphed into surprise, then disbelief, and then, finally, a huge grin. "Oh my God," she said, sitting down on a barstool. "You know, as I've read his books, I've often thought about you and Hank Jr. and how his characters shared a common thread with your lives. Maybe that's why I related so well to his stories. I've thought about where he was and what he was going through. Well, he was putting it all down on paper, wasn't he? We've been reading about his anguish in one form or another for years now."

Hank Jr., as Derek, appeared a little after nine-thirty. As he had done with his mother the night before, he fell into his Aunt Eva's arms. More tears were shed.

But Eva wasn't quite as understanding or forgiving as Mai and Hank had been about Derek's dope smuggling. She lectured him on the loss of lives from drugs.

"I lost a nephew in San Diego to drugs. He was only nineteen. I lost two cousins in Mexico to the cartel wars. The people you work for are some of the most brutal scum who've ever walked this earth. I can't believe . . . ."

"I think he understands all that." Mai put her hand on Eva's shoulder and squeezed gently. "I don't think he's harbored any illusions about what he did and who he did it for. The important thing is that he's back now, and we need to help him."

Still staring at Derek, who hadn't tried to stop her or justify his actions, Eva said nothing for a moment. They were sitting at the kitchen counter. Hank and Norm were in the living room, close enough to hear everything.

"And you think those old men are going to take on the cartel?" Eva asked, gesturing with her head toward the living room. Her tone reeked of skepticism and sarcasm.

"Hellooo," Norm said. "We can hear you. I'm old, but I'm not deaf." He grinned. "Besides, I'm not *that* old."

Eva snorted. "Yeah, and I weigh a hundred and thirty pounds."

"Now, children," Mai said. She gave Eva's shoulder one last squeeze and stepped away. "Let's all sit in the living room and talk this through."

Hank asked Derek if he remembered the people he'd worked with on the last mission. Derek nodded. "I know the guy I connected with in Cabo is related to Raul. According to Raul, the guy who was supposed to take delivery in Long Beach is also related. I'm thinking that if we can find those guys, we'll be a big step closer to finding out what happened."

Norm asked, "So we're going to just ask around for cartel thugs, like we're looking for some long-lost relative, and then approach them and ask if they stole $30 million in cocaine?"

Hank grinned. "I think we'll have to massage that plan a little bit, but yeah, more or less."

"Do you know Raul's last name?" Eva asked.

"Martinez," Derek said.

Eva laughed out loud. "Might as well be John Smith."

"What about the guy in Cabo?" Hank asked.

Derek shook his head. "His name was Guillermo. He talked too much, but he didn't tell me his last name. Said he was from a small town north of Cabo, on the coast. I kind of assumed he and the guy in Long Beach were also Martinezes."

"I still think we should do nothing," Mai said firmly. "The person they're looking for is gone. It sounds like Derek did a good job of covering his tracks. Anything else is just too dangerous."

Music began emanating from Hank's front pocket. A blues riff. He pulled the phone out and looked at the display. No caller ID. "Hello?"

"Is this the person looking for the Vietnamese kid in San Francisco?" The voice had an unmistakable accent.

"Who's this?"

"Doesn't' matter," said the caller. His tone was brusque. "I think I know the guy. What's his name?"

Hank thought fast. "His name is Nguyen Van Duc. I'm an old friend and former private investigator. He has a fairly severe mental illness, and he's been missing for almost two months. I've been asked to help find him." He paused. "What did you say your name was?"

"I said that doesn't matter. The guy I'm talking about is tall for an Asian. He speaks Spanish."

"The person you're describing couldn't possibly be our man. He's only been gone a short time, and he's almost nonfunctional on his own."

There was a moment of quiet on the other end of the line. "Hmm," the man finally said. "Well, it sure looks like a guy I've seen around. But that guy ain't retarded, so I guess I'm wrong. Sorry to bother you."

Hank grunted and hit the end-call button. Then he looked into the expectant and worried faces staring at him. "Well, that kind of makes our option to do nothing moot. That was a guy with a Mexican accent asking about the flyers we put out. He was positive he knew who it was but said he wanted to be sure."

"That was pretty brilliant making up the story about me being mentally ill and nonfunctional," Derek said with a grim smile. "There've been days when that would have described me perfectly."

Norm asked, "Do you think he bought it?"

Hank shrugged his shoulders and exhaled a large breath. "Who knows? But even though the call was to an 800 number I had routed to my cell, I've got to get rid of this phone—smash it to bits. We have to assume they're still on the hunt."

The group went quiet. Clearly, that phone call was a game changer.

It was Eva who spoke first. "I have family in Miraflores, which is north of Cabo. It's a little inland, but pretty much right across the gulf from Culiacán, a hotbed of Sinaloa cartel activity. One of my cousins is a cop in the area. He doesn't interfere with cartel business—he's got a family to think of—but he pretty much knows everything that's going on in the region."

"He on the cartel payroll?" Hank asked.

Eva shrugged. "*Quien sabe?*" Who knows? "But maybe he can help us find out who Guillermo and the other players are."

"Can you reach out to him?" Mai asked. "If he won't police the cartel, why would he talk to us?"

"He may not," Eva said. "But I haven't heard a better plan coming from you geniuses."

Chapter 50

In the stories and novels Hank Jr. wrote as Mike Mann, several involved young men being raised without a father. As Norm had pointed out, it was something of a recurring theme. But in none of the stories or novels did the son ever reconnect with the absent father.

At one time, he'd toyed with the idea and had gone so far as to write several drafts of a scene in which father and son meet up after many years. But Hank Jr., as Mike Mann, couldn't seem to dial in the realistic emotions the kid would have been feeling. Now Mike Mann, as Derek, knew why. His emotions, feelings, thoughts, hopes, imaginings were laid out like a lunch buffet at a Reno casino: joy, anger, terror, indifference, cynicism, skepticism, curiosity, love, even hate—all were laid out on their own emotional platters.

What Derek *didn't* feel like was a forty-year-old adult. Nor did he feel like a world-famous author. He felt like a kid—like a kid in trouble hoping his parents would help him get out of it. He'd been alone his entire adult life. He was smart and he was empathic and he was creative, but he was no longer socialized toward a family setting.

Now he sat on the edge of the bed in his mother's guest room and thought about the old people downstairs debating his future. He knew he hadn't made the best decisions in his life. He'd fucked up almost everything except his writing. But it was ludicrous to think that a couple of seventy-year-old men could take on the Sinaloa cartel.

No, he thought, *the best thing to do would be to slip out tonight and disappear again.* Maybe he'd go to Europe. Or South America.

He was fluent in Spanish, and there were some countries, such as Peru, where Asians were well represented. He'd blend in well.

He heard Hank calling him and went downstairs.

"Come on," Hank said. "We're going to drive out to the boat harbor and talk to whoever is around. Maybe someone saw something the morning after you docked." He looked Derek over. "Bring your sunglasses. I have a ball cap in the van you can use. The one person we don't want anyone recognizing is you."

Derek started to protest, but then changed his mind and nodded. "Let's go."

He could disappear later—if it looked like the old guys were in over their heads.

*   *   *

The smog hung over Los Angeles like a petulant child. It was unrepentant and unmoving despite the small breeze as they got close to the ocean. Hank drove, Norm sat shotgun, and Derek and Stoner, who had made peace with each other, lounged on the couch.

Derek stared out the window at the brown haze, his brain in overdrive. *How nice it would be not to have to run again*, he thought. He'd missed his mother and his Aunt Eva. It would be hard to run again. And he kind of liked his father. The old guy seemed confident and competent. He had been CIA, after all. *Who knows? Maybe he and this Norm guy really can do something.* Still, what were the realistic odds of finding out who stole the load of coke? *Raul knows damn well I didn't take it.*

Derek saw the Alamitos Bay Marina come into view, and he told Hank where to park. When he hopped out of the Sprinter, he immediately saw that the boat he'd piloted from Cabo San Lucas, *Sayonara*, was still in its mooring. The gate to the floating docks was closed, which meant it was locked. He pointed that out to Hank.

"No problem," Hank said. He had something in his hand, but Derek knew it couldn't possibly be a key. Nevertheless, Hank walked to the gate and acted as if he were unlocking it with a key. A moment later, the gate swung open and Hank pocketed whatever he'd used. Norm chuckled as the three men walked onto the dock.

Sayonara was four boats down. There were about ten boats in slips beyond it. Immediately to their left as they walked onto the dock, a ramp led down to another dock, which connected to another, and then another, from which vessels of various sizes and types were nestled in their particular slips.

As they approached the *Sayonara*, Hank called out to see if anyone was on board. Getting no answer, he motioned for Norm and Derek to stay on the dock and then climbed onto the aft deck. He peered through the French doors leading to the salon. It was littered with pieces of cardboard, and the carpet looked dirty. Some of the cabinets were standing open. He tried the doors to the salon, but they were locked.

"Can I help you?"

Hank stepped back from the doors and looked to where the voice had come from. A thin man wearing cargo shorts, a torn T-shirt, and a dirty ball cap was standing on the flying bridge of a boat two slips away, opposite from where Norm and Derek stood. The man had thinning gray hair and dark, leathery skin. He held a can of beer in his hand, and a cigarette dangled from his mouth, even when he spoke.

"Yeah," Hank said. "We were supposed to come by and take a look at this boat to see if we were interested in buying it or one like it. But I don't see anyone here. Do you know if anyone's around?"

The man shook his head. "Haven't seen anyone for weeks. The day after it came in, some guys came with a bunch of big wood boxes. They had a key to the gate. They said they were supposed to replace a bunch of the furniture."

Hank nodded. "Yeah, I heard the owner was replacing some of the furniture, but I can't tell what's been done. Looks kind of dirty in there to me."

The man took a sip of beer and wiped his lips. "Don't surprise me none. The guys looked like thugs to me. But what the hell, most of the kids look like thugs to me nowadays. But they had a key to the gate and the boat, and their van said 'Woody's Marine Supplies,' so I didn't think nothin' about it. They were in and out in about thirty, maybe forty, minutes. Carted away whatever they replaced. Doesn't surprise me if they didn't clean up after themselves."

Hank nodded again. "Well, I'm not going to hang around waiting for someone to let me in. If you see someone, can you let them know that Mr. Winter came by to take a look, and they can give me a call to set another time?"

"Sure thing," the man said. "It's a mighty fine boat. Costs a pretty penny."

Hank started to climb off the boat, but he turned back to address the man. "Do you know the owner?"

The man shook his head. "Nah. Every once in a while a captain and one or two crew come and take her out. They probably pick up the owner or guests in Newport or somewhere swanky. Moorings are tight down there."

"Well, thanks again," Hank said.

Chapter 51

"No such thing as Woody's Marine Supplies, or Woody's Marine anything," Norm said, sitting at the table of the Sprinter with his laptop.

"Surprise, surprise." Hank stared out the driver's window.

"What are you looking at?" Derek asked from the passenger seat.

Hank nodded toward the nearest light pole, on which was mounted a camera.

Derek grunted. "Okay, I see it, but obviously the van will have been stolen—or at least the plates will be false."

"Correct," Hank said. "But I want to get a look at the men." He paused. "Or, I should say, I want *you* to get a look at the men."

Norm asked, "How are you going to get the harbor master to let you view the videos?"

Hank started the car. "Leave that to me."

*   *   *

The next day, Hank, Norm, and Derek were back at the marina. Hank drove the Sprinter out a pier to the Long Beach Marina office. He turned to Derek. "What time did you leave the boat?"

Derek thought for a moment. "I'd say right around six-thirty."

"That's p.m., right?"

Derek nodded. "Yeah."

"Okay, let's go." Hank opened his door and stepped out into the smog-laden air. It felt like it burned the bare skin on his arms.

Once Norm and Derek were out, he locked the van and led the way toward a one-story blue building at the end of the pier.

The receptionist was a mousy woman with bad teeth and dark, stringy hair. She mumbled something that Hank took to mean, "Can I help you?"

"Hi, my name is Hank Reagan. Gene Rodman from HR Security called Bill Whitman to arrange for us to meet."

The receptionist stared vacantly at Hank for a few moments as if she were trying to process what he'd just said. Then she gave a half nod and picked up the phone. Hank still couldn't understand her mumbling, but apparently Bill Whitman could. A few moments later, a door to the office behind her opened and a man stepped out. Probably in his fifties, he was mostly bald, stoop-shouldered, and had a huge beer belly. His white dress shirt had to work hard to keep everything covered.

Hank and Whitman shook hands, and once Whitman acknowledged he'd spoken with Gene Rodman, Hank motioned for Norm and Derek to follow him into Whitman's office.

The office itself was spacious, with a panoramic view of the harbor. The desk was an anarchic mess of papers and binders. Fake wood paneling covered the walls. A window air conditioner whirred, loud and irritating. Two chairs faced the messy desk, but Whitman directed them to a table and chairs off to the side. A laptop computer sat on the table.

"So, I understand you folks are hot on the trail of a fugitive murderer," Whitman said. "Sounds exciting. Who'd he kill?"

"This man's wife," Hank said, pointing at Derek. "This is Clarence Wong. The suspect was the Wongs' neighbor back in Dallas. He fled after the murder, and we've tracked him to California. We had a tip he might be around here, maybe working on boats, which is what he did for a living in Texas."

Whitman looked at Derek, who wore a ball cap and fake clear glasses Hank had come up with. "I'm very sorry for your loss, sir."

Derek nodded his thanks.

"Our tip was fairly specific," Hank said. "If we could take a look at the parking video by the entry to dock number one on July 17, between 6:40 and 8 p.m., and then again for the morning of the next day from 9 a.m. to noon, that should tell us whether we're on the right track."

Whitman rubbed his chin and then ran a hand over his semi-bald pate. "As I told Mr. Rodman, I'm really not supposed to do this without approval from higher up." He paused and gazed directly at Hank. "But given the circumstances and our agreement, I can let you take a look." He pointed to the computer. "We just need to progress the video to . . . what time did you say? 6:40?"

When Whitman had things set up, Hank gave him a look that conveyed his intent to view the video without him looking over their shoulders. Whitman took the hint and relocated to his desk. "Well, I'll leave you to it, then."

Hank didn't want anyone seeing Derek on the video, which was why he'd asked for the time after Derek had already left the marina. He wanted to see if anyone approached the *Sayonara* immediately after he had gone. Derek had told him that Raul's man had supposedly watched him dock and then leave.

Sure enough, at 7:12, a man got out of a blue Ford van that had been sitting in the lot from the start of the video at 6:40. Hank looked at Derek, who shrugged, which told Hank that Derek didn't know the man. As he got close to the dock gate, the man's features were identifiable, assuming someone knew who he was. Hank stopped the video, and with a quick glance back at Whitman, who was reading some papers at his desk, pulled out his iPhone and snapped a few photos of the man on the screen.

When Hank resumed the video, they watched as the man used a key to enter the dock and then walk in the direction of the *Sayonara*. Unfortunately, the boat itself was out of the camera's view. Hank briefly thought about asking Whitman if there was a camera that would have shown the *Sayonara*, but then decided he didn't want to call attention to the specific boat.

At 7:19, the man reappeared on the screen, leaving the dock. He carried nothing. He got in the blue van and drove away.

Hank progressed the video to the next morning. He knew they were looking for a van with *Woody's Marine Supplies* printed on the side, so he fast-forwarded to speed up the process. He stopped whenever someone appeared on the screen, even if they weren't coming from a van. Two men entered the dock before the video showed any van parking close to the gate. Hank glanced at Derek, who shook his head.

Moments later, a white van pulled into a spot close to the gate. Three men got out of the van, which clearly bore the name Woody's Marine Supplies on the side. One man opened the back doors and the three began pulling out large wooden crates, which they loaded onto two dollies. There were four crates in all, three large and one smaller. Two men worked the dolly with the larger crates to the dock, and the single man followed with the other crate. The same man who'd been the driver of the van the night before unlocked the gate, and then all three men worked the dollies, one at a time, down onto the floating dock.

Hank paused the video, glanced back at Whitman, and snapped more photos. When Hank hit the play button, the three men disappeared from view as they headed to the *Sayonara*.

Forty-eight minutes later, the men reappeared on the video feed. They pushed the two dollies with the crates up the ramp and to the parking lot. It was obvious in the video that the crates had been pried open.

"Kind of brilliant," Derek whispered. "I was wondering how they'd get all the packages off the boat without calling attention to themselves. They brought empty furniture crates on board and simply loaded them up with the shit, making it look like they were carting away the old furniture."

"Do you recognize them?" Hank asked, his voice low.

Derek nodded. "The guy in the T-shirt is obviously the guy from the night before. That one in the aloha shirt is Guillermo, my contact from Cabo. I think I've met the third guy once or twice before, but I'm having a hard time remembering when and where and who he is."

"Okay, I think we have what we need," Hank said, standing up. He walked over to Whitman, holding out his right hand to shake. In his left hand he held an envelope that he'd pulled out of his back pocket. He placed the envelope on the desk and shook Whitman's hand.

"Any help?" Whitman glanced down at the envelope.

Hank shook his head. "Looks like a false alarm. No one coming or going in the video was our man."

"Too bad." Whitman slid the envelope into the top drawer of his desk.

Once they were back in the Sprinter, Norm asked, "You bribed him?"

"Yup."

"How much?" Derek asked.

"Five hundred."

As they rolled onto the Long Beach Freeway, Norm muttered, "Talk about stupid. That guy just risked his job for five hundred bucks."

Chapter 52

Hank, Norm, and Derek stopped at an Apple store on the way home from the marina so Hank could buy a new phone. He didn't mention his prior account with Verizon and created a new contract with AT&T. Then they went to a generic electronics store, and Hank bought seven prepaid cell phones.

It was almost dinnertime when they got back to Mai's condo. The smell of freshly roasted chicken wafted out of the open doorway to Eva's condo. Both women had glasses of white wine in hand and greeted the men with big smiles. Stoner greeted them with a happy-sounding bark.

The women had news.

"I was able to get my cousin in Miraflores on the phone," Eva said. "He told me he'd be happy to help us."

Hank asked, "What'd you tell him?"

"Don't worry. I made up a good story about another cousin who was in some kind of trouble and needed to square things with the Martinez family. He didn't want to hear many details, so I kept it vague. We're just trying to find a guy, someone named Guillermo—that kind of thing."

Hank asked, "Did you say which Martinez family you were talking about?"

"Yeah, kind of. I said the one that was involved with drugs. I didn't know if I should let him know I knew they were part of the cartel."

Hank thought about it. "Okay. But we need to be careful here, particularly if your cop cousin is dirty."

"I know, but if we're gonna do this, we're gonna have to take some risks."

"C'mon, Aunt Eva," Derek said, his voice choked with emotion. "I don't want you and Mom getting involved. I swear I'll disappear again if I think that's happening."

Eva put her big arm around Derek. "Don't worry. We'll be fine." She turned to Hank. "What did you find on the cameras?"

Hank accepted a glass of wine from Mai and sat on one of the barstools. He pulled out his phone and found the photos of the men.

"Send those to my printer," Eva said. "Then we can all see who we're dealing with."

"Good," Hank said. "I don't really want to be carrying their pictures around on my phone." He got the instructions from Eva and printed the photos.

"So," Norm said, once they'd all studied the men in the photos and Derek told them what he knew of them, "it looks like Raul's own men stole the load." He looked at Derek. "Am I right?"

Derek nodded. "His own family is stealing from him."

"So all we need to do is let Raul know who the real thieves are, and you should be off the hook," Mai said, looking anxiously at Derek. "Right?"

Hank was moved by the depth of hope in her eyes.

Derek nodded slightly. "Maybe." He paused a beat. "I guess I can try to call him and see if this sets things right."

Hank had been thinking about various scenarios from the moment Derek confirmed that the men in the video were Raul's family. Now he said what had been troubling him.

"What if those guys were actually working for Raul? What if Raul wants to start a war with another family in the cartel, and this is some kind of opening gambit? Maybe he needed this load to prepare for war. In the meantime, he wasn't ready to show his hand, so he needed to make it look like someone else ripped him off." He motioned his head toward Derek. "Derek was the most believable suspect."

It was half a minute before anyone spoke.

"Shit," Norm said.

"That's pretty devious," Mai said.

"He could be right," Derek said.

"Well, let's eat," Eva said.

Chapter 53

The next day, Hank announced that he and Norm were going to go to their condos in Laguna to get some things they needed. They'd spend the night and be back the next morning. "In the meantime, I think we're okay for a while, so relax and enjoy your time together. We can all be thinking about what our options are, but don't dwell on it too much for now. Taking a break will free up our thinking."

Then he brought out ten prepaid phones—three he already had, plus the seven he'd purchased the day before. He handed two phones to each person, including Eva. The phones were all labeled either No. 1 or No. 2.

"Here's the deal. Each phone has each one of us on speed dial. I'm one, Derek is two, Mai is three, Eva is four, and Norm is five. Until you hear otherwise, everyone will keep their phone number one turned on unless we're all together. Keep it with you at all times. Keep number two with you as well, but turned off. If any phone is compromised, we'll switch to number two as necessary. The speed dials on those have been set as well—same order."

"How come I have to be last?" Norm asked in a mock whine.

Eva took her two phones and put them on the kitchen counter. "Does that mean we can't use our regular cell phones?"

"No, they're okay unless one gets compromised like mine did with that call in response to the leaflet," Hank said. "Just don't use them to call any of us. Use the prepaid for all calls among ourselves."

"This is some serious spy shit," Norm said.

"Let's hope it's overkill," Hank said. "But it doesn't hurt to be careful. Remember, these guys are playing for real, and they have cops and feds on their payroll."

*   *   *

The first person Hank and Norm bumped into at the death farm was Tiffany and two other women Hank didn't recognize.

"Well, looky here," Tiffany said. "No one's seen hide nor hair of you boys ever since that exotic woman came looking for Hank. Where'd you boys get off to?"

"We went on a hunting trip," Norm said, without missing a beat. "We wanted to kill some shit and get away from some of the busybodies around here."

Hank followed Norm to the elevators, leaving the speechless women to stare at them as they walked away.

"Good one," Hank said in the elevator.

"Let's go out to dinner tonight," Norm said. "I can't stand the thought of going to the dining room."

"Done. Come down in a little while, and we'll take a few tokes and go to that little Italian place. Mai and I went there—the food looked pretty good."

*   *   *

Once inside the condo, Hank stood in the center of his living room for several minutes, thinking of Becka. He felt her presence—or at least he imagined he did.

"I thought my life was over when I lost you," he said softly into the room. "I thought I would hang around here, playing golf and cards while waiting to die." He paused and looked around. He felt a little bit foolish, but he could also feel the onset of tears. He shut his eyes for a moment. For the first time in a long time, he could visualize Becka's face. When he opened them, he smiled. "I wish I believed you were somewhere where you could see everything that's going on with me because then I'd know you'd be shaking your beautiful head and saying, 'What the fuck?' "

After another moment, Hank pulled himself out of his reverie. He threw his dirty clothes in the washer and pulled out some clean clothes to take with him. Then he went to a dresser built into the interior of the master bedroom closet, opened the bottom drawer, and pulled out a large metal box. He took it into the bedroom, placed it on the bed, punched a code into the box's entry system, and opened the lid. Inside were three handguns. Two were 9 mm—a Glock 17, which held seventeen rounds, and a Smith & Wesson M&P 9, which also held seventeen rounds, but which had the added benefit of being able to keep one round safely chambered. The third gun was a .45 Glock 37, which had a Zev Tech suppressor.

Hank selected the Glock 37 and its silencer. It would have the best stopping power of the three guns. He pulled out the Glock 17 as well. He didn't know if Derek knew how to use a gun, but having been a drug runner, he assumed he did. Norm already had a gun.

Hank put the guns and the ammunition for each in the bag he'd brought his laundry in. Then he closed and locked the metal box and stowed it in the closet. He laid his clean clothes over the two guns.

*   *   *

In Pasadena, Derek and Mai sat at the kitchen counter, sipping coffee. The sliding door to Eva's condo was open, but she was at her restaurant. So far, there had been a few awkward attempts at small talk, but neither had broached any of the larger, elephant-in-the-room type of topics.

Mai wore a magenta ao dai over white slacks. Derek thought she looked both elegant and informal. He wore blue jeans and a plain white T-shirt. He ran a hand through his dark hair and wondered what they should talk about. There was so much he'd done wrong, so many fucked-up decisions he'd made. And now he'd come home and brought life-threatening danger to them all.

"Why did you feel you had to leave, Hank?" Mai asked. Her voice was soft, non-accusatory.

He didn't bother to tell her to call him Derek but simply stared down into his coffee cup as if it held the answer to the events that had transformed both of their lives in the course of a few days.

Moments passed. Mai gave him time.

When he finally looked up, his eyes were glassy, filled with re-strained tears. "I really thought I'd thought it all through. I mean, I shouldn't have gone up to Mount Wilson with those assholes in the first place. But I was writing a story about them, or kids like them, and I thought it would put the final touches on my piece. Then, when Dana showed up, already drunk and stoned, and they started raping her, I felt helpless. Billy Campbell was holding me. Then they tried to get me to rape her, too. That's when I finally fought back, and Billy fell off the cliff. They told me I'd killed him."

Derek paused, wiped a hand across his moist eyes, and breathed out a heavy sigh. "They made it clear that if I didn't keep my mouth shut, they would all claim that I was the one who raped Dana and pushed Billy off the cliff. It would have been my word against all of theirs."

"But the doctors could have determined who raped her from the semen," Mai said, still in a gentle tone.

Derek shook his head. He raised and lowered his shoulders. "I didn't think any of the forensic shit through. I just reacted. I wondered at graduation why no one was talking about Billy's dis-appearance. Now I know it's because he hadn't disappeared—he was in the hospital.

"When I saw Dana at graduation, she obviously knew some-thing had happened to her but didn't know what. I made the decision to take her up to that pastor's place she'd been talking about. I didn't want to bring shame on you. I didn't want to go to jail for something I didn't do. I understand it was a totally self-ish act."

"Sounds more selfless than selfish to me," Mai said. "You know I would have stood by you, no matter what."

Derek nodded, looking down at his cup again. "I understand a lot now that I didn't think about or understand at the time." He looked up into Mai's eyes. "I'm so sorry, Mother. I'm sorry for everything."

Before he could say anything further, Mai was off her stool and had her arms around her son. He buried his face in her shoulder and finally let himself cry.

Chapter 54

Hank and Norm returned to Pasadena shortly before lunch the next day. Hank had stowed the .45 in the Sprinter and kept the Glock 17 in his bag. They'd also replenished their supply of dope.

"One of us is going to have to pretend we need medical marijuana soon," Norm said.

Hank grunted.

"Or maybe we can ask your drug-smuggling son if he knows where we can score. Although come to think of it, he probably only knows how to get a few tons at a time."

"Not funny," Hank said.

"What, just because we face possible extermination by the most dangerous drug cartel on Earth, we can't have a sense of humor?"

When Hank walked into Mai's condo, he could tell that something had changed between mother and son—something good. It was as if fresh oxygen had been pumped into the room. It was more comfortable, more breathable.

Although their reunion had been joyful, naturally there would be a lot of tension, questions, and feelings to work through. Now, Hank sensed a major shift in the comfort level between the two; they seemed at ease and relaxed.

"Everything okay here on the home front?" he asked as he tossed his bag onto the couch.

Mai smiled broadly. "We've had a perfect morning, given the circumstances. How was your retirement home?" Her look turned teasing.

"Made us feel old again," Norm said. He looked around. "Where's Eva?"

"She's down at the restaurant supervising a big lunch for us. She said to come on down anytime after noon."

Derek added, "She also has some interesting news."

Hank sat on one of the barstools. Norm pulled down a glass and began pouring himself a glass of water.

"Those two guys I thought were Raul's cousins aren't his cousins at all."

"Who are they, then?" Hank asked. "And how does Eva know?"

"She faxed their photos to her cop cousin in Miraflores, and he called her back to say he didn't even need to make inquiries. All three men who carried the load off the boat are Raul Martinez's sons."

Hank sat very still. Were Raul's own sons ripping him off? Or was Raul ripping off his own load? And if so, why? Then he had another thought. "From where did Eva fax the photos?"

"I presume from her office in the restaurant," Mai said. "Why?"

Hank didn't respond right away. Finally he said, "I hope she can trust her cousin."

*   *   *

A half hour later, Hank, Mai, Norm, and Derek were sitting at a corner table in Eva's restaurant. The lunch hour was hectic, and Eva was busy working, putting out fires and chatting up customers.

Without their having placed any orders, two waiters brought a tray of margaritas followed by platters of food—enchiladas, chicken mole, chile rellenos, and refried beans. It was as if they hadn't eaten in days, digging into the food with surprising exuberance.

Halfway through the meal, Derek nudged Hank and nodded toward the front door. Two men wearing ball caps pulled low over their faces were talking to Eva. Derek leaned into Hank. "Doesn't the one guy look like—"

Before he could finish his sentence, Eva was being ushered out the front door by the two men. She glanced back toward them once, a look of pure fear on her face.

Hank pushed back his chair. "Norm, you and Derek get the van. Derek, while Norm is pulling it around front, you go up and grab my bag. It's on the living room couch. Mai, go back to the condo. Everyone turn on cell phone number one. I'm going to try to follow them. I'll call Norm and Derek and tell them where to meet me." Then he was gone.

Norm, Derek, and Mai looked at each other in a kind of shock before Norm stood and got everyone moving.

Hank walked quickly through the restaurant and out the front door just in time to see the two men and Eva turn the corner at the end of the block. Thankfully, they were still on foot. He looked around frantically and saw a young man in a Saab about to parallel park.

Hank ran to the car and knocked on the window. "I'll give you five hundred bucks to help me follow someone who's in trouble." He pulled out his well-stocked money clip.

"Fuck off," the man said.

Hank backed away and looked around again. Two doors down, he spotted a red-and-black taxi from which a passenger was getting out. He sprinted to the cab and managed to hop in as soon as the passenger had cleared the door. The cabbie looked back in surprise.

"Start driving," Hank said. "Turn right at the next corner. I'll give you five hundred bucks if you can keep the meter off and help me follow someone who's in big trouble and needs my help." He paused, thankful to see that the burly black cabbie had begun to drive. "We'll probably need to follow a car. I don't know how long it will take. If it's more than an hour, I'll pay you two hundred an hour after that. You okay with keeping the meter off?"

The cabbie, who looked to be in his early fifties, was completely bald. Hank couldn't see much of his face in the rearview mirror, but he saw a glint of humor in the man's eyes.

"You mean, 'follow that car,' like in the movies?" he asked.

Hank saw the two men push Eva into a black Camaro half a block up. "Yeah, exactly like that. See that black Camaro up on the right? That's what we need to follow."

"I can keep the meter off if you slip me another one of them bills for my dispatcher, but I don't want no trouble."

"No trouble, no risk," Hank said. He peeled off another hundred-dollar bill and tossed it and five others onto the front seat. "Once we see where they're going, you'll let me out, and you can get back to work—or take the rest of the day off. You won't get close to them. You won't call the cops. You won't be in any danger. You won't remember this trip at all, in fact. Got it?"

The cabbie glanced down at the bills and then slowed to allow the Camaro to pull out into traffic. "Got it. But what's going on? Is that chick in danger?"

Hank hesitated. "Yes. But the less you know, the better. I'll follow them to wherever they're taking her and then handle it from there."

The cabbie nodded, as if to himself, and then began following the Camaro.

Hank pulled out his cellphone and called Norm. "You in the van yet?"

"Just waiting out front for Derek."

"Okay. They've got her in a black Camaro, and they're turning back onto Colorado Boulevard, heading east. I'm in a cab."

"Got it. We won't be far behind you."

The cabbie was doing a good job. Hank only suggested dropping back a bit once when they were getting too close.

"We're on the 210 now," Hank said to Norm. "Still heading east."

The traffic on the freeway was light, but busy enough to allow them to follow close without fear of discovery. The Camaro exited the freeway at Rosemead Boulevard and headed south. Tailing the thugs became a little more complicated on the busy thoroughfare, but the cabbie handled it well, sliding effortlessly in and out of the traffic while keeping at least three cars between the cab and the Camaro. Hank figured the guy watched a lot of cop shows.

They turned left onto Garvey Avenue. The neighborhood was light commercial, not upscale. Hank relayed the location to Norm, who was still on Rosemead, not far behind.

The Camaro turned right onto a side street. "Take it slow," Hank said.

There was a deserted-looking warehouse on the corner. As they made the turn, Hank saw the Camaro pull in behind the building.

"Drive past," he told the cabbie.

As they proceeded down the street, Hank saw the Camaro stop in a driveway beside a rundown wood-frame house tucked in between the warehouse and a boarded-up dog grooming business. The house was set back from the street, and the front yard was nothing but dirt and weeds and litter.

Hank instructed the cabbie to let him out. "We good?" he asked as he got out of the car.

The big man smiled. "Who you talking to, mister? I don't know you." Then he was gone.

Hank called Norm and filled him in on the location as he watched the two men pull Eva from the car. She was struggling, and it was obvious the one thug had a gun pressed into her wide back. The two men pushed and dragged her into the dilapidated house.

"Stay in the right lane on Garvey and watch for me," Hank told Norm. "I'll be at the corner in a minute. I didn't catch the name of the street I'm on." Then he strolled past the house on the opposite side of the street. He hunched his back and shuffled, so that he looked like a bent old man making his way along the road. Wearing khakis and a checkered, long-sleeved shirt, he was thankful he wasn't overdressed.

Without turning his head to obviously look at the house, he noted one other car parked in the driveway, now blocked by the Camaro. So there would probably be more than just the two hoods in the house. There was a small front porch. He saw no one outside standing guard. From his angle and while trying to feign disinterest, he was unable to tell if there were any side doors. He assumed there was a back door.

He got back to Garvey moments before spotting the Sprinter. He hailed it and pointed to an open parking spot on the corner.

Chapter 55

Hank was sweating and breathing hard when he slid the side door of the van open. His heart pounded, and the smoggy air burned his lungs.

"Okay," he said, climbing into the back. "I think there are at least three guys in a house right around the corner. Probably our *tres hombres*. Two cars in the driveway. Whoever they are, they're pretty amateurish. They've made several mistakes so far." He paused while he reached into his bag and pulled out the 9 mm Glock. He handed it to Derek. "You know how to shoot?"

Derek looked down at the gun. He hadn't held a gun since his attempted suicide. "Just tell me where the safety is."

Hank looked at him quizzically for a beat and then pointed to the safety. "Don't shoot unless you absolutely have to, and then shoot to kill. Pistols are hard to aim, so use both hands, like you see cops do on TV. Aim for the chest. It's the biggest target." Hank then pulled the .45 out of the cabinet and fitted it with the silencer. He looked at Norm. "You have your gun?"

Norm nodded.

Hank wiped his brow and took a deep breath. "Okay. We don't have time for any kind of plan. I'm going straight in the front door. Derek, you go around back if you can. There must be a way in on the other side of this warehouse. Keep yourself hidden from view, even if it means staying on the other side of a fence for now. I don't want anyone looking out a back window to get alerted. That'll get me killed.

"Norm, you follow me to the front of the house but stop at the corner of the warehouse so you won't be seen. You probably won't hear my silencer. So if you hear shots, it means they're shooting at me, and you should probably call the cops. There's no point in all of us getting killed." Hank climbed out of the van. He stuck the pistol in the back of his pants. "Oh, and Norm, lock the van. This isn't a great neighborhood."

As he turned to leave, he heard Derek climb from the van and then felt Derek's hand on his shoulder.

"Hank . . . Dad, you don't have to do this. This is my mess. I'll . . . ."

Hank was still registering the fact that Derek had called him Dad as he patted his hand and moved off toward the house.

Hank went into his old-man walk as soon as he cleared the side of the warehouse. There was no one on the porch, and the curtains were all drawn. No apparent lookout. *Dumb shits.* He heard a car turn onto the street, and he pulled his shirttail over the gun. The car passed without slowing.

Hank turned up the weed-infested walkway to the house. He shuffled along, forcing himself to go slowly. It wasn't hard. His heart was pounding like a pile driver. He could feel the sweat on his brow. His stomach was a tight knot. It had been decades since he'd been in any kind of dangerous situation.

At the front steps, he didn't let himself slow. He walked up the steps and across the porch to the front door. He was glad to see there was no screen. He knocked. He heard movement and then saw the door begin to open. He pulled the gun out.

"Who the fuck—?"

Hank shot the man in the face and then kicked the door the rest of the way open. A second man was sitting on a bright-red couch. He leaned forward and reached for the gun on the table in front of him. A soccer game blared on a television across from the couch.

Hank shot the man three times. He didn't know if the guy was dead, but he slid onto the floor and wasn't going to be a threat.

Hank looked around. He spotted a kitchen at the back of the

house, through a large open arch. He didn't hear or see anyone back there.

To his right were two doors. He could hear movement and what sounded like someone whimpering behind one door. He pushed open the other door. It was a small empty bedroom with a soiled mattress on the floor, which was littered with beer cans and crumpled cigarette packs. A large Bowie-style knife lay beside the mattress.

Hank was about to push open the second door when it opened from the inside, and a man appeared holding a gun. He was wearing the same ball cap he'd worn when he abducted Eva from her restaurant. There was blood on his white T-shirt.

The man mouthed something as he came into the hallway to see what was going on, but Hank didn't hear what he said. He shot the man in the right shoulder and then shot again. His second shot missed the shoulder and hit the man in his bicep. Just as good.

The man's gun clattered to the floor and his expression moved from confusion to pain to fear. He grabbed his shoulder with his left hand. "Who the fuck are you?" He took in his two dead or dying comrades. Then he started to back into the room he had come from, kicking at the door to close it.

Hank stepped forward and kicked the door all the way open. Then he shot the man in the left foot. He kicked the man's gun toward the living room. The man sank to the floor, crying and swearing. His arm was bleeding profusely.

Eva was tied up in a chair, her mouth covered with duct tape. Tears streamed down her mascara-smeared face. A thin line of blood ran down her right cheek. Her eyes were huge with fear and relief.

"Hang tight, Eva. We're here now. You'll be fine. I'll be back in a second. I need to make sure there's no one else here. Then I need to stop this *pinche cabrón* from bleeding to death." He ignored Eva shaking her head and her muffled cries. He saw a stiletto knife on a table next to her. That was what would have made the cut on her face, he figured. It was also what would have been the torture weapon.

"I need some help, man. I'm bleeding to death."

Hank ignored the thug, who was leaning against the wall by the door. He checked the bathroom to make sure it was empty. When he was assured there were only three kidnappers, he opened the front door and called for Norm. Then he went to the back of the house and did the same for Derek. In the kitchen he grabbed some ratty dish towels and a roll of paper towels and went back to the bedroom. He tossed a towel to the thug on the floor. "Here, press this tight against your arm. It's bleeding the worst."

"Fuck you," said the man. "I need medical attention."

Hank ignored him and walked to Eva. He pulled the tape off her mouth as gently as he could. She started to say something but stopped when they heard the front door opening. Hank thought she was about to scream, so he put his hand on her mouth and made shushing sounds. "It's just Norm." His voice was soothing. "Derek will be coming in the back. You're fine now."

When Norm appeared in the doorway, his face went ghost-white. "Holy shit!"

"Don't touch anything," Hank called out. "Here, take one of these towels and open the back door for Derek. No prints. Warn him as well. Then come back here and untie Eva and get her back to the van."

"Holy shit," Norm said again. He looked down at the thug on the floor, trying to staunch the flow of blood from his arm.

Hank said, "C'mon, man. I need you to focus."

Norm nodded and took a towel from Hank and walked to the back. A moment later, Hank heard the door open, and he heard Norm saying something to Derek. He turned his attention back to the thug and the growing pool of blood. If he didn't do something right away, the guy would be unconscious soon.

Hank picked up the roll of duct tape that had been sitting next to the stiletto. He knelt beside the bleeding man and pressed a towel against each of the bullet wounds. Then he wrapped the towels in place with the tape. Just as he was finishing up on the foot, the man took a swipe at Hank with his left hand. It was a glancing blow to the side of Hank's head. Hank grabbed the man's hand and twisted his index finger until it broke. The man cried out in pain, and Hank quickly stuffed a blood-soaked rag into his mouth.

Norm came back and went to Eva. As soon as he freed her, she threw her arms around him and held on tight, sobbing into his shoulder.

Hank asked, "Where's Derek?"

"I told him to go out and check the garage, just to be sure."

A moment later, they heard sounds at the back door. "All clear in back," Derek said as he appeared in the doorway. Then he spotted Eva. "Oh, fuck. Oh, fuck." His face was pale, his mouth slightly open. The Glock 17 was still in his hand, hanging loosely at his side.

"Okay, guys," Hank said. "Get Eva to the van. Norm, you stay with her. Derek, there's a butcher knife in the van's kitchen. I need you to get it. Norm will show you where it is."

Norm asked, "What're you going to do?"

"We need answers from this asshole. I'm going to do what I have to do. Now let's get moving. We don't know whose house this is."

Norm and Derek began walking Eva toward the front door.

Hank called out to them. "If it looks like anyone's coming to the house, hit the speed dial for my phone. Just let it ring once. Then hang up. I'll get the hell out of here. Once Derek's back, Norm, you move the van onto the street but don't park right in front. Be inconspicuous. Just so you have a line of sight to the driveway. Again, if you see anyone coming, ring me once."

As Hank waited for Derek to come back from the van, he forced the wounded man onto the chair recently vacated by Eva. Then, using the duct tape, he wound the man's torso to the chair, leaving both hands free. Hank knocked the ball cap off the man's head. He was clearly one of the men on the video from the boat harbor. He moved the stiletto out of the man's reach.

Hank went into the living room and quickly searched the pockets of the two dead men. He left money and IDs. From the man on the floor by the couch, he extracted a piece of paper with some handwriting on it. He didn't take the time to read it but stuffed it in his own pocket.

"Lay your hands flat on the table," Hank said when he returned to the bedroom. He picked up the stiletto, using a clean towel around the handle.

The man did as he was told, grunting in pain as he pulled his useless right hand up.

Hank pulled the rag from the man's mouth. "What's your name?"

The thug seemed to ponder the question, as if it were some kind of trick. "Roberto," he said, finally.

"Good. Here's the deal, Roberto. You're going to answer my questions, and when we're all done, if you're still alive, I'll want you to go back to Raul and deliver a message. Got that?"

"Fuck you, asshole."

Hank stuck the bloody rag back into Roberto's mouth and then, without missing a beat, slammed the stiletto into Roberto's left hand, the one with the broken finger.

Roberto's howl of pain was muffled behind the rag. The man's eyes were those of a cornered wild animal.

The front door opened. "It's me," Derek said. His eyes grew wide when he saw Roberto sitting in the chair with a stiletto stuck through his hand and into the table.

Hank asked, "Anyone around?"

Derek took his gaze off Roberto and looked at Hank. He shook his head. "Dead."

"No pun intended?"

"Funny," Derek said. "What do we do now?" He dropped the large butcher knife on the table.

"Now we find out what these motherfuckers are up to."

Hank went to the kitchen and a minute later was back with a bowl of ice cubes, which he set on the table. Then he took the duct tape and wound it over both Roberto's wrists and over and under the entire table, twice. When he was done, he used a paper towel to wipe off the pieces of tape he'd touched.

"This is going to get really ugly if Roberto here doesn't start talking right away, so feel free to go out and wait for me in the van."

Derek didn't hesitate. "I'm with you."

Hank nodded and then turned his attention to Roberto. "All right, then, let's get started." He picked up the butcher knife and spoke to Derek, seemingly ignoring Roberto. "There was a sadistic South Vietnamese colonel I knew who loved this interrogation technique. He used it even when he didn't need to." Hank paused and put his hand on Derek's shoulder. "It's truly sickening, but it does tend to work, and we don't have time to fuck around. So forgive me for what you're about to see."

Hank glanced at Roberto, who was following the conversation closely. Tears rolled down his cheeks and snot dripped from his nose.

"Here's what's going to happen," Hank said, still talking to Derek. "Every time Roberto refuses to answer my question, I'm going to chop off one of his fingers. If we run out of fingers, I'll chop off his toes. Your job will be to use one of these towels to pick up the piece of finger or toe and drop it into this bowl of ice. That way, if this piece of shit can get to a hospital in time after we leave, maybe the docs can sew them all back on.

"As soon as you toss the finger or toe into the ice, I want you to stick a piece of paper towel over the stub and then put a piece of duct tape tight over that. You might want to tear little pieces of tape off now so you don't have to mess with it while the finger's bleeding."

His son looked at him long and hard. Hank didn't know what was going on in Derek's head. He wondered what Derek would think of him if he had to make good on his brutal threats. "You okay?" he asked.

Derek nodded and picked up the roll of tape.

Hank turned back to Roberto and studied him for a moment. He looked to be in his mid-twenties. His black hair was pulled back into a small ponytail. There was an expensive Rolex on his right wrist. His face was drawn with pain and fear. Tears and sweat mingled with snot on his face.

Hank pulled the rag from Roberto's mouth. "What's your full name?"

"Fuck you and every whore in your family."

Hank sighed heavily, then raised the butcher knife and chopped down hard onto Roberto's little finger. He stuffed the rag back into Roberto's mouth before the scream could fully materialize. Then he looked at Derek and nodded to the fingertip lying on the table. "You on this?"

Derek moved into action. He picked up the tip with a paper towel and put it in the bowl of ice. Then he stuck some paper towel over the bleeding tip and taped it.

Hank let the pain and shock subside before pulling the rag from Roberto's mouth.

"Roberto Martinez," he said without further prompting.

"You related to Raul Martinez?"

"He's my father, you *pinche viejo*, you old fucking asshole. That's why you're going to be so fucked when this is over."

Hank nodded, as if considering the proposition. "Who're the other guys?" Hank gestured toward the living room.

"My brothers."

"Is one Guillermo?" Hank asked. He glanced at Derek, who shrugged, as if to say he didn't check.

Roberto nodded.

"And the other one?"

"Pablo. My younger brother."

"Any other brothers?"

Roberto shook his head.

"So, tell us why you hijacked your own load of cocaine."

Roberto looked as if he were going to refuse to answer, but he saw Hank pick up the rag and the knife. "My father's taking over the cartel. The load was going to help finance our soldiers."

"Why'd you have to fuck him over?" Hank nodded toward Derek. He'd forgotten what name Derek had been known to Raul by.

"We needed to point the blame at someone while we got our shit together. He was expendable and convenient."

"So Raul knew damn well he didn't steal the shit?"

"Of course."

"Who runs the cartel now? Who is it Raul wants to over-throw?"

Roberto's face was contorted in pain. The dripping snot made him snort. His shoulders shrugged. "My father's partners aren't all one family. After El Chapo was arrested again, there was a power struggle. The compromise was to put three men in power. What do you call it? A tri-something."

"A triumvirate," said Hank.

"Yeah. My father and two others. But my father wants every-thing consolidated under the Martinez family. That way we know who to trust."

"That's not answering my question."

"I don't even completely know. There's a main guy in the U.S. named Alberto and his partner in Mexico named Tito, or at least that's what everyone calls him. I don't know Alberto's last name. He's the most secretive of all. My father knows him, of course. He's the third partner in the cartel. I think they grew up together. But he doesn't even tell us. He says he'll take care of Alberto per-sonally when the time comes. Our cousins in Mexico are going to take out Tito and his main guys."

"Where in the U.S. is this Alberto?"

"I don't know. I'm guessing L.A. or San Diego."

Hank nodded and thought for a moment. "Why did you kidnap this woman?"

Roberto closed his eyes. When he opened them again they were glassy, and Hank could see he was losing him. He rocked the stiletto from side to side.

The pain caused Roberto to cringe, but his eyes came back into focus. "She sent a fax to a cop in Mexico asking who we were. We needed to find out who she was and what she was up to." He nodded toward Derek. "We thought it might have something to do with Danny, but we weren't sure."

"So you're saying that, as of now, as best you know, Alberto and Tito and their side of the cartel have no idea what the Martinez side is up to?"

Roberto let out a huge sigh, expelling spittle as he did so. "I'm in fucking pain, man. I need a doctor. Tell me what you want me to tell my father and then let me go."

"Answer the question."

Roberto shook his head. "So far, they have no clue."

Hank looked at Derek. "Any more questions?"

Derek shook his head.

"Okay, take the knife and what's left of the tape and meet me at the van," Hank said. "I'll clean up here."

Derek glanced at Roberto and opened his mouth to say something, but Hank's phone rang first.

"Fuck. Grab the shit," he told Derek, motioning to the knife and tape. Then he picked up his gun and stepped into the living room. He parted one of the front curtains enough to see an old-looking Chevy pull into the driveway. "Head out the back door. You'll need to show me how you got into the backyard."

Derek nodded and began to move toward the kitchen. Hank walked back into the room and shot Roberto twice in the face. He heard a car door slam as he joined Derek in the kitchen. Together, they walked out into the backyard. Derek motioned toward a chain link fence. One side of the chain link had been cut away. It was a big enough opening to allow a person to slide through.

Derek started toward the fence, but Hank put a hand on his arm. They would be exposed to the driveway and whoever had driven up.

"We need to wait a moment," Hank whispered. He concentrated on trying to hear steps on the porch. He heard nothing, but after a moment, he decided they'd waited long enough. He motioned for Derek to move, and the two of them jogged to the fence. Hank thought he heard some kind of exclamation from the house, but he didn't pause.

He got to the fence and had started to pass through the opening when he felt an explosion in his chest.

Chapter 56

Hank made it through the chain link opening, but that was as far as he could go. The pressure on his chest was unbearable.

"I'm having a heart attack." His voice was so weak that Derek didn't hear him. Hank leaned against the wall of the warehouse and slid down to a sitting position. He tried to call out again to Derek, but he had no voice.

His son had almost reached the sidewalk on Garvey before he turned around and saw his father on the ground. He ran back and knelt beside him.

"Heart attack," Hank choked out. "Call Norm. Bring car around. Need to get to hospital."

Then things went black, and the gun slipped from Hank's hand.

Derek picked up the gun and stuck it into the back of his jeans alongside the gun he already had. He left Hank sitting in the dirt by the side of the warehouse while he went out to the street. When he saw that Norm had seen him, he went back to Hank and grabbed him under his arms and lifted him up. He tried to carry him, but he was surprised at how heavy his seventy-year-old father was. He dragged him through the dirt and across the sidewalk, and with Norm's help, pulled him into the van.

Eva had been on the laptop looking up the closest hospital, and when the van's side door was closed, she gave Norm directions.

Derek laid Hank out on the floor of the van. He could see his father was not breathing. He began CPR, which he'd learned while getting his boat captain's certification. "C'mon, Dad. You can't leave me now. C'mon." Derek's vision blurred as he began to cry, but he didn't stop the chest compressions. He talked to his father and cried. He pumped Hank's chest until he felt the van pull into a driveway and the door was slid open and his father was put on a gurney and wheeled into the ER.

At the hospital, Norm took charge, providing Hank's personal and insurance information. He convinced Eva to hold off on calling Mai until they knew whether he was alive. It wouldn't be long before they would know that much.

In fact, it was less than five minutes before the ER doctor gave the group the good news: Hank's heart had been beating when he was admitted. Derek had saved his father's life.

Chapter 57

By the time Mai got to the hospital, Hank was stable and out of danger. Norm and Eva were in the waiting room; Eva had pretty much attached herself to Norm since her ordeal and refused to be alone. Derek had talked his way past the nurses to stay at Hank's bedside, but visiting hours were ending. Mai asked him to wait outside for her.

Mai found Hank's room in the coronary care unit to be dark and depressing. A nasal cannula delivered oxygen through his nose, heart monitors dotted his chest, and an IV line was inserted in his right hand. His eyes followed her to his bedside.

"Oh, Hank. I'm so sorry. This is all my fault." She took his hand. It felt cold. She had cried all the way to the hospital but thought she had gotten herself under control. Now she started crying again.

Hank shushed her. "No one's fault," he mumbled. "I'll be fine. I need a stent. No biggie." Mai started to say something more, but he shushed her again. "Just sit with me a few minutes. No regrets."

And so the two former, now current, lovers sat in silence, holding hands.

After a couple of minutes, Hank gave her hand a squeeze and smiled. "I'm happy."

When the nurse opened the door, Mai bent over, kissed him gently on the lips, and walked out of the room.

*   *   *

Norm arranged for Hank to be transferred to Huntington Hospital in Pasadena the next morning. His stent procedure was scheduled for early afternoon. The cardiologist told Norm that there wasn't an enormous amount of damage either to the artery or to the heart, but there'd been just enough plaque to block the artery when Hank's heart had overworked itself.

When the doctor asked what Hank had been doing at the time of the heart attack, Norm had to think fast. He said they'd been out for a drive when Hank heard something on the radio about Donald Trump and become highly agitated. He went off on a rant about the candidate and then started to grab at his chest.

The doctor looked skeptical, but after a moment he just nodded.

* * *

That night at Mai's condo, sitting on stools at the kitchen counter, the group was at loose ends. They agreed Eva shouldn't go back to her condo, and Mai shut and locked the adjoining door.

"We just killed the three sons of one of the heads of the Sinaloa cartel," Derek said. "If Raul has any inkling about who did it, then we're at great risk."

"Of course he has an inkling who did it," Eva said. "It was whoever rescued me. So they know it's someone related to me. And they know where I work and probably where I live."

After a few minutes of silence, Norm got up to fix some martinis.

"Think we're safe here?" Mai asked.

Derek was thoughtful for a moment. "At least for tonight," he said. "Tomorrow we should find another place to stay for a few days until we can figure out where we stand."

Norm shook the martinis and poured them out.

"So what exactly happened?" Mai asked. "How did you rescue Eva?" She took a martini from Norm.

The three exchanged glances. Derek spoke first. "Pretty simple, really. Dad followed the bad guys to a house off of Rosemead. Then he walked in and shot the three guys who were holding Eva. But he didn't kill the third guy right off. He got him to talk first."

After a full minute of silence, Mai, her voice so soft it was barely audible, asked, "How did he do that?"

Derek proceeded to tell them about Hank wrapping Roberto's wound with duct tape, impaling his hand with a stiletto, chopping off his little finger, and threatening to chop off the rest of his fingers and toes if he didn't talk.

It was the first time Norm and Eva learned what went on in the house after they'd left.

"Jesus," Norm said.

Eva's breaths quickened, her eyes wide.

Derek's brow furrowed, as if he were deep in thought. "He did what he had to do to find out who went after Eva and why."

"What were you doing?" Mai asked, concern in her voice.

Derek shrugged. "I did what Dad asked me to do. It only took one finger for the asshole to start talking. We had most of what we needed by the time we got the signal from Norm that someone had pulled into the driveway. So Dad shot Roberto and we split. We'd barely made it through the fence when he had his heart attack."

Mai had seen her share of violence and death in Vietnam. She'd watched her parents get blown up in their restaurant. But that was another lifetime. Now she was having a hard time wrapping her head around the fact that her old/new lover had just killed the three sons of one of the heads of an infamous criminal enterprise. Derek was right. They were all in serious danger.

As if reading her mind, Derek said, "Raul wanted me dead just as a matter of strategy. But now, once he deduces that I was involved in killing his sons, the shit's going to hit the fan big time."

No one talked for a long time after Derek disclosed what had occurred at the house off Garvey. They sipped their martinis and thought their own thoughts.

Norm retreated to the couch, and Stoner followed. He patted his lap and Stoner jumped up, resting his head on Norm's thigh. The dog raised his eyes to look into Norm's own Basset Hound eyes.

"You can smell their guilt, can't you Stoner?" Norm whispered, rubbing the dog's head. "Mai brought Hank into her life hoping to find Hank Jr., but his involvement with the drug cartel put everyone at risk and his father in the hospital. Eva's fax to her cousin in Miraflores brought the thugs to her restaurant, and now Hank is a murderer and Derek and I are accomplices."

Norm sighed deeply. After a few moments he placed his empty glass on the coffee table and called to the others, "So what's our plan?"

Derek, Mai, and Eva joined him in the living room.

"We need to figure out a way to let the other faction of the cartel know what Raul's up to," Derek said. "Once we do that, either Raul will be history or the other side will be history. We'll be rooting for the other side, whoever they are. If the bad guys we're rooting for can take Raul and his bad guys out of the picture, we'll be fine."

Norm yawned. "I'm beat. I feel old and tired. Hell, I *am* old and tired. I'm going to bed. Let's all think about it overnight." He looked around the room. "What are the sleeping arrangements for tonight? I'll go sleep in the van so Eva can have my bed."

Eva shook her head. "No way. I'm sleeping with you tonight, Norm. I don't think anyone's feeling particularly sexy, so I think we can safely share a bed." She gave Norm a look that was almost a smile. "I know I'm big, but it's a king-size bed, and I promise not to take up too much room." She paused. "You don't sleep naked, do you?"

Norm grinned. "I do."

"Well, keep your shorts on, and I promise I'll try not to ravage you."

"Really?" Norm asked. "You honestly think you'll be able to keep your hands off me? You know, I've never been ravaged by a plus-size woman. All my wives have been skinny trophy wives."

Everyone laughed for the first time that night.

Chapter 58

Mai stared at her bedroom ceiling. She worried about Eva, who was one of the strongest women she'd ever known, but she hadn't strayed far from Norm all night and now refused to sleep anywhere but in his bed. Mai tried to imagine what Eva must have gone through that day, and although she'd heard the account, she knew she was far from comprehending the terror her friend must have felt. It was sweet of Norm to be so understanding.

It was hard for Mai not to berate herself for what had happened to Hank and Eva. And to her as well. Until she'd recruited Hank to search for Hank Jr., she'd lived an uncomplicated life. Yes, there had been a hole in her heart over the loss of Hank Jr., but she had lived with that for over twenty years and had grown accustomed to it. She had Eva for company, and her business to keep her busy. Other than Eva, she'd had no family to cry over, to minister to, to experience the pain of loss. She'd already lost her son and her one true love. It was as if she had prepaid the anguish she knew all families must face sooner or later. Now they were back in her life, and with them came renewed exposure to pain and the fear of loss.

Mai tried to think about what they should do. They were still at risk. But with Hank in the hospital, it wasn't as if they could all take a vacation in Hawaii until they were assured it was all over. So far the people who were after Derek had no idea who he really was and what his relationship to Eva was. They had no idea that Eva's best friend was the mother of the man they wanted to kill. But Mai knew it wouldn't take a whole lot of sleuthing for them to figure it out. Everyone at Eva's restaurant knew Mai was Eva's best friend. Even though most had no idea Mai had a long-lost son, it would be a natural leap sooner or later to investigate her friend.

God, she wished Hank were there, lying beside her. Hank would know what to do.

*   *   *

Derek was gone in the morning when Mai came down to make coffee. When Eva and Norm appeared, she handed them the note he had left.

> *I'm catching the early flight to San Francisco. I had a thought during the night, and I want to follow up. Hopefully, I'll be able to find out if we're still in danger. Don't worry. I'll call on cellphone No. 1 later.*

Eva read the note aloud.

"Shit," Norm said. "What do you think he's up to?"

No one looked as if they'd slept particularly well. Norm was pensive.

Mai shrugged. "I don't have a clue. But I'm scared to death. You don't think he's going to do something crazy, like sacrifice himself to keep us safe, do you?"

Norm shook his head. "No. I can't see him putting you and Hank through something like that after all you've done for him. I know he feels guilty about putting you all at risk, but I can't see him causing you even more pain by sacrificing himself to the bad guys."

"I agree," Eva said. "He wouldn't do that to you. Or to Hank."

Mai wiped a tear from her eye and nodded slightly. She took a sip of coffee. "Okay. I think I agree. Let's hope you're right. But what else could he be doing?"

Chapter 59

Derek saw the shock on Alberto's face when he walked through the door of Chaco's. But Alberto recovered quickly, and much to Derek's surprise, gave him a big bear hug.

"Fuck, I'm glad to see you," he said in a whisper. "I was afraid you wouldn't get my message that everything was okay—that it was safe for you again."

Derek stared at Alberto with a look of incomprehension. "What do you mean? What message?"

Alberto looked around. "Come, let's go to my office." He led Derek through the restaurant. Derek waved to a couple of dishwashers he knew as he passed through the kitchen.

Once in the tiny office, Alberto explained that he'd been able to get Raul to rescind the kill order and that Derek (as Danny) was no longer in danger.

"I saw a leaflet that was circulating with your picture on it. I called the number to see if it was you. I wanted to get word to you that everything was fine. But whoever answered said the person on the leaflet wasn't you, that it was some fucked-up mental case. So instead, I just put the word out that if anyone saw you, to let you know you were good."

So it was Alberto who called Hank. But he hadn't been safe. Raul had still been searching for him. "Alberto, I'm not sure why you thought everything was okay, but it wasn't. I wasn't safe." He paused, wondering if he could trust Alberto. He decided he had no choice. "Tell me, how are you and Raul?"

It was Alberto's turn to look confused. "What do you mean?"

Derek took a deep breath. "Raul is making a power play to take over the cartel. It was his three sons who stole the shipment of coke I brought in. Yesterday, those three assholes kidnapped a woman who'd been helping me get information out of Mexico about the guys who'd been involved in the shipment.

"A friend and I were able to follow them to a house in L.A. They turned out to be Raul's three sons, all of whom are now dead. I know Raul must know about it, since someone else came to the house while we were still there, and we had to escape out the back door. But before one of the sons, Roberto, died, he told us the Martinez family intended to take control of the cartel. Raul didn't like the three-way power sharing. They hijacked their own shipment to finance their army. They needed to blame me to buy time."

Alberto looked intently at Derek, absently fidgeting with a stack of invoices. His face had turned hard, angry.

Derek thought he had just made the biggest mistake of his life. Strike that—the *last* mistake of his life.

"Get up," Alberto ordered. He stood and came around the desk.

Derek considered making a run for it, but so far Alberto didn't have a weapon in hand. Derek stood up.

"I need to frisk you," Alberto said. "See if you're wearing a wire. I need to find out what kind of game you're playing."

Derek held his arms out to the side. "I'm not playing a game. I'm trying to get Raul off my back, and I'm trying to alert you to his double cross."

Alberto patted Derek down. He made Derek take off his shirt, then put it back on. He then did the same with his pants. When he was satisfied, he motioned for Derek to sit down and then retook his seat. He started riffling the invoices again. "What makes you think I need to be alerted? What does any of this have to do with me?"

Derek shrugged. "If it doesn't, it doesn't. Roberto Martinez told us that his father's two partners in the cartel were Alberto and Tito. He said Alberto was secretive and lives in the States. Tito lives in

Mexico. Alberto had been childhood friends with Raul. I remember you telling me you two had been friends. If I'm warning the wrong Alberto, so be it. If you're nothing more than Raul's friend, then I reckon you'll want to kill me on his behalf. But I'm guessing you tried to protect me by ordering Raul to back off. I'm guessing you had the power to order Raul to back off. Or thought you did."

Derek took a deep breath and let it out slowly. "You knew damn well I had nothing to do with stealing that load of coke. Raul must have assured you he would follow your instructions, but instead, he ignored you. He found my people in L.A., and the shit hit the fan."

Alberto sat silent again, obviously processing the information. After a moment, he nodded, stood up, and walked around the desk. He gave Derek another bear hug. "I'm glad my message didn't get to you. It could have cost you your life. I think it's safe to say that after tonight, tomorrow at the latest, Raul won't be a concern to either of us. I don't see any need to comment on your assumptions, but I can tell you that I do have a certain amount of influence, and you have my absolute guarantee you will never be bothered again."

"The Martinez family made the connection to me through my friend in L.A. Can I be assured that there will be no reprisals from their clan?"

Alberto nodded. "The fact that Raul used his sons for the job of kidnapping your friend tells me your involvement is not widely known. Probably no one but Raul and his boys knew about your friend." He chuckled. "Which was good for you, since those kids are . . . were . . . total fuckups. But whatever the case, rest assured that whatever Martinez family might be left when this is all over, none of them will be looking for you." He smiled broadly.

"So you killed Raul's boys?"

Derek gave him a lopsided grin. "We did."

Alberto looked as if he was going to ask a question, but then he gave a small nod. "I assume you're no longer Danny Lee. Go and be whoever you want to be. Go write your books."

Chapter 60

Hank was already out of surgery and sitting up in bed, surrounded by Mai, Norm, and Eva, when Derek called on Mai's prepaid cell.

She listened a moment. "Okay, we're glad you're safe," she said. "I love you." She hung up and looked at Hank. "Derek said he didn't want to talk over the phone, but he thinks everything's going to be fine. We should know for sure in a day or two. He'll be back in a couple hours."

Hank said, "Thank God."

"Amen to that," Eva said. "Now, Hank, when did the doctors say you'd be getting out of here?"

"Probably day after tomorrow. Everything went well."

"What do you think we should do?" Mai asked. "Do you think we'll be safe in my condo?"

"Let's see what Derek has to say when he gets back," Hank said. "I have a feeling he gambled that the Alberto who is Raul's partner is the Alberto who owns the restaurant in San Francisco—the guy who got Derek into the business in the first place. If so, and if Alberto didn't know what Raul was up to, he'll owe Derek big time."

*　*　*

"Page three in the Metro section," Derek said, dropping the *Los Angeles Times* on Hank's hospital bed. He had just returned from San Francisco. He closed the hospital room door.

"Someone was walking their dog by that house yesterday afternoon, and the dog went nuts. So the guy went to the front door. Apparently he didn't even go in. He could smell the death from the porch and called the cops."

"Before we get to that, tell us about San Francisco," Hank said. "I'm thinking you went to see your friend Alberto."

Derek nodded and sat on the edge of the bed. "Good guess. The more I thought about it, the more I convinced myself that Alberto had to be Raul's silent partner."

"How'd you reach that conclusion?" Eva asked. "Do you know how many Albertos there are?"

"Yeah, but there were a lot of clues once I started thinking. What got me going in that direction last night was my telling these guys how you chopped off Roberto's little finger and threatened to chop off the rest. I remembered Alberto telling me how he and Raul had been childhood friends. He told me a story about how Raul chopped off the fingers of a friend of theirs who'd stolen twenty bucks. Both Raul and Alberto had been working for the cartel.

"Then, of course, there was the fact that he recruited me. Obviously, he was intimately familiar with the business. I remember how Raul was deferential to Alberto whenever he came to the restaurant. I assumed it was just because they were old friends and it was Alberto's place.

"Alberto knew the shipment had been hijacked and that Raul was pointing the blame at me. He told me there was nothing he could do at the time. Why would he think he could do something to protect me if he wasn't in a position of power?"

Hank nodded. "Still, it was a pretty big leap of faith and a huge gamble going there. If you'd been wrong, you'd be dead by now." He paused and adjusted the oxygen cannula. "So did he admit he was *the* Alberto?"

Derek shook his head. "Not in so many words, but it was pretty clear he had no idea what Raul was up to, and he made it pretty clear we'd have nothing to worry about."

There was a lull in the conversation until Norm, standing beside the bed, nodded toward the newspaper. "What are the cops saying about the murders?"

"Drug related. Only one of the Martinez boys was known to the local authorities as being part of the cartel, but that was enough to put the cops on that track." Derek paused for a beat. "Which is good for us."

Mai picked up the paper and began to read. "The story is pretty graphic." She looked at Hank. "I still can't believe you did that."

Hank closed his eyes and saw the picture of the dead man in his mind. He wondered if he should feel worse than he did, but he certainly wasn't going to convey that to the others.

"Not really that big a deal," Hank said. "Especially when you're dealing with dumb-shit amateurs. Those guys are used to the bull-in-a-china-shop approach to violence. The two brothers didn't even have time to register what was going on before I shot them. I got a little lucky with the third in that he was slow to respond, and I was able to disarm him right away."

"Well, you knights in shining armor came just in time." Eva absently rubbed the thin laceration on her face.

"I have a question now that everyone knows what went on in the house," Derek said. "How come you got the bowl of ice?"

Hank smiled grimly. "Hope. I needed the piece of shit to think he had a chance to live. I wouldn't be trying to save his digits for reattachment if I was going to kill him, now would I?"

"Well, I'm just glad you didn't have to keep going," Derek finally said. "I don't know how much longer I would have lasted."

"You and me both," Hank said. "You and me both."

After a long pause, Norm said, "So now we wait for news about cartel-related murders?"

Hank nodded. "We should monitor as many California news sources as possible."

"What if we don't hear anything?" Eva asked.

"Then I ask my man in San Francisco, Tommy Phan, to stop by Alberto's restaurant and see if the guy's still alive," Hank replied. "If he is, I think we can assume his side won the war."

*   *   *

It took two more days before news of a major war within the Sinaloa cartel broke. A *Los Angeles Times* reporter tied the brutal murder of "prominent Bay Area businessman Raul Martinez" to the deaths of his three sons in Los Angeles. The next day, the DEA confirmed that Raul Martinez hadn't been so prominent after all. He'd long been suspected as a major leader in the cartel though his front was that of a beer and tequila importer.

The *Times* reporter then began tying in the murders of dozens of mid-level cartel soldiers in Southern California and Mexico. He got the DEA to admit there was a major power play going on within the cartel although little was known about the non-Martinez side of the leadership. Following the re-arrest of El Chapo, the scramble for power over the cartel had been shrouded in secrecy.

Hank, now back at Mai's condo, ensconced on the couch and constantly fussed over by everyone, including Stoner, asked Tommy to stop by Chaco's in the Mission District to see if the owner, Alberto, was still there. Tommy called back within an hour to say the restaurant was closed. It looked permanent. Tommy offered to ask around about what happened, but Hank told him to drop it.

"It makes sense," Hank said to Norm and Derek. "If he's now the only cartel *jefe* in the States, he probably had to move back down to San Diego or L.A. Or maybe even Mexico. He'd need to consolidate his power. He probably won't be able to be as anonymous as he's been."

"Yeah, but what if that's not what happened?" Norm asked. "What if he's dead?"

Hank shrugged. "Then he's dead. We already know Raul and his kids are dead. After the war started, the only threat to Derek would have been retribution for the deaths of Raul's sons. But with him dead, even if there are still other Martinezes alive, I seriously doubt if revenge against an outsider like Derek would be on anyone's agenda."

"I agree," Derek said. "Although I keep wondering who it was that showed up while we were still in the house. Obviously, whoever it was didn't call the cops since the bodies weren't discovered until the neighbor came by with his dog."

"I've been wondering about that as well," Hank said. "My best guess is that it was one of the Martinez brothers' friends who saw the carnage and went into hiding. He probably called Raul, but he would never have called the cops. So long as he's not a Martinez on the loose, I doubt he's a threat to us."

Derek stood and walked to the window, staring through the sheer curtains. After a moment, he turned back toward the couch.

Norm was now sitting on its far edge. The women sat in the matching leather armchairs.

"What about our exposure?" Derek asked. "Do you think we're safe from the cops? Shit heels or not, we did commit murder."

Hank tried to keep his expression neutral. He'd been worrying about the same thing. He was pretty sure they hadn't left any prints. Even if they'd left something more subtle that would lead to DNA, the authorities didn't have any of their DNA for comparison. The one thing that gave Hank a chill of fear was the piece of paper he'd found in the pocket of one of the guys while Derek was out at the van. It was a handwritten note with Eva's name and the address of her restaurant. Hank's search of Roberto had been pretty thorough, but the search of the brother he'd shot first was cursory at best. What if there'd been something on him that would lead the police to Eva?

Chapter 61

As the days passed, they began to allow themselves to believe they were safe. Eva moved back into her own condo. No one seemed surprised when Norm and Stoner moved in with her. Hank, who had been sleeping on the couch, moved back to Mai's bed.

Derek had bought himself a new computer and was trying to mollify his agent and editor. But he was having a difficult time writing, and it sent him into a funk. Mai finally called him on it one night when Norm and Eva were over for dinner.

Derek gave a slight tilt of his head in response to Mai's question. Then he took a deep breath and let it out. "I guess I'm just having a hard time adjusting. All of a sudden, I have a family—and a dad who was willing to put his life on the line for me before he even knew me. I don't know that I deserve that kind of respect, let alone love. I mean, I can't believe what I put you all through." It looked as if he had more to say, but then he blinked and wiped at the tears spilling from his eyes.

Hank spoke into the silence. "When Norm and I were on the road looking to interview the Mount Wilson crew, we went to an RV park in Kingman, Arizona, where a demolition crew was pulling the side off a double-wide trailer. We asked what was going on and were told that the man who lived there had died and was so huge they couldn't fit his body through the door. So they had to tear the trailer apart.

"The point is, sometimes people build walls around themselves, or simply let walls be built, and breaking free may not always be so easy. It may, in fact, require drastic, even violent, means." Hank looked at Derek. "Your walls were built not just by you, but by disgusting and ultimately dangerous men, so it was inevitable that if you were ever to break free, it would require some destruction. Luckily, we were there to help be the destructive force to set you free."

The room was silent again. After a full minute, Norm said, "And at least you didn't stink like that dead guy did when they pulled the side off his trailer."

EPILOGUE

Three years later

In the three years following the cartel war in which Raul and most of his family were slaughtered, the only one who moved out of the two connected condos in Pasadena was Derek, who had legally changed his name to Henry Reagan Jr. Although he had grown to love his extended family, he had trouble living with other people. He found it ironic that he now yearned for the solitude he had previously found so depressing. Of course, it was different now that he could simply drive to Pasadena to have dinner with his parents. His new, chosen solitude didn't manifest itself in gut-wrenching loneliness like the old solitude had for so long.

He bought a modest house a block from the beach in Venice and began writing again, at first tentatively. It was different writing without the sense of angst with which he had lived since he'd run away at eighteen. The sense of being all alone in the world was gone. The sense of guilt over what he thought had happened on Mount Wilson was gone. And the self-loathing he'd refused to acknowledge over being a drug runner was gone.

And so Hank Jr., as Mike Mann, found it hard to be a writer and be happy. It was so foreign to him that for several months, he'd been unable to work on the book for which he'd been paid a sizable advance. He tried writing some short stories, more as a writing exercise than anything else. He also wrote a few personal essays, which were not meant for publication.

Then one day, after a long walk on the beach during which he'd recalled the discussion about the walls he'd erected around himself, he had an epiphany. He would take his novel in a completely different direction than he had planned. His story would suddenly diverge from the dark and ominous path his protagonist followed, the path his readers would expect him to continue to follow, to a series of events that would give way to a poignant and optimistic dénouement.

The novel garnered rave reviews, and when his next novel was equally as upbeat, the literary world began speculating on what kind of life-changing event could have happened to the reclusive Mike Mann.

*   *   *

Norm, Eva, and Stoner lived in Eva's condo. The two humans engaged in constant, good-natured bickering. Eva made fun of Norm's hound-dog eyes and pelt of body hair. Norm made jokes, albeit delicately, about Eva's plus size.

Eva said Norm was so weird he couldn't even get a date at the retirement home. Norm said he wouldn't marry Eva in case one more trophy wife came along.

And so it went. But anyone who watched the two interact couldn't possibly miss the fact that they genuinely enjoyed each other.

Norm confided in Hank that he'd discovered he'd missed out on good sex for most of his life. "My ex-wives were all so beautiful, so physically perfect, they didn't think they needed to do anything during sex except lie there. Hell, I didn't think they needed to do anything except lie there." Norm grinned and shook his head in wonder. "Man, did Eva show me what I'd been missing."

Hank covered his ears. "Nah, nah, nah, nah," he chanted.

Stoner barked in apparent agreement.

*   *   *

Hank and Mai fell deeply in love for the second time in their lives—their two love affairs separated by forty-one years. Hank joined Mai's gym, which was less than a block away, and felt pretty good for a seventy-three-year-old. He'd stopped thinking about his heart attack, stopped worrying that he would drop dead during sex.

When his condo at Sunrise Adult Community sold and Mai invited him to make their living arrangements permanent, Hank took her to dinner at a beachside restaurant in Malibu. When the wine was poured and Mai proposed a toast "to us," Hank's face turned serious.

"What is it?" Mai asked.

Hank hesitated. "I'm not sure how to say this, so I'm just going to plow ahead. I want to make sure you know what you're doing, Mai. I want to make sure *we* know what we're doing." It looked as if Mai was about to say something, but Hank held up his hand to stop her.

"I'm old. At this stage of our lives, our age difference matters. I watched the only other woman I ever loved wither away and die. I lived and felt her pain. I felt her loss so thoroughly I honestly didn't think I could go on living. Now I'm putting you in a position to be the one who lives through that." He fought back the tears he could feel were forming. "I don't. . ."

"Stop." Mai's voice was harsh and firm. "Just stop it, Hank. I've waited over forty years to be able to love a man again. I mean really love. I've paid my dues, and now I'm going to love you for as long as you let me, and you're not going to mess that up with some maudlin bullshit about death and dying. Yeah, one of us will get sick and die before the other. It will be hell for whoever is still living. But until then, we will have loved. We will have experienced the most precious thing life can give us."

Now Mai was tearing up. "We aren't a couple of pussies. We know what's coming, and no matter how bad it may be at the end, the getting there will be worth it." She paused. "So fuck you, Hank Reagan. The only way you're not moving in with me is if you tell me you don't love me."

Hank looked at Mai and wiped a tear from his right eye. The two made eye contact and held it for several long moments. Then, slowly, Hank let himself smile. "No, fuck you, Tran Xuan Mai. I love you. So I'm moving in."

Although he still had dark moments when he thought about Becka and about mortality, they were few and far between. He still grunted his old-man noises when he sat down or got up out of a chair. He still joked with Norm about being old. But the beautiful reality was that he didn't really feel old.

On one beautiful spring day in Pasadena, Hank walked out of Macy's with a package in hand and stopped, riveted on the sidewalk. He looked down at the Macy's bag and the shoebox inside and realized that while he'd been buying these shoes, the thought that they could be the last pair he ever bought never occurred to him.

The year after the two moved in together, Mai sold her noodle empire, and they began to travel. It was after their second trip to Europe that Mai said she'd like to go back to Vietnam.

Saigon was bittersweet. The two wandered the moped-clogged streets looking for landmarks they would recognize. The building in which Mai had lived during their love affair was still there, although there was now a Kentucky Fried Chicken outlet on the ground floor. The restaurant where Mai had worked and whose owners were on the CIA payroll was gone. It was now an Emporio Armani. The former American embassy had been demolished and was now a park.

Hank kept most of his thoughts about the lunacy of the Vietnam War to himself. After all, he mused, Mai's parents had died simply because so many South Vietnamese muckety-mucks liked to dine at their restaurant. The couple who'd taken her in and given her a job had worked for the CIA, fearing a Vietcong victory would spell the end of life as they knew it. So many people dead. So many families torn apart. And for what?

The two visited Hanoi, which was easier for Mai in that she had never been there and had no physical or emotional memories to intrude on their enjoyment of the now-vibrant city.

Then they met up with Norm and Eva, who had flown in to join them for a week at the Four Seasons in Hoi An. Their villa was on the beach and had a private pool. Every morning, their private butler brought them a selection of international newspapers.

It was from the *Los Angeles Times* they learned that "suspected Sinaloa drug cartel kingpin Alberto Espinoza, whose nickname was La Culebra, the Snake," had been found dead in his La Jolla enclave. According to the article, Alberto had apparently died in his sleep. He'd been found by his personal valet.

Lying facedown on the bedcovers over his belly was an open novel he'd been reading. It was Mike Mann's bestseller *Coming Home*.

ABOUT THE AUTHOR

David Myles Robinson was born in Los Angeles and attended San Francisco State College, Cal State Los Angeles, the University of Hawaii, and San Francisco State University. He obtained his J.D. in 1975 from the University of San Francisco School of Law, where he met his wife, Marcia Waldorf.

After moving to Hawaii, where Robinson's family lived, he became a trial attorney, specializing in personal injury and workers' compensation law, and Waldorf joined the Public Defender's Office before being appointed as a judge, first at the district court and later at the circuit court level. She retired from the bench in 2006, and Robinson retired from private practice in 2010.

Always passionate about writing—including work during college as a staff journalist for a minority newspaper in Pasadena—he completed his first novel, a precursor to *Tropical Lies*, about twenty years ago but he says it was so stilted from his years of legal writing that it was "just awful. That's why my first novel after retirement, *Unplayable Lie*, had nothing to do with the law." He since has completed and published *Tropical Lies* and *Tropical Judgments*, with a new novel set for publication by Terra Nova Books in the fall of 2018.

Robinson's non-writing interests include skiing, golfing, and travel. He and Waldorf have traveled to all seven continents and been to sub-Saharan Africa a dozen times. Two of his travel stories were honored in the eleventh annual Solas Awards competition for Best Travel Writing.